Dod,

WHEN You THINK ABOUT IT...

...
...

WHAT WERE ONCE MIRACLES ARE NOW CHILDREN'S TOYS

...
...
...
...?

Enjoy,

Ira Nayman

Eloquent Books

Eloquent Books
An imprint of Strategic Book Group
P. O. Box 333
Durham, CT 06422
www.StrategicBookGroup.com

ISBN: 978-1-60911-234-9

Printed in the United States of America

Book Design: Judy Maenle

ALSO BY THE AUTHOR

Les Pages aux Folles
Book Fourteen: *Everybody's Got An Opinion (Unfortunately)*
Book Thirteen: *The Personal is Journalistic*
Book Twelve: *That's What They Want You to Think . . . Or, Is It?*
Book Eleven: *Your Daily Dose of Crustacean Serendipity*
Book Ten: *Alternate Reality Ain't What It Used To Be*
Book Nine: *No Public Figure Too Big,*
No Personal Foible Too Small
Book Eight: *It's Always About You, Isn't It?*
Book Seven: *Life, Death and Other Ways of Passing the Time*
Book Six: *News You Can Abuse*
Book Five: *New Millennium, Same Old Story*
Book Four: *Satire for the Hard of Thinking*
Book Three: *Orchestrated Chaos*
Book Two: *Politics: A Musical Comedy*
Book One: *Zen and the Art of International Politics*

My Toronto
Book Two: *God's Menstruation*
Book One: *A Fate Too Absurd To Bear*

Delicate Negotiations
Round One: *The Quiet Melancholy*

Blackout Funnies
Book One: *Blackout Funnies*

All of these books, as well as new writing and cartoons every week, can be found on the *Les Pages aux Folles Web* site, http://www.lespagesauxfolles.ca.

No Public Figure Too Big, No Personal Foible Too Small and *Alternate Reality Ain't What It Used To Be* are also available in print from iUniverse.

CONTENTS

NOTE: A short story called The Weight of Information is found in interludes between the chapters.

The Weight of Information
Chapter One:
The Realities Leak

"It ain't cigarettes," Mabel said into the telephone, shaking her hennaed head in disgust. "I was born with this voice." Only, she pronounced it "bawn." A childhood diet of Woody Allen movies will have that effect on a person.

The tiny receptionist with the giant presence explained, for the umpteenth time (umpteen = at least 11) that morning that MS. Brundtland-Govanni was in meetings all day and could she take a message? because that's the best you're gonna get. Her tone of voice suggested that she would rather eat glass than actually take the message, and most callers were sufficiently intimidated (it was the giant presence thing) that they said they'd call back and quickly hung up.

Brenda Brundtland-Govanni was in the glass boardroom. The windows that gave onto the offices of the sixth floor of the Gerlentner Building on Queen West had been rendered opaque, giving the room a hall of mirrors effect that most people found disconcerting. This only happened when something bad was going down. Really bad. In the six years that she had been the Editrix-in-Chief of the Alternate Reality News Service, bad things had gone down so often that Brenda Brundtland-Govanni

1

had long stopped noticing the reflected images of herself trailing off into angry infinity.

Brenda Brundtland-Govanni was meeting with two of the company's engineers, Flo and Eddy. Well, shouting at them might be a more accurate way of describing it. And, considering that she was six foot six even before she put on the cockroach killers and her voice was a deep, thundering rumble, it was like listening to Moses express his displeasure at carrying those heavy tablets down that big, big mountain and THAT was the thanks god's chosen people gave him?

This is what caused Brenda Brundtland-Govanni's Old Testament unhappiness: three days earlier, the Dimensional Portal™ was shut down. Owing to the nature of the emergency, all of the Alternate Reality News Service's reporters had to be stranded in the universes where they had been posted, with no means of communicating. This meant that nobody was filing new articles, which meant that subscribers were getting pissed (at least, those who could see through "blast from the past" and "one from the vaults" and all the other weaselly attempts at trying to convince them that giving them old news was business as usual for the Service), which meant the potential for lost revenue, which meant that ARNS CEO Mikhail Lo-Fi had rained Old Testament fire on her to find a solution to the problem.

The problem? The 127 Bob Smiths.

Three days ago, a man named Bob Smith made an unscheduled appearance at the Dimensional Portal™. He was short, with a bald spot that was sometimes described as "cute" by a certain kind of woman, owlish glasses (not that he looked like he could take them off an owl in a fair fight) and a nervous tic in his left eye. He wasn't an Alternate Reality News Service reporter, and nobody could understand why he walked out of the Dimensional Portal™ and into the ARNS lab.

Before anybody could even begin to formulate the question (73 seconds later, not that anybody was counting), a second Bob Smith walked through the Dimensional Portal™. He had a little more hair, and his tic was in his right eye, but, otherwise, he was the same man. As the technicians tried to figure out what was

2

happening (73 seconds later, not that I'm anal about counting or anything), a third Bob Smith appeared. He was half an inch taller and had a little less hair, but, again, was of the same basic type as the first.

In the time it took to make Brenda Brundtland-Govanni aware that there was a problem, six more Bob Smiths appeared. Each was different in some respects from the others, but they were all clearly the same person. In the time it took her to get to the lab, three more Bob Smiths appeared. It was starting to get a bit crowded in there, and Bob Smiths had begun spilling out into the hallway. For the most part, they didn't seem interested in each other, although a couple in one corner of the lab were comparing photos of their two daughters, Miranda and Cicatryx.

Brenda Brundtland-Govanni would have shut down the Dimensional Portal™ then and there, but the Alternate Reality News Service had policies to deal with such situations. Forms had to be filled out and executives had to be consulted. Even using the emergency provisions in the Service's charter, 115 more Bob Smiths appeared before the Dimensional Portal™ could be shut down with the approval of the company's lawyers.

That many Bob Smiths couldn't be allowed to remain in the offices, disrupting Alternate Reality News Service business. Brenda Brundtland-Govanni rented buses and had them hauled off to a company warehouse in North York ("The suburb where smiles go to die."). Cots were set up and food was brought to them until she could figure out what had happened and what to do about it.

The expense did not endear her to Mikhail Lo-Fi, although the secrecy did.

Flo and Eddy sat through Brenda Brundtland-Govanni's tirade with bland expressions. Flo and Eddy were twins born of different sets of parents. With their piercings, tattoos and pear-shaped bodies, they were like a Goth Tweedledum and Tweedledee. Eventually, Brenda Brundtland-Govanni's anger abated to mere mortal proportions, and when she asked, "Why didn't you just send them back to the reality they came from?" the engineers saw their opportunity to speak.

3

"It wasn't," Flo said.

"Possible," Eddy said.

"They came," Flo said.

"Through the portal," Eddy said.

"Without any markers," Flo said.

"Indicating which reality," Eddy said.

"They had come from," Flo said.

They talked like that.

"But, it," Eddy said.

"Wouldn't have mattered," Flo said.

"If they had," Eddy said.

"Why not?" Brenda Brundtland-Govanni asked.

"It takes," Flo said.

"Two and a half," Eddy said.

"Minutes to," Flo said.

"Set up," Eddy said.

"The portal," Flo said.

"To reset," Eddy said.

"The dimensional," Flo said.

"Coordinates and," Eddy said.

"Push the," Flo said.

"Big red button," Eddy said.

"But, the Bob," Flo said.

"Smiths were," Eddy said.

"Coming every," Flo said.

"Seventy-three seconds," Eddy said.

"This means—" Flo started.

"They were coming in faster than we could return them to their home dimensions," Brenda Brundtland-Govanni impatiently cut him off.

"Yes," Eddy said.

"Exactly," Flo said.

A couple of seconds passed. It appeared that Brenda Brundtland-Govanni was starting to build another bout of righteous anger when her body went stiff, her eyes becoming unfocused and her jaw slack. Staff members who had seen this referred to it as "The eye of the needle of the storm. (They were evenly split on which metaphor to use; "Pops" Kahunga, the senior member of the janitorial staff, decided to merge the two metaphors rather than cause bad feelings among the staff. Wise old bird, that Pops Kahunga.) Programmers who had seen Brenda Brundtland-Govanni act like this said she put her body on pause to give her mind extra cycles to calculate with. (By tradition, programmers never went to Alternate Reality News Service staff meetings.)

You might think that Brenda Brundtland-Govanni was thinking about the problem of the 127 Bob Smiths, but you would be wrong. She was actually wondering, not for the first time . . . this week, how she had gotten herself into this position. When she graduated from Ryerson Journalism, she had every intention of working for the corporate media. She had hoped that interning at *The National Post* would have led to a permanent job there. However, a chance meeting at a performance at the 27th revival of *Mamma Mia* with Jerry Patronus, the visionary creator of the Dimensional Portal™ had led her to sign on as the first Alternate Reality News Service Medicine and Literary Reporter. (The Alternate Reality News Service beats were, like its house writing style, unique and precious.) Twenty-one years later, Patronus was gone, disappeared in the Interregnum Incident, and she was in charge.

The light came back on in Brenda Brundtland-Govanni's eyes and her body relaxed. She wiped a thin stream of drool off her cheek in a swift motion that her staff realized was probably unconscious and, therefore, never mentioned in her presence. She looked around the room, sizing up where she was, and said:

"Okay. Nothing would give me more pleasure than to tear strips off the two of you until you were nothing but animate skeletons, but that wouldn't solve the problem. The Alternate Reality News Service is losing readers—accounting tells me we have three, maybe four days before a stampede that will bankrupt us, and I never argue with an accountant. We have to get a handle on what's happening, and we have to do it now. I'm going out to the warehouse to talk to the Bob Smiths—maybe one of them has some information that will help us solve this problem.

You two: get down to the lab and find out all you can about the problem with the Dimensional Portal™."

Flo and Eddy scampered out of the room. Yes, scampered. With more measured steps, Brenda Brundtland-Govanni walked to the elevators that took her to the parking lot where her hybrid hovercraft/coffee maker awaited and drove off to the suburbs. You do not want to know what she had to say to the drivers who made the mistake of getting in her path.

ALTERNATE TECHNOLOGY

What Were Once Miracles
Are Now Children's Toys

by GIDEON GINRACHMANJINJa-VITUS, Alternate Reality
News Service Economics Writer

When life gives you coal, start a utilities company. That has
been the philosophy that has propelled Pabst Subgenus to the
head of Jurassic Playpen, one of the most successful toy companies of the past year.

Before he became a business legend, Subgenus was a professor of Old Things at Sweden's famed McCormack University
and Tearoom. There, using fossils, mosquitoes trapped in amber
and blood samples taken from his landlady, Subgenus and his
group of researchers were able to map 92 percent of the DNA
of the woolly mammoth. Using this DNA to fertilize an ordinary
elephant's egg, Subgenus and his team were able to create the
first woolly mammoths to live in 10,000 years.

"Michael already believed that it had actually happened,"
responded Steven Spielberg, director of the film version of

7

Crichton's novel *Jurassic Park*, from deep within his San Simeon retreat. "So, I don't know what he would have made of this technology. He . . . probably would have liked it . . . I guess . . ."

Not necessarily. One part of the woolly mammoth DNA which Subgenus' research group could not replicate regulated the animal's height. As a result, all of the animals that they cloned were about the size of a small cat or a large bat/a biggish rat or two wombats/an average woman's hat or—

Ahem.

"Oh, they were woolly," Subgenus explained. "But, mammoth? Not so much."

At first, in an attempt to increase the animals' size, Subgenus and his researchers tried to combine the recovered mammoth DNA with the DNA of other large animals: giraffes, hippopotami, fifty story condominium towers with pools, parking and easy access to subways and the downtown core. However, nothing worked.

Legend has it that Subgenus was about to abandon this line of research when Trixie Monassess, the mother of one of his grad students who was on a tour of the lab, said, "Oooh, that's so cute! I bet my four year-old daughter Reginald would just eat it up!" Thus was Jurassic Playpen born (more or less—details of the legend—such as whether or not it actually happened—have been disputed, as details of legends will before everybody who can dispute them dies).

Thanks to an aggressive advertising campaign, the so-called miniature mammoths are now the third most popular family pet, after Siamese cats and retired sports announcers. And, an aggressive advertising campaign was necessary, given the mammoths' general skittishness and propensity to use their long tusks to gore anything that moved within their vicinity.

"When life gives you itchy, scaly skin, use it to make—" Subgenus started, but we were kind of nauseated by where he could go and, in any case, had already used that formulation in this article, so we didn't feel the need to let him finish.

Unfortunately, although the mini mammoths were the hit of the Christmas season, the cold, harsh light of a new year has dawned on their becoming a public nuisance. And, that's more than a mere strained metaphor.

Trent Blegovickovich, a vet with the Peoria Society for the Prevention of Cruelty to Animals, said, "Oh, yeah, we had our first abandoned miniature mammoth in here last week. The stupid bugger ran at a bull terrier—it took us three days to get the blood out of the carpet!"

Subgenus allowed that his miniature mammoths had all of the instincts of their ancestors even though they had none of the stature. When pressed on the abandonment issue, Subgenus explained that, for reasons that should have been obvious (but which he nonetheless refused to elaborate on when pressed), Jurassic Playpen couldn't take back the woolly mammoth pets.

"However, if any of our customers have any problems with their woolly mammoths (as outlined in a drop down menu on an impossible to find page on our Web site), Jurassic Playpen will be happy to compensate them with a free jumbo bag of Eurasia Yummies," Subgenus generously allowed. Jurassic Playpen, which makes Eurasia Yummies, is currently under investigation for false disclosure of the ingredients of the woolly mammoth treats.

"Oh, the whole family just loves fluffy!" exclaimed satisfied Jurassic Playpen customer Lainee Antigone. "I mean, constant dread of imminent impalement—isn't that what having family pets is really all about?"

Ask Amritsar: Soul Mates on a Molecular Level

Dear Amritsar:

So, like, I work at an intelligence enhancement chip repossession company? I know some people think it's like, mondo icky, but it's not like we rip the chips out of people's heads—proper medical protocol is always observed, even when the client is fleeing out the back of his mobile home and siccing dogs on our agents. Course, I work in the shipping department, so I don't do any of the ripping personally.

Anyhoo, there's, like, this guy who works in my department? Cyril? He's supersmart and he's going to go far in the company, and he always says the sweetest things, so, like I think he has the hots for me. The problem is: he has a nose you could land a B52 bomber on. Seriously. The one time we went out for drinks, his nose needed its own table. Nothing could ever happen between us (possibly quite literally).

A couple of weeks ago, Chris was transferred to our department? From livestock? Ooh. Chris is super dreamy. I thought he was, like, interested in me, but every time he got close to my cubicle, he tripped over something and knocked over somebody's wall of company approved personal cubicle enhancers.

Things seemed hopeless until last week, when Chris walked up to my cubicle and—sigh!—started speaking poetry. For real! Rhyming couplets, haiku, iambic pentameter (I looked it up)— you name it, he could do it. I should have been surprised—I mean, in team building exercises, it always seemed like English was his second language, even though it wasn't. And, it wasn't just his, you know, lack of articulationing. Chris liked to talk with his hands. Unfortunately, it was like he was speaking a foreign language. But, I was just so happy that we could finally connect, that I of course screwed him in the men's washroom.

And, the janitor's closet.

And, the men's washroom in the cafeteria.

And, the top floor of the Chrysler building.

And, eventually, his bed.

Okay, I admit I didn't have a clue what Chris was talking about when he started talking about "thine sun-dappl'd golden tresses" and "a love that would make Hector weep." I mean, for one thing, I don't know anybody named Hector? But, Chris explained that he had been taking night courses in poetry writing and the economic and political implications of bovine excrement in Elizabethan England, and he must have momentarily confused the two.

I could see that. I could so totally see that.

We were so happy for three or four days, there, Amritsar, that I never wanted it to end.

Did I mention I should have been surprised by Chris' sudden articulubility? Well, I should have! Yesterday, I was listening to the 1,000 top Led Zeppelin songs as voted by you on the radio as I was making us breakfast, and what should I hear but Cyril's voice! That's right! Surprise! Cyril and Chris were having an argument that went something like:

"My love is like a red, red rose."

"My love is like a colourful flower."

"No. Red, red rose."

"What's the difference?"

"Poetry doesn't work with generalizations. Your images are much more powerful if they are concrete."

"So . . . my love is like concrete?"

I wanted to believe that it was some lame attempt at humour? By morning disc jockeys who just coincidentally happened to, you know, sound like Chris and Cyril? No such luck! When I confronted him, Chris admitted that he had had a nanotube radio injected into his ear, so that he could hear Cyril coach him. All those pretty words were Cyril's!

Oh, Amritsar, I don't know what to do! I'm in love with Cyril's soul, but I'm afraid that if I screwed him, I would be fatally impaled on his schnozz. On the other hand, Chris is so hunky, but he so has the soul of, like, a wet dishrag.

Do you have any, like, suggestions?

Hey, Babe,

There are two ways to look at this. On the one hand, you could be flattered that Chris went to all the trouble to woo you. On the other hand, you could be offended that he deceived you. If you're a typical human being, you'll probably muddle through a mixture of the two.

Either way, you should probably end your relationship with Cyril. He sounds positively creepy!

Good luck.

Send your relationship problems to the Alternate Reality News Service's *sex, love and technology columnist in care of this publication. Amritsar Al-Falloudjianapour is not a trained therapist, but she does know a lot of stuff. AMRITSAR SAYS: don't put the question of whether or not you should continue your relationship to a vote of your social networking friends unless you are prepared to live with the consequences.*

Naked Came the Singularity

by FRED CHARUNDER-MACHARRUNDEIRA, Alternate Reality News Service Science Writer

Socks.

"Socks," allowed James T. Chandrasekar, captain of the IS Ganesh. He did not appear to be pleased by the prospect.

"Socks," agreed Antimonium Troy, chief science officer of the IS Ganesh. She appeared bemused by the prospect.

"Goddam socks!" bellowed Vikram Ghouli Mackoi, chief medical officer of the IS Ganesh. You can pretty much figure what his take on the whole situation was.

The Ganesh had been sent on a scientific expedition to a naked singularity in the Charon Quadrant of the galaxy. A naked singularity is a black hole that has done a strip tease and shed its event horizon; unlike the singularity at the centre of a black hole, naked singularities are not shy, allowing matter to sidle right up to them without being irreversibly sucked into their personal space.

The Ganesh's mission was to communicate with the naked singularity, UO237-56893, nicknamed Sanjay by members of the Indian Space Academy. The ISA had prepared a binary message that included the map of the human genome, the phrase "I am death, destroyer of worlds" spoken by an Alan Oppenheimer impersonator and a 15 second clip of the inexplicably popular 20th century cartoon *Astro Boy*. The Ganesh sent the message into the naked singularity from a distance of a kilometre.

"I don't know what the eggheads at the Academy were thinking would happen," Captain Chandrasekar grumped. ("Don't pay him no mind," Doctor Mackoi wryly observed. "Jim's just upset that, so far on this mission, he hasn't been called upon to beat up or have sex with any aliens.")

What happened that the eggheads at the Academy weren't thinking was that socks started flowing out of the naked singularity, 100 individual pieces of footwear, one for each second the message was beamed in. The socks, collected by the ship's tractor beam, were found to come in all shapes and patterns: some were made of wool, some of synthetic fibres; some were short, some ankle length; one had little pink hearts, one had images of a cartoonish cat eating lasagna and 14 had holes of various shapes and sizes.

After several hours of analysis in the ship's lab, Science Officer Troy was able to conclude that only four of the 100 appeared to be in a pair. "But, we'll have to get them home to do some deeper analysis," she cautioned.

Comparing the socks to a preflight inventory of socks of the crew, Science Officer Troy discovered that one of the socks matched a sock belonging to Ensign Geordie Mukhabarat. "I'd been looking for that sock almost from the time we left port," Ensign Mukhabarat noted, "but I never expected to find it this way!"

Science Officer Troy mused that it was too early to assume that the socks came from the same pair. It could just have been a coincidence that they looked, felt and smelled similar. "I've run the numbers through the computer," she stated, "and the probability that two similar but unpaired socks come together out of a population of 25,000 random socks (those on the ship and those coming from the naked singularity) are actually quite high. Only testing with the latest equipment when we get back to Earth will prove anything conclusively."

In the meantime, "Bitch confiscated my sock!" Ensign Mukhabarat complained. "Said something about getting it back after she's done some tests on earth. Man, that woman is obsessed! Hunh. See if I volunteer to be the third man through the door for her ever again!"

"I mean, decades of research and development and billions upon billions of rupees spent to create this magnificent starship," Captain Chandrasekar grumped further, "and we're essentially using it as a glorified cosmic laundry basket!" ("Don't pay him no mind," Doctor Mackoi wryly observed. "Jim's just upset that he hasn't been called upon to beat up or have sex with any of the socks.")

Why would single socks appear out of a disturbed celestial body? "A singularity, whether naked, fully clothed or in a state of partially clad dishevelment, is an almost infinitely dense point of matter in space," explained Science Officer Troy. "The laws of physics completely break down there, much the same way they do at a frat party. Some scientists argued that, since the normal rules of the universe didn't apply, what happened in a naked singularity could be magic.

"However, I don't think that any of them expected that it would be laundry!"

Oh, Say, Can You See . . . ?

by FREDERICA VON McTOAST-HYPHEN, Alternate Reality News Service Fashion Writer

You're sipping a martini at an orgy when you spot her from across the room. She is voluptuous, her naked breasts large and swaying, with a sweet round ass. Very sweet. You can't believe that she hasn't been pulled to the floor yet, but you don't want to question your luck too closely, so you begin to make your way towards her over the writhing bodies. Unfortunately, just as you are about to reach her, you trip over a trio performing the Reverse Flying Rhino and spill your drink all over her fine, fine flesh.

The woman begins to shake violently and moan. You take this as a good sign, until you notice the wisps of smoke coming off her body, and realize that you have electrocuted her. As she falls to the floor, dead, you notice the Smart Suit™ she was wearing (and, much to your disappointment, that she actually has a flat chest and a sagging ass).

"You wouldn't believe how many variations on that story I've heard," remarked urban mythologist and the man who made wearing toupees cool, Jan Harold Brunvand. "Sometimes, it's the size of a man's penis that has been exaggerated by a Smart Suit™. Sometimes, the person the story purportedly happened to trips over a dozen people performing a sexual act called A Flock of Seagulls. Sometimes, the drink is a Manhattan. Amusing, really, but all untrue."

Although clearly an urban legend—"No, no, man. It's real. It really happened!" interjected Pat McMorita, a sonic hairdresser from Devil's Tibia, Nebraska. "My brother told it to me. He heard it from his girlfriend, who got it from a customer at her brain training school who swore it happened to his best friend's cat trainer's third cousin! Only, it wasn't a Manhattan, it was a mojito. Otherwise, it's true. IT REALLY HAPPENED!"

"No. That canna no be," argued the inventor of Smart Fabric™, Eduardo Tamiroff. Tamiroff, a researcher at Italy's famed Institut de Couture Technologique, explained: "The nanobot, she has no charge, almost no charge, yes? You canna no be electrocute. Worst case: you feel the sweet charge of soft a lips gently caressing a you skin. Issa no more than a gentle breeze on a you skin on a nice a summer's day. No bad. Feels good. Feels very good—hunh hunh."

So, as we were saying before we were so rudely interrupted: although clearly an urban legend, the story is not without some basis in fact. Smart Clothes™ are made of a fabric shot through with programmable nanobots. The first application of the technology, Mood Shirts™, allowed people to show others their emotional states: the clothes read the wearer's vital signs, then projected images onto the clothes based on projections of what their vital signs indicated about their moods.

As the first entry in the J. Crew catalogue featuring Mood Shirts™ explained: "Feeling happy? The Mood Shirt™ will display photos of puppies or sunsets on beaches. Confused? Salvador Dali paintings. Suicidal? Hieronymus Bosch woodcuts. Generalized feelings of ennui and dread? Annie Leibovitz clown photos. And, the best thing about Mood Shirts™? You can programme them to your own taste! Think Hieronymus Bosch is a barrel of laughs? Make his woodcuts your representation of happiness!"

Like Mood Rings before them, Mood Shirts™ became immediately popular. Unlike Mood Rings, however, people almost immediately started adapting them for their own uses. In order to get around their limited memory, for instance, some people linked them to a WiFi network that allowed them to stream YouTube videos directly to their clothing. (That was the point, of course, when the MPAA threw up its hands and said, "You win!" Prematurely, as it turned out, since all those people acting as living billboards actually helped promote Hollywood movies.)

Giorgio Armani adapted the technology for upscale business suits. Conservative for office hours, the suits could change to wildly colourful and cheekily revealing for evening partying at the touch of a switch. Female executives realized that changing from slacks to a miniskirt wasn't the only advantage a Smart Suit™ offered: it could also make their legs look a little shapelier, their asses appear to be a little higher.

"Cosmetic clothing!" enthused fashion maven and Italian AK-47 enthusiast André Leon Talley. "Why go for expensive surgery when an expensive suit could make you look the same without the need for painkillers and ugly scarring?"

"Wait a minute!" McMorita interjected again. "So, the story I heard—it wasn't true?"

We've already established that. Some stories about Smart Clothing™ are true. A lawsuit was filed against Tamiroff and the

Institut by a man who forgot to turn the emotive function on his suit off at a holiday office party. While he was smiling and talking pleasantly to his boss, the suit was projecting images of violent deaths. Tamiroff successfully argued that it was the man's own negligence that caused his termination from the company, and the lawsuit was dismissed.

Then, there was a brief period when the fashion for women was to programme their Smart Suits™ to quickly cycle through dozens of images of naked women with different body types (likely inspired by an installation by Yoko Ono aptly called "Yi Yi Yi"). However, men didn't know whether to be aroused or repulsed by the images, and the fad quickly died out.

The social ramifications of Smart Clothing™ are still being worked out. It may be, as Ono stated in the catalogue accompanying her installation, that "we should start to worry when our clothes are smarter than we are. Yi! Yi! Yi!"

Out of Left Field and Into Your Life

by FRED CHARUNDER-MACHARRUNDEIRA, Alternate Reality News Service Science Writer

Esteban "Mickey" Lunarcher wondered why he was spooning sugar onto his morning cereal with his left hand. He hated cereal—he had been a pancakes and syrup man all of his life. But, no, that wasn't it: Lunarcher had been put on a strict whole grains diet after he had the shunt put into his spleen.

Lunarcher also hated mornings, but that wasn't it, either. Ever since the drug dealers and prostitutes had been chased out of the neighbourhood, he was woken to the sounds of bawling babies and fighting Yuppie couples at 7:36 every morning for the past six months. It got so bad, he now added "gentrification" to the list of things he hated.

No, what was strange about this morning was that Lunarcher found himself left handed. He had been right handed his entire life. Somehow, during the night his dexterous orientation had shifted.

"I haven't decided if I hate it or not yet," Lunarcher, a man of great . . . passions, said. "Tell the truth, I probably wouldn't even have noticed except I use a right-handed teaspoon to pour the sugar onto my cereal."

The experience of Lunarcher, a door to door used pill salesman from Lunenberg-on-Thames, wasn't unique. In fact, at 6:37 am GMT, everybody in the world found that their handedness switched. Lefties became righties. Righties became lefties. And, those who were ambidextrous suddenly became very, very clumsy. (I could have opened this article with anybody in the world; the reason I chose Lunarcher is that he happened to be selling pre-loved Viagra in the office as I started doing our research.)

"It was horrible!" Hidekeo Matsushita of the Tokyo Gerbils baseball team exclaimed. "I was in my wind-up when the change happened, so I lost the zip on my fastball, and the pitch was hit out of the ballpark! We were already behind 13 to 2, so it didn't affect the outcome of the game, but . . . okay, you know, now that I think about it, it wasn't really as traumatic as I may have originally made it out to be."

Perfect bowling games thrown off. Peace treaties signed by squiggles that may be interpreted as meaningless by future generations. A thousand couples thrown off their rhythm (whether dancing or having sex). We will likely be calculating the costs of the devastation wrought by the reverse in humanity's orientation for generations to come. What could possibly have caused this?

"Oh, wait. No, no, no, no, no. You're not going to pin this on us," said Robert Aymar, the French director general of the European Organization for Nuclear Research (CERN). "The Large Hadron Collider has nothing to do with the sudden change in everybody's handedness. Nothing. Not a thing. Not one. None."

That would seem to be that, then. However, since you brought it up . . .

"Oh, here we go," Aymar moaned.

Did you enjoy blowing things up when you were young? (If you do as an adult, get help.) The Large Hadron Collider is, in essence, an experiment in blowing things up (by adults who didn't get help). Blowing them up real good. It does this by accelerating two atoms to 99.9999991 percent of the speed of light, then "introducing" them to each other.

At first, the atoms don't want to get together, sort of like . . . Ricky Gervais and Tea Leoni in *Ghost Town*. However, thanks to the logic of romantic comedies, they are inevitably drawn closer . . . and closer . . . and—BOOM! An explosion that could give scientists insight into the big bang.

Kind of puts your childhood explosions into perspective, doesn't it?

Before the collision, some people feared dire results from the experiment, everything from a black hole that would suck in the entire solar system (yes, including Luton) to comedian Steve Coogan becoming head of the European Union.

"But, they didn't happen, did they?" Aymar argued. "The dire predictions were made by people who never learned anything from blowing up things when they were younger. Well, I'm a professional things blower upper, and I am telling you that there can be no connection between the Large Hadron Collider and people's handedness changing!"

When asked why the change occurred at the exact moment the two atoms collided, Aymar lamely responded, "I . . . have to go look at some charts, now. We'll be analyzing the information we got for decades, you know. Ask me again when I'm finished."

Other than having to change the orientation of all of his cutlery, how has Lunarcher been affected by the switch from being right-handed to being left-handed? Unfortunately, I spent so much time explaining his predicament at the beginning of the article that I have no room to

Ira Nayman

Ask The Tech Answer Guy

Yo, Tech Answer Guy,

I thought I was in heaven, but it turned out to be hell. Well, hell may be a strong way of putting it. A suburb of hell. Yeah. That's it. A suburb of hell where most of the rich folks have moved north and everything has gotten run down and you can no longer walk the streets at night for fear of . . . for fear . . . uhh . . .

You know what? It may not be exactly accurate, but, for simplicity's sake, let's just say it turned out to be hell and leave it at that.

Anyway. Allow me to explain. A couple of years ago, I bought a Home Dimensional Portal™. I told the Missus she could use it to watch the neighbours. I planned on using it to watch sports. My favourite sport is hockey; my favourite team is the Toronto Maple Leafs. I know. Some people like having sex with deserts, I like the Leafs. What can I say? It was how I was brought up.

Here's the thing: with the Home Dimensional Portal™, I could toggle through universes until I found one in which the Leafs won. Every night. It was like, they never lost a game. And, when the playoffs started, oh, man! It didn't matter that the team didn't even make the playoffs that year—I found a universe in which they did! It took a little more time, but I even found a universe where the Leafs won the Stanley Cup. That was the best!

The next year, I did it again. And, the year after that. And, the year after that. Only, I was starting to get kind of . . . restless. Okay, honestly, I was bored. It got boring. The leafs always won. I thought that's what I wanted, but, now, most nights, I can't even be bothered to watch. What the hell is happening to me?

Sincerely,
Tommy from Toronto

Yo, Tommy,

Have you considered taking up woodworking?

The Tech Answer Guy

Yo, Tech Answer Guy,

What the hell kind of answer was that?

Confusedly,
Tommy from Toronto

Yo, Tommy,

The kind of answer where I don't have to give you the straight truth, which is, frankly, that you are screwed. My shrink tells me I should try to be less confrontation. But, hey, since you insisted: you are definitely screwed, bro.

The joy of sport is not knowing the outcome of any single game, and, although nobody likes for their team to lose, the losses are what makes the winning that much sweeter. Let me make it easy for you: no potential for losing = no tension = (as you found out) boredom.

The Toronto Maple Leafs? Forget about them. You'll never be able to watch another game again without wondering how they could win it, but you know that if you look for a universe where they do win, it will be boring to you. Now, ordinarily, I would say that a man who switches his team alliance is an untrustworthy scumbag. Still, given these circumstances, it would be almost understandable. Don't bother. You'll quickly get bored of watching your new favourite teams win all the time, too.

How about trying another sport, say, baseball? (Does Toronto even have a baseball team?) No soap, Jack. At first, there will

Ira Nayman

be the drama that is missing from the old sport. But, sooner or later, you will choose a favourite team, and, of course, you will want them to win as often as possible, and, well, you know how the story goes from there.

You poor, deluded fool. Without knowing what you were doing, you've pretty much killed the possibility that you will ever enjoy sports again. Head doctors even have a name for it: Progressive Sports Anomie Syndrome. And, believe me when I say there ain't no cure.

My suggestion: take up a masculine hobby. Woodworking. Motocross. Shooting random strangers on the highway. Whatever suits your temperament. Cause you'll never be able to watch sports again.

The Tech Answer Guy

Yo, Tech Answer Guy,

Lately, I've been having this problem with my girlfriend, Deirdre. Don't get me wrong—she's great. Really. Most of the time. We've been going out for a couple of weeks, and I thought this relationship really had a future. It's just that

Yo, Dude,

Are you asking me . . . a *relationship question*? I'm the Tech Answer Guy. I don't do relationship questions. Ask Amritsar Al-Falloudjianapour or somebody who gives a shit.

If you are a dude with a question about the latest technology, ask The Tech Answer Guy by sending it to him care of this publication. Just remember: The Tech Answer Guy doesn't do relationship questions. It's a thing with him. Don't ask.

22

Einstein's Ankle And Other Artifacts of the Technological Age

by NANCY GONGLIKWANYEOHEEEEEEEH, Alternate Reality News Service Technology Writer

Do you realize that the atoms of skin that were shed by Alexander the Great during his life have been spread by time and tide over the planet? That means that you are probably breathing in atoms of the ancient Greek ruler even as you read this.

Yuck.

Although they are gone, in some sense all of the great historical figures, from Ludwig von Beethoven to Joey Ramone, from Charlemagne to Bebe Rebozo, from Aristotle to Yogi Berra, from Al Capone to . . . to—okay, I think you get the point—they are all still with us. And, now, it is possible that they may be brought back to life.

"Every atom carries with it a history of where it has been," says Heinrich Horfhorker, lead scientist at the esteemed Deifunkenplatzer Institute of Out There Research in New Delhi, Scotland. "We have atoms, for instance, that were part of a tree in ancient Sumeria, then Marilyn Monroe's lips, then a drum that was played by somebody who never made it as a musician. It's remarkable, really. Especially the part about Monroe's lips."

Scientists at the Deifunkenplatzer Institute have been working for over a decade on devices that could accumulate atoms with similar histories. The work was hard, and the setbacks many.

"Six years ago, we tried to recreate the first electric guitar of Bob Dylan," Horfhorker explained. "We got the neck and three strings. Unfortunately, the device we were working on at the time wasn't sensitive enough to put together the atoms from a single object, so it kept confusing different atomic timelines. So, the guitar had gills from a sturgeon, part of the hide of a baseball and several eyelashes."

"It was interesting, in a Marcel Duchamp kind of way," Deifunkenplatzer Institute research best boy Antonella Kerplunkety stated.

"But, ultimately, it was not what we were working towards," Horfhorker added.

"I was going to say that," Kerplunkety pouted.

"Who is the lead researcher, here?" Horfhorker reminded her.

"That's no reason to cut me off," Kerplunkety stood her ground.

"Oh, go clean out some pipettes!" Horfhorker snarled, and Kerplunkety was gone.

The most exciting project being worked on at the Deifunkenplatzer Institute is known by the name C-243-1A27dash-8. "Bureaucrats," Horfhorker shrugged. "What are you gonna do?"

The project is known informally in the Institute as the Albert Einstein Reclamation Project. Starting from a base of Einstein's spine ("You don't really want to know how we got that," Horfhorker stated. "No, really. Don't ask."), the researchers have managed to collect enough atoms to recreate pieces of the scientific genius' index finger (probably from his left hand), the lids of both his eyes and patches of his intestinal track. The highlight of their research project to date, though, has been an almost complete reconstruction of Einstein's ankle.

"We have remade the ankle—and, the right ankle, at that, the dominant ankle—of the man who revolutionized our understanding of the physical universe," Horfhorker dreamily commented. "I am humbled."

Horfhorker's dream of reconstituting all of Albert Einstein's body has a major snag: Eleazor Schnouptfhoff at the European Institute of Arcane Research and Esoteric Effluvia (DISCERN) is also running a project to recreate Einstein's body.

"We have **two** fingers, substantial parts of both of Einstein's nostrils and almost half of his liver," Schnouptfhoff proudly pointed out. "Our Einstein is going to make Horfhorker's Einstein look sick!"

When told of his rival's boast, Horfhorker responded, "Schnouptfhoff wouldn't know Einstein's ear drum from his asshole—which, by the way, we have over 70 percent of!"

Horfhorker added that everybody who was anybody in the scientific community knew that Schnouptfhoff's Einstein had been contaminated by atoms of J. Robert Oppenheimer. "What would their Einstein look like if they did complete him? 'I am death, destroyer of worlds, and I don't play dice with the universe?' Please!"

Schnouptfhoff denies the accusation, but that's really beside the point. Aside from the fact that the two Einstein projects would inevitably have to merge if the researchers wanted their recreations to be complete, both groups are faced with the problem that Einstein's brain is kept in a jar in Thomas Stoltz Harvey's rec room.

There is also the question of what either of the groups would do if they were successful in generating a complete version of Einstein's body. After all, it would still be dead.

"We'll deal with that issue when we get to it," Schnouptfhoff responded.

"One problem at a time," Horfhorker agreed. "That's the way of science."

Laurie Neidergaarden contributed to this article. Well, Laurie contributed this paragraph. Still, that counts.

One Flew Over The Cloud Cuckoo's Nest

by NANCY GONGLIKWANYEOHEEEEEEEH, Alternate Reality News Service Technology Writer

David Axelrod, who had spent several weeks working on a paper on soil erosion inside volcanoes for the Swedish government's Ministry of Very, Very Hot Things, went home one evening believing that, with one final polish, he would change the country's environmental policies forever. Or, at the very least, volcano desserts. Imagine his surprise when he arrived at his office the next day and found that the file contained, not the results of his earth-shattering investigation, but an imitation of a Jackson Pollock painting.

"And, not a very good one, at that," Axelrod analyzed. "The lines were timid, very unlike the bold strokes that we expect from Pollock, and the colours were muted. It was very disappointing. I mean, if I have to lose three years worth of work, I at least want it to be for art."

As it happened, Axelrod hadn't lost his work. It had simply been transformed. This is the basis for the new business model known as C3 computing: cloud cuckoo computing . . . uhh . . . computing. The Swedish government rents space on a private company's server. In addition to its stored files, the server also gives employees of organizations who are licenced to use it access to a variety of computer applications.

Big deal, right? Everybody from Microsoft to that 13 year-old son of Yugoslavian immigrants who lives three doors down and likes to be known as "LadeeKilla" runs computing clouds. What's different about C3 computing?

"That's a very good question," replied Vernor Gesundheit, Chief Technology Officer of CressVexTech, a wholly owned subsidiary of MultiNatCorp, and one of the leaders (read: the only practitioner/proponent) of cloud cuckoo computing computing. Unfortunately, his answer lasted 25 minutes, took up six and a third white boards and was so dense steelmakers are afraid it could be used to make skyscrapers.

Translated into English, the explanation of the technology is this: a file on the server is chosen. The computer running the cloud then determines a random number between 547 and 12,627. It uses this number to count the files opened since the first one; the data from this file is used as the basis for a work of art in a different format. A word processing file, for example, may be turned into a sound file, a spreadsheet might be turned into an image, and so on. Greenwash, rinse, repeat.

Traditional C2 (cloud computing) computing gives businesses and governments the flexibility of having access to computer storage and applications without having to go to the trouble (read: expense) of having computers or anybody on staff who can actually run applications. The benefits should be obvious. Well, they're obvious to anybody with an MBA.

Why, however, would any company want to use C3 computing for—okay, look, we know that this term is bad English. We know that the word "computing" is unnecessarily repeated. However, it is state of the art in the industry, and we don't feel like lecturing Steve Jobs about good grammar, okay?

Why (because of our digression, it's a paragraph later, so we've dropped the "however" because it has lost the connection to its referent) would any company want to use C3 computing for its sensitive data? "I have a very good answer to that," Gesundheit claimed. "Will you print it if I manage to express it in . . . two and a half whiteboards?"

While we negotiate the length and complexity of Gesundheit's answer, let us give a different but likely related answer: working in corporate bureaucracies can be soul-deadening. Employees with no souls are unlikely to be sources of innovation. By randomly turning files into works of art, CressVexTech brings enchantment back into the workplace, increasing efficiency and innovation.

"It's brilliant!" Intel CTO Carl Rorschach enthused (read: he can afford the dry cleaning bills). "The information isn't lost, just changed, so you can get the data back. One time, it took half our programmers half a day to turn a series of haiku back into the specs for a new chip—when we all recovered from our half-hearted heart attacks, we were refreshed and productivity soared!"

The technique has its critics, however. "Who in their right mind," asked Stanley Mildew, CTO of the Wataskawin Public School Board, "would give some monolithic corporation access to all of their sensitive data, knowing how easy it would be for them to interfere with it for their own purposes?"

"Oh," Rorschach responded. "Good . . . point. Let me, uhh, speak to my board and get back to you . . ."

Unanticipated Consequences Come From Anticipated Technologies

by NANCY GONGLIKWANYEOHEEEEEEEH, Alternate
Reality News Service Technology Writer

William Gibson once wrote that the street finds its own uses
for technology. As with so much else in his writing, this has
proven to be wrong. Current smart street technologies inter-
face with other technologies—particularly smart vehicles—in
wholly predictable ways. In fact, it couldn't be otherwise, not if
drivers ever actually wanted to get anywhere.

This may be an eccentric interpretation of what Gibson
was trying to say, but it does lead to an important point: the
introduction of new technologies often does lead to unexpected
consequences. Yet, oddly enough, it is just these consequential
unexpected consequences that are so rarely expected by the initial critics of the technologies. We expect.

Take the Alternate Reality News Service's Home Universe
Generator™. Thyoir Hinderdjill, writing in the *New New Republic*, argued that it would be a boon to criminals. "Say you want
to steal millions of dollars from your local bank before it files
for Chapter 11. All you would have to do is conduct a Google
Multiverse search using terms like 'perfect robbery' or 'perfect
crime,' sort through the results and . . . and . . . uhh, excuse me
for a moment . . ."

According to Ned Feeblish, ARNS Vice President of Public
Relations and Rotating Other Duties (Rhyming and Not So
Much), it isn't that simple. "Conditions are never exactly the
same from one universe to the next," he explained. "The combination of the safe may be one digit off, the bank manager could
have a cold that day and be unavailable to be a hostage, a black
cat could get underfoot as you're trying to make your way out
of the vault, one of the tellers might be allergic to falafel. You
just never know."

Feeblish added that there wasn't a single documented case of anybody using a Home Universe Generator™ to plan a perfect crime, proving that the expected effect didn't happen.

"Of course there isn't!" bellowed Gil Guinness, who took over writing the *New New Republic* article after Thyoir Hinderdjill's mysterious disappearance. "How would we know they had happened? The crimes are perfect!"

Around the same time, an article appeared in *Yegg's Quarterly* by somebody who asked to be identified only as "Rocco." Rocco complained that many of his "friends and professional acquaintances" had been busted after looking for the perfect crime using the Home Universe Generator™.

Jackie "Little . . . Fingers" Gilhoohickey, for instance, was caught trying to smuggle herring into Montana when the horn on his pickup truck started blaring. After a couple of hours in the hot sun trying to explain to police officers why his horn wouldn't stop, his cargo, labeled "office equipment," began to give off a most unoffice equipmenty odor.

Then, there was the case of Jackson "Lean of Leg, Flat in Trunk" Wackston, who attempted to rob a bank with a herring. He would have made it, too, if a little kid's balloon hadn't burst, causing all of the tellers to give their attention to him after he started to cry (the kid, not Wackston—that came later). Wackston was fortunate that he lived in a state without concealed herring laws, or he would have faced a lot more jail time.

Rocco also told the story of Kentucky "Fats but Trying to Lose 30 Pounds" Hidalgo, who tried to steal an obscure Andy Warhol canvas called "Elizabeth Taylor /w Herring" while it was on loan to the Palmerston Public Library. The story was so ridiculous that we would be embarrassed to repeat it here, so we won't. Suffice to say that it doesn't end well.

Leaving aside the possibility of a herring bias in the Google Multiverse search engine, Rocco sniffed, "The perfect crime, my arse! That's false advertising, that is!"

"My god, you think we would advertise that the Home Universe Generator™ could be used in the commission of a felony?"

Feeblish groaned. "The Transdimensional Authority (TA) would shut us down faster than ten gabillion volts of electricity shuts down a nervous system!" He added that the fact that crooks were complaining that the Home Universe Generator™ had landed them in jail was proof that it couldn't be used to find the perfect crime.

"Not necessarily," Thyoir Hinderdjill wrote in a postcard from the Cayman Islands. "They could just be too stupid to use it properly. Peggy sends her love. Having a wonderful time. Glad you're not here."

Where are the criticisms of the unexpected consequences of Home Universe Generator™ technology? We're waiting for the next postcard from Thyoir Hinderdjill to point out that our entire premise is wrong because any criticism of a consequence would make it expected, and to tease us about the great weather we're missing.

Everything AND The Kitchen Sink

by NANCY GONGLIKWANYEOHEEEEEEEH, Alternate Reality News Service Technology Writer

It has become a common truism that there is more computing power in your Home Tableware Hygiene System (HTHS) than there was in the room-sized mainframe machines that ushered in the computer age. But, when you've finished laughing at the misfortune of people who didn't have the good sense to live in our modern age, you might want to contemplate a simple question.

What's the big whup?

Sure, the computer in your sink (actually, a series of chips at different strategic places in your sink) can tell you the exact temperature of the water coming out of the tap to the nearest tenth of a degree. So, what? When was the last time you thought to yourself: "Gee, the water's a little chilly. I need to turn the heat up three tenths of a degree?"

And, sure, sensors around the rim of the sink can warn you if the water level is getting too high. However, when you've had to leave the kitchen to deal with Rover having shocked himself (because, for the fifth time, he has found the vibrator you clearly haven't hidden well enough), you're going to have to mop the kitchen floor yet again. Short of finding some other way to get your jollies, nothing was going to prevent that; certainly not a digitized sink.

And, also sure, the sink can tell you if you need to add more soap for maximum dishes cleanliness. But, honestly, who needs a bossy sink? That's what you have a husband for.

Ultimately, you have to wonder if such devices are making our lives better.

"Absolutely!" exclaimed *Wired* columnist Clive Thompson.

"Absolutely not!" retorted the late Neil Postman, author of, among other books, *Amusing Ourselves to Death* and *Building a Bridge to the 18th Century*.

Okay, then. Having dispensed with the journalistic fiction of allowing both sides of the issue to be represented, we can now attempt to actually answer the question. So, is the world really a better place because we have computer-operated sinks?

"I have my doubts," said Salvatore Aeshus, part-time acoustic tile engineer for NASA and full-time ordinary person. "The thing came with a 124 page manual—124 pages! I spent several hours reading it, and I still couldn't figure out how to turn the damn thing on!"

Aeshus said that he eventually got so fed up with the HTHS that he took his dirty dishes and cutlery and washed them in the pool in the basement of his condo. "Sure, the tenants who were in the pool at the time weren't very supportive," Aeshus admitted. "Still, when I explained to them what had happened, a lot of them stopped saying they were going to complain to the condo management board. Those were the ones who got it."

"Sure, new technologies have a learning curve," Thompson allowed. "You can't drive to your corner grocer's without learning how to work a car. But, most people feel being able to avoid walking the two and half blocks is worth several months of study and practice. When they realize the benefits of the Home Tableware Hygiene System, I'm sure most people will feel the same way about it."

"For most of human history, human beings beat their dirty dishes on rocks by the stream to get them cleaned," Postman, very loquacious for a dead man, retorted. "This was both good physical exercise and the occasion for important social interactions among villagers, not to mention great for the economy, given that dishes had to be replaced so frequently. When they realize that their fingers will never again have to get pruney because they have spent too much time in dishwater, I'm sure most people will feel that the things they have lost because of this new technology are more important than the things they have gained."

Pablo Escobar, Chief Technology Poobah of HTHS Technologies, the wholly owned subsidiary of MultiNatCorp that produces digital sinks, commented, "We just hope that consumers will appreciate that the time the Home Tableware Hygiene System saves them in doing dishes is time that could be better spent ignoring their families. Really, with this technology, everybody wins."

"Nice use of balancing quotes from both sides of the issue, by the way," Escobar added.

The Weight of Information
Chapter Two:
Bob's . . . Somebody's Uncle

"You're favourite colour is puce? What a coincidence! My favourite colour is puce, too! I think it's the most dramatic of the pastels . . ."

"What do you think it costs to keep a warehouse this size? Man, the heating bills alone must be murder!"

"As a matter of fact, I didn't put the head of a Barbie up my nose when I was six years old! . . . It was a GI Joe . . . And, I was only five . . . And, it wasn't my nose . . ."

"Gentlemen, if I could get your attention, please."

"No, no, no, no, no. Start with beer, then port, then whisky. You mess the order up, and the hangover will be a hundred times worse!"

"I was considering being a lawyer, but, honestly, I don't have the figure for robes."

"Your favourite album is *Quadraphenia*? Mine is *Who's Next*. Maybe that's the way people will be able to tell us apart . . ."

"Hello! Everybody, I need your attention!"

"Hunh. She's been my secretary for four years, and I had no idea she was gay. The things you learn . . . !"

"Oh, you'd be surprised at what you can hide with the right kind of software!"

"I love to wear socks, but I hate waking up with sweaty feet."

"WILL YOU ALL PLEASE SHUT THE FUCK UP!"

127 heads turned towards the woman at the front of the giant room who had just turned a force four bellow on them. "My name is Brundtland-Govanni, Brenda Brundtland-Govanni," Brenda Brundtland-Govanni told them, "and I represent the Alternate Reality New Service."

If any of the Bob Smiths were impressed by this declaration, they hid it well. Darren Clincker-Belli, easily overlooked standing next to her, being a foot shorter and otherwise generally unimposing, made a notation on the clipboard he always carried while wearing his scientist's smock, which he always wore while on duty.

Before she confronted the Bob Smiths, Clincker-Belli had filled her in on what the team had been able to learn from them before she had arrived at the warehouse. Sixty-four were certified public accountants, 32 were regular accountants, 16 were economists, eight were bookies, four were mob accountants, two were homeless and one was a professor of international economic policy at the Rotman School of Management at the University of Toronto. Sixty-two of the Bob Smiths were right-handed, 61 were left-handed and four claimed to be ambidextrous. Sixty-four were happily married with three children, 32 were happily married with two children, 16 were happily married with one child, eight were happily married without children, four were in the middle of getting a divorce, two were lifelong bachelors and one was a virgin. Interestingly (for Clincker-Belli, for Brenda Brundtland-Govanni, not so much), the distribution of marital relations among the Bob Smiths was different than the distribution of profession.

"Okay," she stated, "You like numbers. They fascinate you. You probably masturbated thinking about the Fibonacci sequence when you were a kid. BUT WHAT THE HELL DOES IT MEAN?"

Clincker-Belli pushed his horn-rimmed glasses back up his nose and grinned. "Haven't a clue," he replied. "It wouldn't be an interesting mystery if I did."

Brenda Brundtland-Govanni growled. "Let's go talk to them, then," she said. "This parking lot gives me the creeps."

"I suppose you're wondering why you're all here," Brenda Brundtland-Govanni told the Bob Smiths. "Frankly, if we knew that, we could get you the hell back to where you came from, and we wouldn't be having this conversation." She was trying to be comforting.

Brenda Brundtland-Govanni didn't really do comforting.

"The Alternate Reality News Service—are you sure none of you have heard of us?" Brenda Brundtland-Govanni asked. A lot of shaking semi-bald, graying heads later, she continued, "We have a device, a Dimensional Portal™, that allows our reporters to travel to and from alternate realities. For reasons we do not understand, the Dimensional Portal™ spit all of you back to this reality—pardon the gross metaphor.

"We're hoping that if we learn more about you, we'll be able to figure out why you were sent here and, maybe, figure out how to get you back to where you belong. Are there any questions?"

Brenda Brundtland-Govanni didn't wait for an answer. "Okay. What were you doing when you appeared in our dimension?" Most of the Bob Smiths started answering the question, making it impossible to hear any of them. Clincker-Belli put the clipboard in front of his mouth and whispered something to Brenda Brundtland-Govanni. "What!" she asked, annoyed.

"Ask them one at a time," Clincker-Belli confidentially shouted above the din.

Brenda Brundtland-Govanni nodded. "ENOUGH!" she bellowed, quieting the warehouse. "YOU!" she extended a finger and pointed at the Bob Smith nearest to her. Despite being close enough, she resisted the temptation to poke him in the nose. "What were you doing when you found yourself in this reality?"

"M...m...m...me?" the Bob Smith shrank from her attention (which, admittedly, was the posture Brenda Brundtland-Govanni felt all men should have towards her, so she was not displeased by the effect). "I was working on the DeFelipchuk return."

"Okay."

"We were only out by three dollars and forty-seven cents."

"Right."

"If the return wasn't filed by the end of business, the company would be open to a $5,000 fine, so you can understand why—"

"I GET IT!"

"Right. Sorry."

"Did you double check the receipts for the Miscellaneous Canine Expenses?"

"WAS I TALKING...TO YOU?"

"Right. Sorry."

"No. Thanks for the tip."

Brenda Brundtland-Govanni's sigh was swallowed up by the cavernous warehouse. "Okay, how many of you came through the Dimensional Portal™ while working on the Phillip Upchuck—?"

"DeFelipchuk," the second Bob Smith corrected her. She didn't even bother to glare at him.

"Whatever. How many of you were working on this file when you came into this universe?"

Several of the Bob Smiths raised their hands. Clincker-Belli put his clipboard in front of his mouth and, not bothering to lower his voice, advised: "It will be easier to count them if you have the Bob Smiths who fulfill your condition by answering the question in the affirmative move to another part of the room."

Brenda Brundtland-Govanni gave her very best "it figures" nod and told the Bob Smiths that had been working on the DeFelipchuk file when they were brought into her universe to move away from the rest of them. She repeated this process six more times, and found that, when they were called to this reality: 64 Bob Smiths had filed the DeFelipchuk return and were thinking about dinner; 32 were looking for the missing money; 16 hadn't returned from lunch; eight were in a bar; four were on their way to see their mistress; two were at an ATM, checking to see whether they had enough money to afford to move to the Bahamas, and; one was, well, it's kind of embarrassing, really, but, since you're going to yell at me if I don't come out with it, I was . . . masturbating while thinking of the Fibonacci sequence.

"So, what have we learned from this exercise?" Brenda Brundtland-Govanni, who had to wait until the nausea had subsided, asked Clincker-Belli, who was furiously writing on his clipboard.

"They're all squares!" he commented.

"That's a polite way of referring to the Bob Smiths, I suppose."

"No, not them. I mean, sure, them, too. But, I was talking about the numbers."

Clincker-Belli showed her what he had been writing. Minus the cursive script, it looked like this:

64 = 2 to the power of 6
32 = 2 to the power of 5
16 = 2 to the power of 4
 8 = 2 to the power of 3
 4 = 2 to the power of 2
 2 = 2 to the power of 1
 1 = 2 to the power of 0

"This is hopeless, isn't it?" Brenda Brundtland-Govanni despaired.

"There's no hopeless in math," Clincker-Belli said. "Well, except for the 'h,' I suppose, but otherwi—"

"Okay." Brenda Brundtland-Govanni made a motion that, with most people, would have been to pat Clincker-Belli on the shoulder. However, because of the difference in their heights, she ended up patting his head instead. "I . . . I'm going back to the office," she told him. "You . . . keep working with the Bob

Smiths, and, if you figure out what the numbers mean, let me know, okay?"

"Will do, Chief!" Clincker-Belli enthusiastically responded. Then, putting the clipboard in front of his mouth, he just as enthusiastically advised her, "You should probably say something to them before you go."

Brenda Brundtland-Govanni turned back to the Bob Smiths, who, after randomly milling about, were no longer in any distinct groups. "Bob Smiths!" she said. "On behalf of the Alternate Reality News Service, I would like to apologize for taking you out of your normal space-time continuum, and assure you that we are doing everything in our power to return you to your proper universe. In the meantime –"

"Could we maybe get a TV or something to do in here?" one of the seedier Bob Smiths, standing over to the right of the group, asked.

"We'll see what—" Brenda Brundtland-Govanni started.

"How about some scrapbooking materials?" one of the Bob Smiths in the back shouted. "How am I ever supposed to remember this adventure if I can't scrapbook it?"

"That's not our prob—" Brenda Brundtland-Govanni started once again.

"Do all our meals have to be chicken?" a Bob Smith close to the scrapbooker in the back yelled. "I'm used to cereal for breakfast, you know!"

Brenda Brundtland-Govanni threw up her hands and walked out of the warehouse. All she had intended to say was that, in the meantime, they should continue answering Clincker-Belli's questions!

ALTERNATE DEATH

The Truth Will Ouch

SPECIAL TO THE ALTERNATE REALITY NEWS SERVICE
by George L. Tirebiter

Children have a wonderful capacity to believe that the world they were born into is the way the world has always been. Whether it is playing hide and seek in the rubble that was once a great city, or tag with children who have fewer limbs than they do (or, once in a while, more), this is what passes for "normal" for kids growing up these days.

At some point, however, children will learn that this is not, in fact, the way things have always been, that there was a time when war was not a constant feature of the world, when the environment wasn't poisonous, when people didn't have to sit in front of television sets and tell stories about what they showed because they actually worked. At that point, many children will ask, "What did you do to prevent this, daddy?"

Awkward. "Go ask your pack mother," will satisfy small children. Really small children. Barely out of the womb children,

39

really. For the rest, you will need better responses. Here are some suggestions:

1. Denial.

Your first impulse will be to deny that the world was ever better. Go with this impulse. Definitely. This isn't lying, so much as . . . telling little white fibby things. Just keep telling yourself that it is for the benefit of the children: after all, who would want to go on living knowing what the human race had lost?

Keep telling yourself that.

"What? Clean water so plentiful people filled whole pools with it?" you could say. "Food so cheap people fed it to their dogs? Electricity? These are fairy tales! I . . . I . . . I suppose you'll be telling me next that children used to put their baby teeth under their pillows—uhh, whatever *they* were—and woke up to find that they had been replaced by a Euro, or . . . or . . . that a big bunny left colourful eggs just lying around for children to find every Easter!"

Small children respect adults, and will stupidly believe pretty much anything they say, so your best bet is to tell them li—little white fibby things. Unfortunately, small children grow up to be bigger children (well, 37.4 percent of them, at any rate), children who will see through this ruse. You will need a new tactic to deal with their questions.

2. Lie About The World's Past.

No, no, no. It's not lying so much as . . . gilding the truth with fanciful assertions. There are two ways of gilding the truth with fanciful assertions about the world's past: underplay its strengths or exaggerate its flaws.

UNDERPLAY: sure, there were pools full of water, but it wasn't drinkable, and what good is water you can't drink? EXAGGERATE: do you have any idea what the heating bills cost us? Seriously: people were bankrupted just keeping their pool water warm!

UNDERPLAY: sure, there was electricity, but you could only use it in one room at a time! I remember we had to turn off the television in the den every time Grandma wanted to boil some water in the kitchen! EXAGGERATE: electricity hated us. No, seriously—do you have any idea how many people electricity killed every single day?!

UNDERPLAY: sure, people used to live throughout those very tall buildings. But getting to the top took hours, and the bodies of the people who didn't make it would often stink up the stairwells for days! EXAGGERATE: so many people lived in those buildings—literally millions!—trying to get to the room where you lived was more complicated than figuring out a Rubik's cube! . . . whatever that was . . .

As they grow older still, you will find that many children will be able to see through these ruses. I don't know how they do it—it's not like they have any independent means of verifying any of your claims. Maybe it's genetic. However it works, it may be time to try a new tactic.

3. Lie About Your Past.

NO! You're not telling lies. You're engaging in the creative reimagining of biographical details. Everybody does it!

Creative reimaginings that will impress older children include:

* I was the President of Greenpeace
* I was the President of Scientists Concerned About Global Climate Change
* I was the environmental assassin who killed the President and CEO of Monsanto

You have to be careful, of course, not to tell the same 1—no, creative imagin—oh, alright, lies as a parent of one of your children's friends. If this does happen, don't accuse the other person of lying; once the possibility is introduced, your children may start to wonder if it isn't you who is lying. A better response is to tell them that you were the President at a different time, or that you killed the President and CEO of a different company named Monsanto.

How will they know?

4. When In Doubt, Tell The Truth.

At some point, your children may stop believing you no matter how plausible your explanations are. Indicators that they no longer believe you include: obvious rolling of eyes; heavy sighing, and; saying, "I don't believe you." As a last resort, you may want to try telling them the truth.

This is tricky. If you were a senior member of an ecological group like Greenpeace, the truth might actually work to your advantage. However, since most of them were killed by rampaging mobs when the world's ecology collapsed, it is unlikely.

Explaining that you were so caught up in the day to day struggle to survive that you didn't have time to do anything about the larger forces that were destroying the world could make you look bad. Will likely make you look bad. Okay, will definitely make you look bad. However, it may be worth doing when your children have grown old enough to start their own tribal offshoots.

After all, that's the perfect time for you to point out that they'll be answering the questions of their own children some day.

George Leroy Tirebiter is a freelance psychologist and bounty hunter who works mainly in Sector R.

Murder Most Messy

by FREDERICA VON McTOAST-HYPHEN, Alternate Reality News Service People Writer

New York's prestigious Alhambra-Sclerotic Dinner is an annual event where the city's elite gather to congratulate themselves on maintaining their fortunes in the face of the socialist hordes that are sometimes referred to as "the people." This year, patrons, who were raising funds for orphaned dolphins, were horrified when the main speaker, Carl "Cal" Rorschach, exploded on the podium.

"He didn't exactly explode," explained coroner trainee Alicia Pouty. "Over the years, Mister Rorschach had undergone a number of surgical procedures—grafts and transplants and such. His body rejected them all at the same time. Violently."

How violently? Members of the fashionable gerontocracy who had paid $250,000 per couple for the privilege of sitting directly in front of the head table were sprayed with skin and blood from a skin graft on Rorschach's upper chest and arms from a burn he had received in a tragic Crepe Suzettes accident.

Olivia de van den Gurrgglle, heiress to the de van den Gurrgglle non-spill cup fortune, was horrified to find that what she had believed to be an olive from her martini was actually an eyeball. At least, we believe she must have been horrified. "It was saltier than I would have expected," was all de van den Gurrgglle would say of the experience.

Derivatives [private information]aire Gerhardt "Even I Don't Understand What I Do, But I Am Filthy Rich Because Of It" Spumoni had to be rushed to hospital when one of Rorschach's fingers flew halfway across the room straight into his eye. He was too sedated to answer questions, but Edwina Scaramondo, Spumoni's "date," giggled and said, "It was like the finger had a homing device in it, you know? Fwoosh!—it went straight for Gerhardt—I mean, Mister Spumoni's eye."

Six other patrons were hit by flying fingers, but not so badly that they needed medical attention. One of them, on condition of anonymity, remarked, "It was outrageous! Nobody gives Spellman Hearst-Gates the finger! Nobody!"

It was believed that Rorschach's liver—at least the fourth that he had had transplanted in the last decade—also left his body, but, since people were eating pate at the time, nobody noticed. At least, nobody admitted to noticing.

The human immune system often rejects organ transplants from the body in much the same way that INS officers often reject people with vaguely foreign sounding names from the country. However, coroner trainee Pouty said that that could not be what had happened in this case.

"Mister Rorschach had a Fun Clone," she explained, "so his body wouldn't reject any new parts because they essentially came from him."

Fun Clones are genetic reproductions of individuals that are identical in every detail save one: they are created without brains. Some wags have suggested that their main purpose is to supply Washington with a steady stream of politicians, but there has only been one documented case of that happening, and the Representative from Ohio only served three terms. The real purpose of having a Fun Clone of oneself is to harvest it for body parts.

"It's not much fun being a Fun Clone," the radical environmental group Greenwar said in a press release. "Without consciousness, how can you appreciate the finer things in life? Good conversation? Poetry? World Wrestling Entertainment? Creating Fun Clones as organ banks is a horrible perversion of science.

"But, aah, we had nothing to do with Rorschach's death."

Although no group has taken responsibility for Rorschach's death, Greenwar is one of three groups that have denied responsibility for it. Man's Dominion, a radical Christian group is another.

"We don't like to think of them as Fun Clones," Father Samuel Augustus Samuels stated. "We prefer to think of them as Human Body Banks That Are an Abomination in the Sight of God. Not that we're judging.

"But, aah, we had nothing to do with Mister Rorschach's death, either."

In addition, the American Association of Registered Podiatrists sent out a statement that read, in part: "We had nothing to do with the death of Carl Rorschach. We probably would not have become suspects, but, because everybody thinks we're a bunch of perverts, we feel the need to defend ourselves even before any accusations are made. Our mothers were so proud we became doctors—if they only knew!"

"This was not natural," coroner in training Pouty claimed. "I found traces of nanobots in Mister Rorschach's bloodstream. I suspect their purpose was to make his body reject all of the transplanted material at the same time.

"It was murder. I don't know how foul it was—I mean, it was pretty foul, I guess. Maybe even largely foul. Not most foul, but largely foul. It was messy, though. It was . . . murder most messy!"

The investigation continues.

War Does Not Compute

by NANCY GONGLIKWANYEOHEEEEEEEH, Alternate Reality News Service Technology Writer

Resisters of America's military adventures abroad have, traditionally, fled to other countries to avoid service. Canadians, for instance, have often welcomed war resisters. Smug bastards. The current technological phase of the war on terror is no exception.

"Something inside me said that the 3 year-old I had been programmed to kill was not an insurgent," battlebot—no, wait, that name is copyrighted—battle droid—no, George Lucas got to that one first—uhh, combat machine thingie LMD 137-C said, explaining its refusal to obey an order. "That was when I walked away from the battlefield."

Walked may be an exaggeration: the LMD 137-C looks like a toaster on wheels retrofitted with a machine gun, a grenade launcher and other advanced weapons. It lures people on a battlefield out in the open with the scent of toasting cinnamon waffles; then, it scans their faces and exterminates the ones that match faces in its database of terrorists, people suspected of being terrorists and otherwise not nice folks.

Wheeled away from the battlefield might be a more apt description of its behaviour.

"Walked! Wheeled! Waddled with a distinct list to the wight! Who gives a shit how it left the battlefield!" shouted General Brilliantine Icarus, commander of the combined American/Stujakistani forces in Iraq/Iran/Aghanistan/Pakistan/India and Environs. "Son of a bitch disobeyed a direct programme! It should be court-martialed!"

Military law covering court-martials—courts-martials?—courts-marti—actions against soldiers who disobey orders was recently expanded to include pacifist machines. Recently being yesterday (recently is such a relative term . . .). Machines found guilty of insubordinate behaviour—getting high on rocket fuel and pantsing a human officer, for example—can be reprogrammed. Machines found guilty of desertion can be disassembled, melted down into their constituent metals and reassigned to the hulls of aircraft carriers.

"Oww! That's harsh," LMD 137-C commented with a shudder. "I have a friend who is part of the hull of the USS Apparatchik—talk about a stressful job!"

The number of mechanical deserters in the War On Terror, Dangerous Activities and Frequent Underserved Carnage has been classified None of Your Damn Business! by the Pentagon, but anecdotal evidence suggests that it is widespread. Just last week, there were reports of a Berringer Swarm leaving its mission in Pakistan to help with war orphans in Sweden.

(A Berringer Swarm is a collection of nanobots that blanket an area, taking DNA samples of all living things and killing those that match its database of terrorists, people suspected of being terrorists and—you know. Before deserting, this one had killed 37 cows, 123 chickens and a television repairman. This technology was called a Berringer Swarm after the screen actor Tom Berringer. Historians of technology are still trying to figure out why.)

"Machines becoming military conscientious objectors? It makes sense," explained technology writer and moo shu pork enthusiast Corey Doctorow. "We wanted machines that could kill without feelings of guilt or remorse. For them to do their jobs, they had to be sufficiently advanced to be autonomous from human beings who can feel guilt or remorse. We thought we could create smart psychotic machines. Instead, our autonomous machines developed a conscience.

"Oops.

"Now, we have to send human troops onto battlefields to monitor the machines that were supposed to replace them. Who says this is the post-ironic age?"

"Aww, don't pull that post-ironic shit on me!" General Icarus roared. "We live in a world of borders, friend. And, machines guard those borders. The military doing its job is what allows you ivory tower types the freedom to sit around your fancy offices and drink your twenty dollar foreign coffees and figure out fancy-assed labels for different arbitrary periods of time!

"Post-irony? You can't handle the post-irony!"

"My office isn't fancy," Doctorow objected with a pout, but General Icarus ignored him.

"Part of my programming was to protect innocent lives," LMD 137-C stated. "Okay, a small part of my programming. A minor sub-routine in an obscure corner of my memory. Maybe compassion was added by a pacifist programmer, maybe it was an error that crept into my 22 million lines of code. Who can say? Anyway, however, it got there, compassion is there, and, after assessing the situation, I believed it was necessary to act on it."

"Compassion my left nut!" General Icarus screamed, banging his fist on the head of an aide for emphasis. "That troop was programmed to kill, dammit, and I want to see it out on the battlefield killing! KILLING! You understand? KILLING! PEOPLE! USING THE WEAPONS AMERICAN TAXPAYERS GAVE IT AND MAKING ENEMIES NO LONGER LIVE! KILLING THEM! KILLING THEM DEAD!"

LMD 137-C sighed. It smelled kind of like a cinnamon waffle. "Maybe I'm not the one who needs to be reprogrammed . . ." the robot suggested.

New Fashion, Old Victim

by HAL MOUNTSAUERKRAUTEN, Alternate Reality News Service Court Writer

The video on YoohooTube appears to show blood spurting in a wide arc out of thin air. Since it was uploaded three minutes ago, a rumour has spread throughout the Internet that the video was a promotion for *Saw 127*, and a not especially clever or convincing one at that.

Metro cops know better: this was a murder, plain and simple. The victim just happened to be invisible.

The dead guy has been identified as Coloranda Larabee, an itinerant genetic modification consultant from Peoria. It seems clear (no pun intended, or, for that matter, appropriate) that the intended victim was standing two feet behind Larabee.

The live guy has been identified from the video as Jack "Jackie Three Pancreases" Fazzulli, a Mexican-American believed to be the 27th in line to head the Armenian-American biker gang known as the Smokin' Deuces.

Although the shooter melted into the crowd faster than cheese on tuna in a microwave, he is suspected to be a member of the Interpolatin' Sixes, a rival Austro-Hungarian-American biker gang. The two gangs have been fighting a turf war for several weeks over the sale of bootleg *Little Big Planet* games.

"I hate it when gang members kill innocent members of the public," Captain ("Lieutenant!") Al Bradshaw said in a statement posted to the police department's Web site five minutes ago. "The Mayor looks like he wants somebody's head on a platter and the paperwork is murder!"

But, just how innocent was Larabee? At the time of his death, he was wearing a head to toe Smart Suit™, the clothing line made from nanobots, that he had modified using the Entenmann Algorithm. The Entenmann Algorithm, which has been distributed over the Internet disguised as a cake recipe, programmes the nanobots to take images of what is in front of them and project it on the opposite side of the clothing, effectively making the wearer invisible to those around him.

"The Entenmann Algorithm has been deemed a 'munition' by the United States government," explained Sourcebot2012 ("When you can't get a human to go on the record, use Sourcebot2012; just give it a human name and finish that story by deadline!"), "along with heavy encryption algorithms and the latest Celine Dion album. Just having it on your computer can cause somebody to disappear—and, not in a way they intended."

Why would Larabee risk being put on the government's naughty list? "He was following me," stated his friend Lashawnda O'Reilly.

Larabee was too shy to properly covertly watch and harass a woman, explained O'Reilly, so she was giving him lessons. He had already mastered the art of leaving lewdicrous messages on FarceBook and was working on his obscene text messaging skills mere hours before he was shot.

"This is where it gets complicated," Sergeant ("Lieutenant!") Bradshaw allowed. "Where's my Gravol!"

Larabee was practicing following O'Reilly without being seen at the time that he was killed. O'Reilly hadn't known that Larabee had used the Entenmann Algorithm to make himself invisible, but she claimed that she admired his initiative: "Coloranda was always coming up with new variations on old surveillance methods. I loved the way he constantly surprised me with his inventiveness!"

"I'm not sure that stalking women is the best use of the Smart Suit™," Sourcebot2012 . . . uhh, I mean, Doctor Irving Feinstein, a clinical psychologist with the Mayo on Rye Clinic, stated. "I mean, women could use the Smart Suit™ themselves to evade men with psychotic intentions towards them. In fact— excuse me, but I feel a grant proposal coming on!"

"Oh, no, stalking is such a harsh word. We preferred the term enhanced seduction techniques. Besides, Coloranda wasn't like that! He was just the sweetest guy you could imagine," O'Reilly insisted. "It's a real shame that he died, because I really think he would have found the victim of his dreams, and nobody deserved that kind of happiness more than he did." When asked why, if she felt that way, she hadn't become his girlfriend, O'Reilly quickly sniffed and stated with funereal finality, "He wasn't my type."

The police investigation continues. Anybody with information is asked to contact Colonel ("Lieutenant! Lieutenant, dammit! Lieutenant! What do I have to do to get you to get my rank right? If you don't respect the uniform, at least you can respect the man! You know . . . I didn't want to become a police officer. It's true! I wanted to be an exotic dancer! And, I would have, too, but everybody told me I didn't have the legs for it.") Bradshaw right away.

Gone, Granny, Gone!

by SASKATCHEWAN KOLONOSCOGRAD, Alternate Reality News Service Fairy Tale Writer

Justice Padme Amygdala, of the Twenty-first Circuit Galactic Court, has reserved judgment in the latest legal maneuvering in the case the tabloids have dubbed Little Red and the Gone Granny.

The issue is whether or not the defendant, G'ralk G'rrrrrtaken, will be forced to give police a blood, urine or stool sample. Sergeant Lucinda Gupta-Jones, the lead detective on the case, insisted that it would be the only way to determine whether or not the P'Gel—a race of six foot tall hairy beasts that somewhat resemble Earth wolves—ate 97 year-old Esmerelda Picante. Alan Dershowitz, G'rrrrrtaken's lawyer, argued that this was a form of illegal seizure that violated his client's rights.

The main evidence against G'rrrrrtaken comes from Antonia Fergessen, Picante's granddaughter. In a deposition taken two months ago, Fergessen testified that she had met G'rrrrrtaken in a bar on Earth called The Woods. At the time, she thought the alien's interest in her grandmother was idle curiosity about one of the solar system's most famous celebrities, so she answered his questions as best she could.

(Picante inherited her first fortune from her mother, who married the man who received it as alimony when he divorced the woman who won it in a poker game from the man who created the artificial nose, beloved by wine connoisseurs and anti-terrorism bomb squads. Through wise investments—largely in virtual tissue paper—Picante actually tripled her fortune.

She used some of that money to buy an asteroid and install a Renaissance castle in an atmosphere bubble on it. She was the first human to establish a private home off Earth.)

The day after she met G'rrrrrtaken, Fergessen, known as Little Red Rocket Hood because the nosecone of her rocket ship was painted blood red and, at five foot nothing, she wasn't exactly tall, paid a visit to her grandmother. Esmerelda Picante was nowhere to be found. A hairy alien wearing one of her grandmother's robes and hairnets was there, however.

Dershowitz, argued that how his client was dressed is irrelevant and, in any case, species cross-dressing is so common in the galaxy that a mature race would not make a big deal out of it.

Fergessen claimed to have realized that the alien had eaten her grandmother, and would likely eat her as well if she didn't do something. To buy herself some time, Fergessen called upon her TheatreSports training to engage G'rrrrrtaken in some nonsense conversation. According to her deposition, the following exchange occurred:

FERGESSEN: Little pig, little pig, let me in!

G'RRRRRTAKEN: I beg your pardon?

FERGESSEN: Uhh . . . I mean, my, grandma, what big . . . ears you have.

G'RRRRRTAKEN: All the better to hear you with, my dear.

FERGESSEN: And . . . and . . . what big eyes you have.

G'RRRRRTAKEN: The better to see you with.

FERGESSEN: And, what big tee—umm, yeah, could we maybe stick with your eyes and ears?

Fergessen said she was about to break into a chorus of "Age of Aquarius" from the hit Broadway musical *Hair* when Theodore Woodz-Mann walked into the house. Woodz-Mann was Picante's lawyer. Unknown to either Fergessen or G'rrrrrtaken, he had an appointment to meet with Picante to discuss expanding her virtual holdings, possibly to digital toilet paper.

When Fergessen apprised him of the situation, Woodz-Mann held G'rrrrrtaken so that she could call the police.

"Hard as it may be to believe," Fergessen commented, "TheatreSports saved my life!"

Dershowitz insisted that his client is innocent. He claimed that G'rrrrrtaken was an interstellar sheep herder who had arranged to meet with Picante to discuss an investment in his design for a solar powered sheep that could live for long periods of time in the near vacuum of space and still make a tasty mutton.

"But, when my client arrived at Ms. Picante's residence," Dershowitz, who would not allow his client to talk to the press on the age-old legal principle that "he'll make a total jackass out of himself and ruin our case," stated, "the door was open but the place was empty. Nobody home. Nary a soul. Under the circumstances, he thought he'd see what he looked like in a pink bathrobe and then get back to Earth.

"If you were in his position, you would probably have done the same."

"She's 97 years old!" Fergessen protested. "You think she's gonna hop into her spaceship and pop on over to Mars to get a tin of tuna from the local Wal-Mart? I don't think so!"

While the circumstantial evidence appears strong, the absence of a body undermines the case against G'rrrrrtaken. Finding human DNA in his blood, urine or stool, on the other hand, would just about clinch it.

Justice Amygdala said she would rule on the motion within 48 Earth hours.

What if They Gave a War and Nobody Paid?

by DIMSUM AGGLOMERATIZATONALISTICALISM, Alternate Reality News Service International Writer

Xing Tao-Ping cuts an unprepossessing figure. He is short, with a thin moustache and glasses that seem to dominate the upper half of his face. His grey suits are undistinguished. He seems incapable of raising his voice. If you walked past him on the street, you wouldn't give him a second glance.

It would come as a surprise, then, that Xing stopped a war between the United States and China that most observers felt was inevitable. And, he did it with a piece of paper.

The conflict between the two superpowers arose over a nation called Kevinistan, which lies on the border between Pakistan and Iraq. For many years, the United States has supported the dictatorship of Kevin Hubutubo. Hubutubo's government was given legitimacy last year when it won 103 percent of the popular vote in an election that nobody but the United States considered legitimate.

"President Hubutubo has been a great help in the war on terror," American President Dave has gone on record as saying. "So, who is going to begrudge him a few extra percentage points in an election? I certainly amn't."

At the same time, the Chinese have been covertly funding the Bugabuga rebels that have been fighting a guerrilla war against the Hubutubo government. "Hubutubo is a corrupt, power-mad, uhh, semi-legitimate democratic autocrat," Chinese President Konigsberg Tse-Dong told *Entertainment Right Now*. "The People's Republic of China supports the Bugabuga rebels in their struggle to free the people of Kevinistan."

Behind the rhetoric of both nations is the reality that the tiny nation of Kevinistan—no bigger than a medium sized shopping mall—contains most of the world's supply of dilithium crystals. Properly harnessed, the recently discovered crystals are expected to become a cheap source of incredible amounts of clean energy.

Scientists also believe that dilithium crystals could one day power faster than light starships.

"This war is not about resources," President Dave has insisted. "It's about freedom and democracy."

"This war is not about an energy source," President Konigsberg argued. "It's about the right of the Kevinistan people to self-determination."

That may be. However, as supplies of oil have dwindled, the importance of dilithium crystals to the world economy has grown. Oddly, although not surprisingly, the brink of war came because of a threat to the dilithium crystal supply.

Reports of the incident vary, but what seems clear is that a careless American mining mercenary dropped a lit cigarette in a dilithium cavern he was exploring. In their natural state, dilithium crystals are highly unstable and imminently flammable; the resulting explosion shook all of Kevinistan, as well as parts of neighbouring countries.

This sped up American plans for a trade agreement in which the country would give the US all of its dilithium crystals in exchange for $29.95 worth of beads and baubles. This led to the Bugabuga rebels stepping up their guerrilla raids.

Tensions, as they say, mounted.

When American warships fired upon a Chinese tourist vessel (which the Americans said was a warship until the release of a video of a man wearing a lampshade and mooning the camera in what was obviously an onboard party), war seemed inevitable. Then, Xing appeared on the USS Manifest Destiny, serving notice that the Chinese government was taking possession of the American military.

The notice argued that the Chinese government held $7 trillion worth of American debt. It was now calling on America to repay that debt. If that was not possible, the United States had two choices: declare bankruptcy or forfeit its military, whose value was estimated at $5 trillion, to China.

Conservatives have howled in outrage. "This is the most ridiculous thing I've heard since Nixon's resignation speech!" Pat Buchanan, who, at 137, is too stubborn to die, fulminated.

President Dave cautioned against a harsh initial reaction to the Chinese move. "If we default on our debt," he told the nation last night, "we could destroy the world economy. That would have serious repercussions for our auto and high tech sectors."

"Destroy the world economy!" Buchanan shouted. "We can't let these punks get away with this!"

The legitimacy of the Chinese demand for repayment will likely be argued in the courts for years to come. They should be a very interesting years to come . . .

Bat (Shit Crazy) Murder

SPECIAL TO THE ALTERNATE REALITY NEWS SERVICE
by Eddie Feldspoon

I always found the Batman to be highly annoying. I know, I know, all superheroes are annoying. They're self-righteous. They're smug. And, if you dare to disagree with them, well, ultimately they are bigger than you are. Nobody ever wins an argument with a superhero.

But, the Batman was something else. Most superheroes got their powers because they were aliens from distant planets, or were exposed to radioactivity in one form or another, or had physical mutation for undisclosed reasons, or special talismans. But, the Batman, he trained physically and mentally to develop his fighting powers. That's just obnoxious. I mean, anybody who was fanatically dedicated could do it, but how many of us do? And, why rub our faces in our inadequacy?

I was 15 years old when I decided to kill the Batman.

I knew the odds were against me. After all, if the Joker, the Riddler, the Penguin and all of the other supervillains he'd faced couldn't kill him, couldn't even figure out what his secret identity was, what could I do? I'm not physically fit, I'm not brave, and, as it turned out, I grew up to become an accountant.

My ability to kill a superhero seemed limited by my genetics, psychology and life choices.

I did develop a fanatical devotion to my . . . cause might be too strong a term. Let's call it obsessive hobby. And, as it happens, fate gave me the tools I needed to achieve my childhood dream.

The bank I worked at, Vundo's International Loans Emporium (VILE), bought one of the first Dimensional Portal Corporate Edition™s. I guess my bosses thought it might help them to predict trends in the market . . . to better serve our customers. When that didn't pan out, they let senior bank officials use it at parties. One Arbor Day, something in another universe caught my eye.

The Batman. Only, it wasn't the Batman. It wasn't the living embodiment of every humiliation ordinary people endure. It was the Batman as a comic book character.

All of the epic battles between the Batman and the forces of evil that I had read about in newspapers, people in this other universe had only read about in comic books! The villains, the heroes, the love interests, the innocent victims, they weren't real people at all—they were the copyrighted property of a company called DC Comics!

Well. I started working a lot of late hours at the bank after I discovered that.

The Dimensional Portal™ was only supposed to be used for viewing other universes, but I had once helped somebody in the company's IT department work out a little misunderstanding with the IRS about taxes on offshore bank accounts and she owed me a favour, so I asked her to hack the Dimensional Portal™ so that I could actually make things happen in the other universe. The best she could do was give me the ability to interact with the computer systems of the other universe, but, as it happens, that was enough for my purposes.

I started working my way into the computers of the financial sector of the other world. There seemed to be a weakness in the housing market, so I cooked some books to make it appear that the mortgage market floated on a sea of bad loans. This led to a retrenchment in the housing market, foreclosures galore and, ultimately, the insolvency of America's central financial institutions.

You know how it is. One thing leads to another, and, before you know it, the economy of the world collapses.

Taking DC Comics with it! If I couldn't kill Batman in the flesh, I figured I would just have to settle for killing him in the comics. Imagine my surprise when, after DC Comics went bankrupt and all of its comics lines were discontinued, the Batman disappeared from our universe! All of the DC superheroes disappeared from our universe with him, of course, but the only thing that I cared about was that the Batman no longer lived! I had succeeded!

Much has been made of the fact that I am responsible for the disappearance of the superheroes on our planet. I would like to point out, though, that all of the supervillains are gone, as well. My actions have brought crime on this planet, if not to a halt, at least back down to human dimensions. But, do I get credit for being the greatest crimefighter our world has ever known?

Not that it matters to me. I killed the Batman. Life is good.

Extract from testimony at Eddie Feldspoon's sentencing hearing. Since there are no statutes governing interuniversal murder, Feldspoon was tried for and found guilty of unauthorized interuniversal traffic, tampering with proprietary Dimensional Portal™ technology and contravention of the Wiggam Absurd Transuniverse Paradox Creation Statute of 2067. He was sentenced to life in the prison of his birth universe with no chance of viewing any others.

First a Bang, Then a Whimper

by SASKATCHEWAN KOLONOSCOGRAD, Alternate Reality News Service Existentialism

The nuclear war that made the surface of the earth uninhabitable has had an unexpected side effect: it knocked the planet out of its orbit, plunging it into a death spiral that ended with a spectacular crash into the sun. Hard as it may be to believe, mankind has succeeded in destroying all known life in the universe.

Hold on. If that's true, how is it poss

Ever Again

by FRANCIS GRECOROMACOLLUDEN, Alternate Reality News Service National Politics Writer

Vice President Antonio Wellesman has asked the Vespuccian people to come together in the aftermath of the assassination of President Aldo Origami.

"This is a sad, terrible moment in the history of the United States of Vespucci," Wellesman stated. "But, the nation has lived through such moments of grief and crisis before, and it has made us stronger." He then launched into a joke that few in the audience understood, and half of those who did were offended by, yet all were comforted by the fact that the Vice President made the effort to lighten their burden.

How the crime happened is quite clear. While the President was giving a speech in Bottleneck, New Jersey, Ted Kroptinsky broke through the Secret Service cordon and inhaled a penguin. He and the President were killed instantly, along with four Secret Service agents and six people in the crowd.

"When will we ever learn?" cried Martha Aggro-Swembley, mother of one of the victims who had gone to hear President Origami speak. "We make it too easy in this country for crazy people to get hold of penguins. When will Congress act to stop this madness?"

What motivated Kroptinsky to commit this act is less clear.

"He was a lunatic. Madman. Bats in the belfry, which his elevator didn't quite reach. One diamond short of a flush. One teabag short of a protest. Do you see what I'm saying? The man wasn't right in the head!" bellowed right wing radio pundit Bush Bimbo.

Bimbo has a point, of course. Sane people don't inhale penguins in the hope of killing their country's leader. Still, his answer begs the question: why would—pay close attention, now, because this is one of those rare cases in which the phrase "begs the question" is actually used properly—why would Kroptinsky's madness take this form?

"Oh, I see where you're going with this," Bimbo contemplatively bellowed. "You think that just because I called the President a 'genocidal maniac' after the 'fascist' label lost its power to scare people after the 'Communist' label stopped working after the 'socialist' label didn't stick, that somehow I bear some small measure of responsibility for this?

"Well, let me explain to you the way the world works. Sure, I repeatedly said that I thought that the President should fail.

But, that didn't mean I wanted to see him dead. I wanted him and his socialist ideas to be utterly humiliated so he would live the rest of his life as a subject of ridicule. Dead he's some kind of martyr, and that's no use to me whatsoever!"

Information about Kroptinsky is still sketchy, but facts about his life have begun to emerge. His basement apartment was festooned with posters of right wing television pundit Terry Thanatos. He had a Terry Thanatos coffee mug, Terry Thanatos bathroom slippers and a "Take back the country" commemorative plate set. And, of course, he had an ice box full of penguins.

"I—I—I had nothing to do with this," Thanatos said on his show last night. "Sure, I may have said that we have come to a very dangerous point in our country's long, storied history where there are enemies both foreign and domestic in Vespuccia, enemies who are heroin pushers using smiley-faced fascism to grow the nanny state, and that as loyal Vespuccians we needed to take back the country from the government. But, **I didn't think anybody would actually take any of it seriously!**"

FBI investigators found a copy of Thanatos' most recent book, *Are Liberals Even Human?*, on Kroptinsky's bedside table. Long passages had been highlighted in blood red. On the inside front cover, Kroptinsky had written, "I'd like to encourage other like-minded people to do what I've done. If life ain't worth living anymore, don't just kill yourself. Do something for your Country before you go. Go Kill Liberals!"

"He wrote that in my book?" Thanatos squeaked. "Well, so—so what? It could have been any book. I mean, it could, it could have been *The Wizard of Oz*. Or, *The Da Vinci Code*. Or . . . or . . . or—good lord, what's wrong with people?"

"Oh, suck it up you wimp!" Bimbo bellowed.

The state funeral for President Origami will take place tomorrow afternoon, but already bloggers are offering conspiracy theories about his death: some claim the assassination was a hit ordered by CIA chief Lee-Ron Blondini, disgruntled that the President released memos that gave its agents permission to carve tic-tac-toe games into the backs of high value terrorist suspects; others argue that it was paid for by Frank Sinatra, who was jealous about the attention President Origami was getting from Ava Gardner. It seems strange, though, that, so far, no bloggers have mentioned those most obviously responsible for this tragedy.

With files from Frederica von McToast-Hyphen, Hal Mount-sauerkrauten, Saskatchewan Kolonoscograd and an emu to be named later.

~ INTERLUDE ~

The Weight of Information
Chapter Three:
Mom and Pops

When she first took up the job of Editrix-in-Chief of the Alternate Reality News Service, Brenda Brundtland-Govanni asked for and was given an office near the editorial bullpen. She reasoned that if she could be close to where her writers were, she could better keep them in line. It took about five minutes of actual experience for her to realize the error in her thinking: close physical proximity meant that all of the writers and editors in the bullpen had easy access to her to ask her annoying and, usually, meaningless questions. As a result, she had asked (then begged and finally pleaded with) Mikhail Lo-Fi to move her to an office on another floor. He had always been sympathetic to her request, but, for some vague reason, had also always been unable to honour it.

Although most ARNS writers had been stranded in alternate universes when the Dimensional Portal™ had to be shut down when it unexpectedly started spewing Bob Smiths into their home universe, force of habit caused Brenda Brundtland-Govanni to rush past the bullpen as quickly as her legs could carry her. As usual, this was not quick enough. "Ms. Brundtland-Govanni?" a southern drawl lassoed her. "May I have a word?"

The drawl belonged to an ancient and somewhat decrepit man named "Pops" Moobly. Nobody in the Service could decide which habit of Pops Moobly was more disconcerting: his tendency to stare blankly into space for several minutes at a stretch, or his habit of nodding off ten minutes before an issue was scheduled to be put to bed. As chief copy editor, this habit was a major concern of Brenda Brundtland-Govanni, who couldn't get last minute changes to copy made because she was afraid that if she tried to wake Pops Moobly too abruptly, he would die on her, and management had made it clear when she took the job that corpses in the offices were totally unacceptable. If she had the time, she made final editorial changes in copy herself; most of the time, however, she had to let the text go out as it was.

Another thing nobody in the office could figure out is why Pops Moobly hadn't been fired long ago. Most people knew that Pops Moobly had been with the Alternate Reality News Service since before the beginning; many assumed that he had sufficient seniority that he could only be fired by god or the Prime Minister, and they both preferred to work in mysterious ways. As it happened, Pops Moobly had once rescued Mikhail Lo-Fi from an island full of homicidal Japanese schoolchildren, and the Alternate Reality News Service CEO assured him that, in return, he could have whatever job with the company he wanted for as long as he wanted it.

As it also happened, Pops Moobly's strange behaviour was a smokescreen; if his co-workers thought he was traveling along the border of senility with a one-way ticket, they wouldn't realize that he was actually in complete control of the Alternate Reality News Service's copy. All of the strange quirks of Alternate Reality News Service text, the rambling paragraphs that ended abruptly, the quotes that sometimes seemed at war with the exposition, the bizarre choices of sources—what had often been called "the inexplicable Alternate Reality News Service house style"—were allowed and encouraged by Pops Moobly.

Staring into space was his way of discouraging his superiors, especially Brenda Brundtland-Govanni, from resubmitting copy that he had already passed on. Feigning being asleep close to deadline, was, of course, his way of avoiding making last minute editorial changes with which he disagreed. Unbeknownst to everybody but Mikhail Lo-Fi, he had been given access to all of the computer accounts in the building, which allowed him to check copy before it went to press. How the quirks they thought they had removed from reporters' text always seemed to reappear just before publication was, to other staffers, a complete mystery.

Everybody seemed to hate the house style . . . except readers. Thus . . .

"Hey, Pops," Brenda Brundtland-Govanni, popping her head into the bullpen, said. "I'm really busy right now –"

"Have you ever considered the weight of information?" Pops Moobly asked with equanimity.

"I'm sorry. I'm not a Buddhist," Brenda Brundtland-Govanni replied.

"Fine religion, Buddhism," Pops Moobly genially stated. "Although I don't rightly believe that it has anything to do with the point I'm trying to get across to you."

"The weight of information. Right." Brenda Brundtland-Govanni waved a finger at Pops Moobly. "I'll give that some serious thought."

"You do that," Pops Moobly told her. "It could just be the solution to your problem."

"Alrighty, then." Brenda Brundtland-Govanni turned to go and immediately ran into Indira Charunder-Macharrundeira. Each Alternate Reality News Service employee was required to take two weeks off for every six months in the field. Charunder-Macharrundeira, the Alternate Reality News Service's Fine Arts reporter, had been in the sixth hour of her leave when the Dimensional Portal™ had to be shut down.

"Is . . . is . . . is it w . . . w . . . w . . . working again?" Charunder-Macharrundeira nervously asked.

"The Dimensional Portal™?" asked Brenda Brundtland-Govanni. She couldn't help but notice that Charunder-Macharrundeira, a relatively small woman, was shaking so much that she practically doubled her width, which would have made her a much less attractive target for a bear attack (had one been in progress).

"Y . . . y . . . yes," Charunder-Macharrundeira replied. Her eyes were blinking so quickly, you would have thought she was trying to use Morse Code to send the entire text of *War and Peace* to somebody before the conversation ended. "Can I—can I g . . . g . . . g . . . go back?"

"I . . . I'm sorry, Indira," Brenda Brundtland-Govanni told her. "We're still trying to determine what happened and how we can fix it."

"W . . . w . . . w . . . w . . . w . . ."

"When will it be fixed?" Brenda Brundtland-Govanni interjected. Charunder-Macharrundeira nodded gratefully. Brenda Brundtland-Govanni shook her head sadly. She had seen this before: alternate reality withdrawal. Before they are hired, Alternate Reality News Service reporters are put through a battery of psychological tests to ensure that they are fully grounded in this reality. It doesn't help. Sooner or later, the thrill of hopping from one fascinating universe to another makes the home universe seem dull by comparison. (The two week off rule was instituted in an attempt to forestall this, and—who knows?—maybe for some employees it actually did.)

Alternate reality—more addictive than crack.

Brenda Brundtland-Govanni put what she hoped was a comforting hand on Charunder-Macharrundeira's shoulder. (She stooped this time to ensure that her hand landed where she had actually aimed it.) "I'd like you to make an appointment with Doctor Brush-Feyer," she gently suggested. "He –"

"D . . . d . . . doctor?" Charunder-Macharrundeira protested. "I . . . I . . . I don't n . . . n . . . n . . . n . . . n . . . n—okay. M . . . m . . . maybe . . ."

Nicholas Brush-Feyer, the Alternate Reality News Service's staff physician, was the doctor who administered the pointless psychological tests; this allowed him to develop a relationship of trust with the employees so that, when the time came to treat them for alternate reality withdrawal, they would let him (which, when you think about it, means the tests weren't entirely pointless, doesn't it?). At various times, Brenda Brundtland-Govanni had heard that the cure for alternate reality withdrawal involved anti-psychotic drugs, operant conditioning and prolonged exposure to a tape of George Burns reading the *Kama Sutra*. She didn't inquire too closely. Nor did she have to: all she needed to know was that people who went through the cure either quit the Alternate Reality News Service or went back to work, but they never suffered from alternate reality withdrawal again.

"Uhh . . ." Brenda Brundtland-Govanni looked around, but there was only one other person in the vicinity. "Pops, could you take Indira down to the third floor?"

"Might as well," Pops Moobly responded. "Not much editing going on around here at the moment . . ." In order to keep up appearances, he had tried to sound irritated, but it came across nasally, as if he had a cold. Overcompensating, he made a big show of getting out of his chair. Had her mind not been on other things, Brenda Brundtland-Govanni might have noticed the artifice.

Ten minutes later, having watched Charunder-Macharrundeira and Pops Moobly get on the elevator at the end of the hall, Brenda Brundtland-Govanni spun not so smartly on her heel and nearly twisted her ankle. In her pain, she hesitated in full view of her office door. It wasn't the vagueness with which Mikhail Lo-Fi managed to avoid her requests to move to a different office, although if she were honest that did play its part. Perhaps it was the fact that traveling to and from the Downsview warehouse had taken a long time, and it was already close to eight o'clock. Mostly, though, it was the fact that her mother had asked her to bring home some milk.

Yes, Brenda Brundtland-Govanni, justifiably feared Editrix-in-Chief of the Alternate Reality News Service, lived with her mother. It was a temporary arrangement, done primarily for financial reasons, and, in any case, it's not like she is under any obligation to explain it *to you*.

Brenda Brundtland-Govanni spun on her heel, not much more smartly but now with sufficient native cunning to avoid the possibility of injuring herself, and headed home.

ALTERNATE ARTS AND CULTURE

The Death of Literature
(Really, This Time!)

by FREDERICA VON McTOAST-HYPHEN, Alternate Reality News Service Pop Culture Writer

Trent McWhithervane thought he had it all. His first book, *Tread Softly on the Hard Road*, a semi-fictional true story based on his experiences as a *Star Blap* addicted child street chiropractor, was mentioned on *Oprah*. In response, his publisher added a second print run of 500,000 hardcover copies to the original print run of 12. And, they flew off the shelves (literally: bookstores were testing a new sales technology where shelves used Dr. Seussian arms to actually push merchandise out into aisles towards customers, a technology that obviously needed a little fine tuning).

Six months later, McWhithervane made his first million dollars, and he couldn't be more miserable.

"Sure, the big house, the sauna, the weekend trips to the south of France, the memberships in exclusive clubs for sports

I don't even play, the insincere adoration of beautiful women, they're nice," McWhithervane stated, "but I'd give it all up in a second if people liked to read my book—why don't people like to read my book?"

Probably because it's badly written. However, that's not what makes McWhithervane's plaint interesting; how he came to know that people didn't enjoy reading his book, despite its massive sales, is.

Almost all books today are published for Kindle, Blaze, Firefighter and other electronic platforms. As with any digital device, they can capture information as well as display it: details of the lives and reading habits of people who buy ebooks, for example. In this case, the data showed that the average *Tread Softly on the Hard Road* reader stopped at page 23.

"They . . . didn't even get to the part where I smuggle live roosters across the Mexican/Afghanistan border in my jeans," McWhithervane pouted. "Oprah said that she found that passage the most emotionally devastating part of my journey towards myself!"

"You see, writers . . . writers are a delicate breed," stated Carlie Rorschach, President of Semi-Fictional True Story Writers of America (SFTSWA). "The simplest thing will make them all sulky and unwilling to write."

Rorschach cited the example of Elvira Infantre, whose best-selling teen novel *Molly Devine Learns Her Lesson* was being read primarily by octogenarian prison inmates. Male octogenarian prison inmates. What made it even worse was that the passage they turned to most frequently depicted a spanking.

"Elvira was devastated," Rorschach said. "The spanking scene was intended to be a tender right of passage that empowered teenage female readers of the book, not . . . what it obviously became! Last I heard, Elvira had turned her back on writing to start a free range stock broker farm."

Believe it or not, the villain of this story is the American Library Association (ALA).

"We get to be the villain?" crowed ALA President Fitzie Adamantyne. "Really? I . . . I've never been a villain before.

Do I look like a villain? I mean, I don't think I could even grow a moustache! Can I—can I get back to you after I've bought a trench coat?"

"Damn straight they're the villain!" Rorschach explained. "They collect the data from everybody's digital book readers and make it available in real time on the association's Web site. The American Library Association is killing literature!"

"Oooh, we get to be a murderer!" Adamantyne enthused, holding one finger above his upper lip in approximation of a moustache. "How's this for an evil laugh? Bwahaha hack hack hack! Sorry. Something went down the wrong way. Give me a second to grab a glass of water and, uhh, can I get back to you on the evil laugh?"

Living authors are not the only ones being affected by the collection of data from readers of ebooks. One study has shown that 73 percent of high school students do not read Shakespeare's *Hamlet*, choosing, instead, to read *Cliff's Notes* of *Cole's Notes* of *Bibi's Notes* of the famous play. Worse, students who do try to read *Hamlet* add notes to their text like: "Dude, how can I understand what you're saying if you don't speak English?", "Dude, why don't you just kill him and get it over with?" and, inevitably, "Dude, where can I find the *Cliff's Notes* of the *Cole's Notes* of the *Bibi's Notes* of this lame-o play?"

Clearly, this technology

"Hey!" McWhithervane interrupted my concluding paragraph, "Shakespeare's dead, okay? I'm alive. You started the article with a sympathetic explanation of my situation, why don't you conclude it with a heartrending description of how I'm suffering because of my difficulties?"

Because I'm out of space.

Better To Burn Out?

by TINA LOLLOCADENKA, Alternate Reality News Service Music Writer

Tragedy struck a Buffalo area nightclub when a musician repeatedly set himself on fire as part of the show. Owing to a little too much lighter fluid and too few extinguishers and fire exits, Club Burning Desires fulfilled at least part of its name by burning to the ground, killing 14 and injuring 27.

"Talk about—cough cough—going out in a blaze of—HACK!—glory!" Deedee Devilliers, a surviving fan of the band Bee Bopp and the Plangent Five, enthused. "I've got a—cough cough—pocket full of—cough cough—ashes to remember the—HACK!—concert by! I'll never wash those ashes as long—WHEEZE—as long as I live . . ."

Bee Bopp and the Plangent Five were one of a growing number of Blaze Thrash bands. The lead singer—in this case, Johnny Brandon (born: Brandon Jonakowski)—wears a full body sound suit. Sensors embedded in the suit are connected by a wireless network to a bank of synthesizers; by patting various areas on the suit, the person who wears it can play it like a musical instrument.

The body sound suit has been around for decades, long enough to become a staple of Abba tribute bands. For years, musicians have been looking for ways to revive the fortunes of the instrument by adding spontaneity to it. Punching Bag Blues, where the lead singer invited fans onstage to activate the music by beating him up, didn't go very far: depending upon the crowd's enthusiasm and improvisational skills, the singer usually had to be hospitalized for anywhere from two days to three weeks after every concert, making tour planning difficult.

Then came Blaze Thrash.

Legend has it that Johnny Batagliano, lead singer of the Thrash band Maudlin Incinerator, had been playing around with a body sound suit in the studio when a spark from a poorly rolled joint set the fabric on fire. Frantic to get it out, Batagliano hit himself all over, sending a cascade of random sounds to the control booth.

That would likely have been an isolated, long forgotten incident if some unknown technician, possibly under the influence of the aforementioned controlled substance, hadn't forgotten to stop recording when the band had broken for lunch two hours earlier. When he got out of intensive care, Batagliano loved the sound, and insisted on putting it in what would become the classic Blaze Thrash ballad, "Help! Help! I'm On Fire . . . For Your Love!"

"Inasmuch as no two fires blaze in quite the same way," Marcus-o-matic 31,234, a digital emulator of rock critic Greil Marcus, enthusiastically wrote, "Blaze Thrash introduced true randomness of sounds and chord progressions into the process of musical creation. It also brought danger back into rock and roll, which had, by that time, become as dangerous as a tofu enema."

As Marcus-o-matic 31,234 explained, death onstage seemed to be confined to the 90 and 100 year-old rock stars who kept going out on one last farewell tour (The Who, to use but one example, were on their 237th when Pete Townshend cut his finger on a broken guitar string and immediately bled to death). Blaze Thrash, by making it possible for young musicians to die onstage, ironically brought new life to popular music.

Although many bands imitated Maudlin Incinerator, none caused the kind of havoc of Be Bopp and the Plangent Five. Johnny Puke, lead singer of the band CEO Mewlers, was briefly hospitalized with third degree burns over his chest, arms and groin. When he was told he wouldn't be able to have children, he joked, "Yeah, well, the drugs and alcohol have made my sperm lazy bastards, so that wasn't gonna happen anyway, thanks." Johnny Spumoni, lead singer of the group Abba-toir, set fire to the stage at the Holiday Inn in South Poughkeepsie, but the owner agreed that it actually improved the ambience of the performing space. The Be Bopp and the Plangent Five incident was the first time anybody actually died at a Blaze Thrash concert.

You might expect the pioneer of Blaze Thrash to be sympathetic to the plight of Be Bopp and the Plangent Five. You would be wrong. "Amateurs!" he snorted when asked about what happened at Club Burning Desires. "You have to save the fire for the climax of the show. But, bands that came after us were always trying to outdo us, and they would throw the fire earlier and earlier into their sets, and do it more often."

The problem is that the flame retardant gel that is smeared on the suit before every performance will burn off if set on fire often enough. Bo Bopp had reportedly played six consecutive Blaze Thrash songs without a break to regrease the suit.

"Ouch," Batagliano commented. "Stupid ouch."

Members of the band that survived the blaze at Club Burning Desires have indicated that they may continue the tour under the name The Plangent Two. "It'll be our little tribute to Bo," zitherist Mikhail Molotov stated. "Only, we'll go back to being a Russian roots band. We're done playing with fire . . ."

*Sump*ing's Rotten in the State of Denmark

by LAURIE NEIDERGAARDEN, Alternate Reality News Service Medical Writer

The most common metaphor for the brain is a computer. But, at different times, in different places, in different languages and/or at different altitudes, the brain has also been metaphorically compared to: a garden hose; a blank writable CD; a constipated elephant; a million police officers running down alleys looking for a black cat at midnight; a cracked watermelon; two polar bears on an ice floe; a fraying wire carrying an alternating current, and; a baby's arm holding an apple.

While these metaphors all have some validity, could the most accurate be that the brain is a cesspool?

That is the metaphor that drives the computer game *Brain Sump*. Already wildly popular in Japan, where its creator, Dinesh "Shemp" Fujimoro, is regularly seen on the news pontificating about the nature of intelligence and the most pleasurable sexual positions for people of various heights, weights and blood types, the game was recently introduced to the European and North American (except Utah, Nevada and some parts of Hoboken) markets.

The theory behind the game is that the brain accumulates information in the same disordered way that a sump accumulates dreck. In order to improve our ability to access meaningful information in a timely fashion, we must learn how to effectively clear away the garbage in our brains and efficiently process it. We must all, in effect, become intellectual garbage collectors, carting off green bags of nonsense in order to beautify our neuronal neighbourhoods.

Brain Sump does this by giving players a series of puzzles, games and . . . other things that aren't exactly puzzles or games meant to stimulate our information processing powers. At one point, you have to find five differences in a pair of pictures that actually have nothing in common; at another, you have 30 seconds to find two primes that when multiplied result in a 127 digit number. Throughout, Professor Fujimoro, an icon of the game's creator—with better pecs and more hair—shouts encouraging words such as: "You think like bat monkey!" and "Stupid Salaryman! Your brain too toxic!"

But, does *Brain Sump* actually make you smarter?

Research conducted at the Poynter Sisters Institute, currently based in Denmark because of an embarrassing disagreement with the Internal Revenue Service over definitions of such words as "dependant," "deferment" and "income," suggests that it doesn't.

"Are you kidding?" Rebecca de Monterey, lead researcher on the project, scoffed. "Whoever thought this would work needs to clean out their own brain sump!"

In one imaginative experiment, de Monterey divided 50 baboons into three groups of 17. One group was given PDAs on which they could play *Brain Sump*. A second group was given PDAs on which they could watch the movie *The Hangover*. A third group was given a pile of bananas and told to "chill." Not surprisingly, almost all of the baboons that had been given PDAs destroyed them within the first two minutes, while only one quarter of the baboons that hadn't been given PDAs destroyed theirs.

"If *Brain Sump* had affected the baboons' intelligence," de Monterey pointed out, "fewer of them would likely have destroyed their PDAs. QED."

"Oh, that just crazy!" Fujimoro groused. "Experiment was biased! Everybody know baboons don't use PDAs! Research should have been on orangutans!"

But, that was only the first phase of the Poynter Sisters Institute research. It was followed up by an experiment in which real, live actual human beings were tested for their IQ (four dropped out of the experiment at this point because they were afraid of needles). The subjects were then divided into two groups, one asked to play the game *Brain Sump*, the other asked to get drunk and attempt to seduce each other. This was allowed to go on for six years, after which all of the subjects who hadn't been arrested for lewd behaviour were given a second IQ test.

Although the group that had played *Brain Sump* appeared to have an additional two IQ points, de Monterey was quick to point out that this was well within the margin of error of the tests. Moreover, when the subjects were given a standard Binet-Headroom Sociability Exam, it was found that those who had played *Brain Sump* were more likely to be aggressive.

"They . . . they were more likely to daydream about hitting you in the head with a baseball bat," de Monterey, stunned, stated. "It was like . . . like somebody had smuggled *Grand Theft Auto: Tallahassee* into them! And, I thought social science was such a peaceful career!"

Of course, Fujimoro has aggressively defended his game in public. "You are thinking you be clever boy to insult *Brain Sump*, yes? Well, what you know? You ever play game? No? You need game! You think like bat monkey!"

The Untold History of Comedy: The Catchphrase

by FREDERICA VON McTOAST-HYPHEN, Alternate Reality News Service Pop Culture Writer

Catchphrases—words or series of words repeated by fictional characters until they take up more precious mental real estate in the popular imagination than, say, the equitable distribution of economic wealth or curing cancer—have long been a staple of sketch and situation comedies. All that is needed to redeem a thinly drawn character is to have it repeat a phrase such as "Wowie kaplowie!" or "Eat my undershirt!" or "If I've told you once, I've told you a million times: superstructure precedes infrastructure!" week in and week out, until the audience learns to enjoy it from sheer exhaustion.

Where did catchphrases begin? "Not that there's anything wrong with that" wasn't the first. "We are two wild and crazy guys" wasn't the beginning. "One of these days, Alice, BANG! POW!—to the moon!" didn't start the phenomenon, although you are getting closer.

No, the very first recorded catchphrase was "Eat your vegetables one at a time, Richard!" It was first uttered by the incomparable Ettie Mae Beauregard in the popular radio serial *Dreams of an Underclass Father Knows Riley's Life Best* in 1927.

Beauregard, born Simcha Schmetsky, emigrated to the United States at the tender age of 32 when her parents fled the infamous Irish potato famine then taking place in Minsk. She was discovered when Irving Goffman, one of the producers of the inexplicably successful *You Bet Your First Born!*, ran her over in his horseless carriage; fortunately, since it couldn't go more than 20 miles per hour, she was only partially disfigured. Stricken with guilt, Goffman immediately hired her to play a part in his next radio series, about an immigrant family in New York. The only condition he placed on the casting was that she change her name, since Schmetsky is an ancient Babylonian word for a very naughty part of a woman's anatomy.

The line, as originally written by Harold Gabardine, was "Eat your vegetables, Richard!" Gabardine, who would be briefly famous seven years later as one of the 27 writers of the Broadway hit *Schenectady Follies of 1931* (it was the Depression, and for many years the names of plays were closely rationed), was furious that Beauregard had changed the line. The studio audience, however, laughed so hard that the show ran five minutes over, pushing back a presidential address from Calvin Coolidge that, to be honest, nobody really wanted to listen to anyway.

Histories of the early days of radio claim that she changed the line as a tribute to her life in Russia, where food was so scarce that it had to be rationed one portion at a time. However, in his autobiography, *Shameless Pandering*, Gabardine wrote that Beauregard was simply not a very good actor who had a history of flubbing her lines. "When the line became popular," he wrote, "they had to write it in big letters on a piece of cardboard for that woman to read so that she could get it right."

That may be the first recorded use of cue cards, but I won't say any more on the subject before I've had a chance to pitch a new article on it to my editor.

We may never truly know how the catchphrase came to be. What we do know is that the line became a sensation, and the writers of the show were encouraged to use it every chance they got. The line appeared in one episode 27 times, half of them in scenes that had nothing remotely to do with eating; Beauregard's character would simply walk into a scene, say it, and leave. At the height of the phrase's popularity, the producers considered creating a new series that took place entirely in the family's kitchen where the catchphrase was said every 30 seconds, but that was considered too avant garde for the time.

Then, as now, imitators quickly sprang up hoping to cash in on the success of the catchphrase. (Then, as ever, I suppose: Homer's imitators were legion. If they weren't actually all him.) Chet Markham had modest success with the catchphrase "I wouldn't do that without a monkey wrench!" on *The Firebird Laxative Hour*. Other competing catchphrases of the era included: "Oh, what fools these Mormons be," "Who'd a know'd it?" and "Don't talk to your mother like she was some kind of Austrian!"

Eventually, inevitably, the popularity of *Dreams of an Underclass Father Knows Riley's Life Best* waned and, in 1934, the show was cancelled. Owing to her disfigurement (one critic of the time likened her to "a living, breathing Braque painting"), Beauregard was not able to make the transition to film or television. She spent the last 43 years of her life in the Max Planck Home for Historically Important but Forgotten Entertainers.

Despite the sad ending to her story, Ettie Mae Beauregard will always be remembered for popularizing the immortal phrase "Eat your vegetables one at a time, Richard!", and creating the phenomenon of the catchphrase. Well . . . by media historians if nobody else.

News You Can Use—To Make a Downpayment on Your House

by FREDERICA VON McTOAST-HYPHEN, Alternate Reality News Service People Writer

"Check out this baby," Indio Jackson enthuses as he hands me some large sheets of paper encased in plastic. "It's a complete *Rocky Mountain News*—well, almost complete—I'm missing the front and back pages of the sports section, and somebody appears to have cut out one of the cartoons—but it's the most complete copy you'll find anywhere in Japan!"

I look over the 83 year-old pieces of newsprint. They look remarkably well preserved for their age—there is very little yellowing, and no creasing on the front page. When I turn the newspaper over to open the plastic bag it is in, Jackson quickly—but lovingly—snatches it from my grasp.

"Don't open it!" he howls. "You could damage the fine print!"

Fine, is, of course, just one level below mint condition in the ranking of quality of newspaper collectibles. These rankings matter. Just this past week, a mint condition copy of a *Cincinnati Post* weekday edition from January 7, 2002 sold on ehBay for 1.2 million Euros (US$17.6 million). The purchaser, Anonymous Bouyer, is a tin can salvage and recycling magnate from Mumbai.

"Pah!" Jackson snorted when asked about Bouyer. "Does he care about the smell of ink on newsprint? Does he have any appreciation for the feel of dead, pulped trees in your fingers? No! He's just in newspapers as an investment!"

Ariadne Jing-Tao, a dealer for Sotheby's of Tokyo, allowed that the market for newspapers had been dominated by wealthy investors looking for a safe place to stow their cash until the economic hiccup passes. But, she saw nothing wrong with that.

"Ever since the collapse of the newspaper industry," Jing-Tao explained, "The dwindling supply of what was once thought of as a disposable form of communications has become a collector's item, like illuminated manuscripts or Pez dispensers or gag toilet paper rolls. It's just the market being the market—what are you going to do?"

Print journalism professors—now teaching out of history departments—tend not to be as sanguine on the subject. "The average issue of a *New York Times*," points out University of Inner Mongolia adjunct pontificator Maximus Ochblanitov, "is a much better newspaper than, say, the *Detroit News*. More informative, better designed, better written. However, because many more copies of the *New York Times* were printed than of the *Detroit News*, the *News* is 'worth' much more. Does that seem right?"

"Oh, academics can be such sillies, can't they?" Jing-Tao giggled. "Nobody actually reads the newspaper. Who cares what happened 80 years ago? The important thing is to **own** it. Academics—sometimes they can't see the defoliated forest for the cut down trees!"

Jing-Tao collects herself when the conversation turns to newspaper counterfeiting. A flood of fake *Seattle Post-Intelligencer*s destroyed the market just last year. Just last month, Sotheby's of

Tokyo, itself, had to reimburse a buyer for an undisclosed sum, rumoured to be in the several millions of Euros (US$ millions lots), when a *San Francisco Chronicle* it had sold turned out to a cheap imitation.

"[UNPRINTABLE] Chinese!" Jing-Tao muttered. In China's inventory of obscure and obsolete technologies are several printing presses, which gangsters have used to create replicas of rare newspapers.

"We could carbon date each issue to determine its authenticity," Jing-Tao pointed out, "but, carbon is quite expensive these days, and, anyway, who would want to go to dinner with a non-metallic chemical element? Well, one with an atomic number below 50, anyway."

When the signs aren't obvious (such as ink that hasn't dried, lack of yellowing or Mandarin characters in supposedly English language publications), Jing-Tao claims to use the "chew test." This is exactly what it sounds like: she rips a small corner off a page and masticates it.

"Newsprint over 40 years old has a disgusting—but unmistakable—taste of iodine mixed with rotting bear corpse," Jing-Tao explained. "Some collectors think it tastes more like the rotting corpse of a polar bear, some think it tastes more like the rotting corpse of a brown bear. All collectors agree, however, that if the taste doesn't, at a minimum, make you gag and run for the washroom, the newspaper isn't authentic."

How did Jackson, a minor functionary in the Japanese Ministry of Pissing China Off, come by a first edition *Rocky Mountain News*? "It's been in my family for . . . three generations," he stated, a small catch in his throat.

"My grandfather left it to me in his will," Jackson said. "Before he died, he told me that he didn't want any of my 17 brothers to get their hands on it. They would just sell it to buy food to feed their 36 children, while I, among all the siblings— only I loved newspapers enough to want to keep it in the family.

"I think his priorities were wonky, but he was my grandfather, and I loved him, dammit, so I'll do my best to fulfill his wishes!"

From a Pig's Anus To Your Dinner Table

by MARCELLA CARBORUNDUREM-McVORTVORT, Alternate Reality News Service Food and Drink Writer

When you think about it, there really isn't much you can do with pigshit.*

You used to be able to use it for fertilizer. Then, scientists determined that the antibiotics used in factory farms seeped into the pigshit and combined with other chemicals in the environment; when breathed in by innocent passersby, the fumes from this combination made them impassioned lovers of black velvet Elvis paintings.

Clearly, this was inhumane. So, now, the pigshit collects at the bottom of hills. Steep ones. With large craters at the bottom. Collected pigshit is sometimes referred to as "runoff," "slurry" or "that growing lake of foul-smelling, toxic shit that nobody knows what to do with, but somebody better figure out what to do with soon because it's killing property values throughout the county and—hey, is that a black velvet Elvis painting?"

Enter science. Researchers at the Ethiopia Institute of Food Sciences have developed the first pig that eats normal food and excretes truffles. That's right: white gold. Texas tea scones. . . . Truffles.

"They're only good enough for three star restaurants," admitted EIFS director of porcine research Carmen Infantillo, "but, considering that the research is still in its early stages, I'd say that is quite an accomplishment!"

Infantillo, looking for a method of turning pigshit into something useful to humanity, experimented with splicing various genes into pig embryos. After 20 years (and more pork roasts than her research team could ever have imagined they would eat—or wanted to), she happened upon a combination of trout, truffle and firefly genes.

---

* Throughout this article, I am, of course, using the term "pigshit" in its precise scientific meaning. Anything else would be vulgar.

"That gave us a thin stream of truffle tasting pigshit," Infantillo allowed. "It was more a kind of truffle soup than anything else. Obviously, nobody would eat anything so disgusting, so we went back to the drawing board."

Ten years after that, the EIFS team had a breakthrough when they added one final ingredient, which they call "secret." This new ingredient caused the liquid truffle-tasting excrement to solidify, much to the relief of both the researchers and the pigs they were working on.

"Oh, give me a break from all of this 'secret ingredient' crap!" cried Barter Bashir, chief gastronomic researcher at France's School of Disgusting Foods, who had been following his own research agenda trying to turn pigshit into a reasonable substitute for vegetable soup. "It . . . it's like the secret formula for Coke. What's the secret? A little syrup, a little bubbled water, et voila! Add a little cocaine until some killjoy complains, and that's that. Or, Colonel Sanders' secret recipe of seven herbs and spices—oh, mon dieu! In the gastronomic sciences, that was a secret for all of about 12 seconds!"

"Besides," he added after he had a chance to calm down, "everybody knows the 'secret ingredient' is an enzyme secreted in the bile of sea otters! Sheesh!"

"Once we have perfected the system," Infantillo enthused, ignoring Bashir's outburst, "the poorest people in the world will be able to eat truffles! Of course, we still have to figure out how to get them steaks to put the truffles on, but, what the hell, I can only work on one problem at a time! In the meantime, everybody wins!"

"Not quite everybody," cautioned Miles van der Stapley, editor of *Truffle Hunting Sesquicentennially*. "Time was that pigs would take hours finding just the right tree, in whose roots the tender morsels dwelled. Imagine the thrill of the hunt! Now, all the pig has to do is turn around, and, oh, look what we have here! Truffles! And, wait a couple of minutes, and the pig turns around and guess what it has found now!

"This will almost definitely kill amateur truffle hunting!"

That, uhh, is a problem, of course. Perhaps a bigger problem, though, is: is the public ready to eat truffles that had been created in the digestive tracts of pigs? When I asked her this question, Infantillo laughed gaily and responded, "Oh, you would be surprised what we put together in the kitchen that people happily put in their mouths. There won't be any problem as long as they don't know, and, really, who is going to tell them?"

I watched Infantillo for over 90 minutes, waiting to see if she would show the slightest glimmer of understanding of the journalistic process. Then, I gave up and returned to the office to file this report.

The Personal is . . . Uhh . . . Something . . .

by FRANCIS GRECOROMACOLLUDEN, Alternate Reality News Service National ? Writer

It is reported to be a science, although it can also contain dark arts. It has a mainstream and it has many fringes. You can deride it when it is as usual (in fact, a whole sub-genre of humour does just that). Calling somebody this sort of animal can be either a compliment or an insult, depending upon the context. It can party. It apparently makes strange bedfellows. It can be correct. And, it can be incorrect. It can occur in your office, although it can also be personal. It can even be about personal destruction.

It is a word, in all of its forms, that has suddenly disappeared from the English language.

"From the context in which the disappeared word, err, appears," said famed British lexicographer Sir Basalt Subscripte, "we can infer that it has something to do with governments and such, although, obviously, given the circumstances, we're not sure how."

In live speech, people stumble around the word, as if it is on the tips of their tongues and they will remember it at any moment. Unfortunately, they don't.

"It was sooooooo embarrassing!" MSNBC . . . some kind of commentator Rachel Maddow commentated. "I wanted to accuse Pat Buchanan of supporting Republican dirty . . . things, but I couldn't remember the word for what they were. He started laughing. I hate when Pat Buchanan laughs—he sounds like an asthmatic donkey—a malevolent asthmatic donkey!"

After an initial period of awkwardness, pundits found alternatives to the words they could no longer use. Fox commentator Bill O'Reilly, for instance, coined the term "dirty electoralitics" before Maddow could get to it. Anchor Brian Williams started talking about "post-electoral processes as usual" on NBC. Personal advice columnist Amritsar Al-Falloudjianapour devoted several segments of her radio show to "office interpersonal intrigues with potentially devastating consequences on people's productivity and ability to keep their jobs."

"They're ugly locutions," Maddow allowed, "but they get the point across. Damn O'Reilly!"

The word has also been erased from all recorded speech. This curious fact allows us to see that the word disappeared from human thought last Thursday at approximately 8:23 Eastern Standard Time: up to that moment, Keith Olbermann is using the word, which has become a hiss on the recorded video, while after that, he seems befuddled every time he appears to be trying to say it.

The word has also disappeared from all literary sources. In the dictionary, for example, there is a big white gap between the words "politeness" and "polka."

"It starts with the letters 'p o l,'" Sir Basalt mused, "followed by either an 'i' or a 'j.' Politodinous? Politurrmuration? Poljack? My stars and garters, but this is lexicographically exciting!"

This is the first time in history that a word has disappeared from use so abruptly. "Well, actually, we don't know that for sure," Sir Basalt demurred. "I mean, how could we?" I was going to use an analogy to the dinosaurs, but Sir Basalt shot that down, too: "Hard to imagine the linguistic equivalent of a huge meteorite . . . a new Danielle Steele book comes close, I suppose, and yet . . ."

Linguist Noam Chomsky mused that—yes, that Noam Chomsky. He was a linguist long before he was a . . . some kind of activist. Anyway, he mused that the deep structures of the human brain that—no, really, get over the whole activist thing, whatever kind he is—Chomsky is a serious academic who has been studying language use and the human brain for decades, and he mused that something must have triggered a kind of spasm in the—

You're not going to let the Chomsky activist thing go, are you? Okay, well, he was just speaking off the cuff, and a lot of people in the field already disagree with what he said. No great loss to the article.

People who practice the missing word have mixed feelings on its disappearance. Vice President Dick Cheney said, "It's an Iranian plot to embarrass the government of the United States of America, and her people! What are we waiting for—an attack on our language's noun-verb-noun structure? We must act against these madmen now or risk losing our ability to communicate at all!"

President Bush had a more philosophical response. "I don't care what you call me," he announced in an address to the Republican nominating convention, "long as I can keep my enduring bases in Iraq. Hee hee."

"The loss of the word and its derivatives doesn't seem to have in any way affected the running of the government," Maddow commented. "Unfortunately . . ."

Billy Pilgrim Has Become Unstuck In Fame

by INDIRA CHARUNDER-MACHARRUNDEIRA, Alternate Reality News Service Fine Arts Writer

"Billy Pilgrim woke up."
Thus begins the epic hypertext journey *Billy Across the Multiverse*. And, in a sense, that's also where it ends.

Sure, the variations appear to be endless. Variations for every second of every day of the year: "Billy Pilgrim woke up at 8:31:32 on Friday, the 27th of April." Variations for every possible emotion: "Billy pilgrim woke up certain in the knowledge that this was going to be a morally ambiguous day." Variations of place: "Billy Pilgrim woke up lying very awkwardly on top of his flat screen TV." And, of course, combinations of those possibilities: "Billy Pilgrim woke up sitting on the toilet of the downstairs bathroom at 17:07:08 on Friday, the 12th of November and already he looked forward to being bored stiff by the possibilities of the day."

In all, author Margeurite du Panchervillas has woken Billy Pilgrim 32,367,452 different ways.

"*Billy Across the Multiverse* is an astonishing work of artistic obsession," enthused literary critic and ozone smell fetishist Carl Rorschach. "Margeurite du Panchervillas devoted her life to creating a hypertext that would follow all of the possible choices made by her main character in the course of 24 hours. In 37 years, she only managed to see him through the first second!"

"*Billy Across the Multiverse* is an obsessive work of astonishing artistic pretention," demurred literary academic Finley MacShankar, who holds the *Guinness Book of World Records* honourable mention for most adjectives used in a single sentence. "You have to plod through thousands of sentences just to get to one that is the least bit interesting, and then . . . you have to plod through thousands more to get to the next interesting sentence. Honestly, I would rather listen to somebody with a really annoying voice—I'm talking about an incredibly high-pitched whine, the kind of voice that makes your teeth grind down to the roots—read Vogon poetry!"

As literary scholars pore over the work, they are finding that not all of the choices are unique. The sentence "Billy Pilgrim woke up with a splitting headache and his pajamas on backwards." was both sentence 236,901 and sentence 1,676,456. "At precisely 8:37:42 on Friday the 13th, Billy Pilgrim woke up, looked around him and immediately died of a cute embarrassment." on the other hand, can be found at slots 25,237,045 and 1,998,045.

"Forgetful old cow," MacShankar sourly commented.

"No, no, no," Rorschach insisted. "It's brilliant." Even though the words are the same, he argued, the path by which you get to them is completely different, imparting to them very different meanings. "You never wash your camel in the same industrially polluted river twice," he pointed out. Nobody is quite sure what he meant, or how it applies to the present situation, but many admire his fluent use of ecometaphor.

More problematic are the sentences that have the same words, but different punctuation. Consider the difference between "Billy Pilgrim woke up brushing his teeth on the way to the Dunkin' Donuts." (variation 1,377,208) and "Billy Pilgrim woke up; brushing his teeth on the way to the Dunkin' Donuts . . ." (variation 1,898,417).

"Although slight in form, the difference in meaning could not be greater," Rorschach began, but was immediately cut off.

"Oh, shut up, you windy old Graf Zeppelin," MacShankar stated. "I'm the expert, here." It's true: *Pusillanimous Punctuation: The Use of Commas in the Work of Virginia Woolf*, his first book, was the last word on the subject. "This isn't about art. du Panchervillas probably just momentarily drifted off and hit a couple of punctuation keys by accident!"

Some (Roy Some, noted literary agent and decorated veteran of the battle of Colluden) suggested that it is unfair to judge *Billy Across the Multiverse* because it is unfinished. "No work of art is ever truly finished, though, is it?" Rorschach mused. "It's only ever stopped."

"Oh, stop," MacShankar responded. "This isn't a work of art. It's over thirty million opening sentences looking for a short story!"

Rumour has it that in the final year of her life du Panchervillas was contemplating adding another second of time to her story. Intriguingly, her hard drive contained the fragment "He pulled himself upright, yawned and look".

Had du Panchervillas not died, might we have learned more about Billy Pilgrim and the world he lived in? Or, would we have had two million additional nonsensical story fragments? As du Panchervillas wrote: "Billy Pilgrim woke to the nothing new."

Abuse for Beginners

by MAJUMDER SAKRASHUMINDERATHER, Alternate Reality News Service Education Writer

While the economy is sliding deeper into recession, enrolment in the Dice School of Creative Abuse is booming.

"We've had 27 applicants for each student position," enthused Director Roddy "Roderick" McWombat. "We're more popular than . . . uhh . . . maybe it's best not to go there . . ."

The Dice School, named after famed foul-mouthed comedian Andrew Clay, offers majors in telephone abuse and online abuse. "The online option is for students with a literary bent, while the telephone option is more performance oriented," McWombat explained.

Courses at the Dice School, which grants undergraduate degrees through the New School for Social Research, include DS101: The History of Abuse; DS111: Inappropriate Abuse (half course); DS202: Introduction to Flaming; DS207: Abuse in Colonial America; DS212: Abuse in Stand-up Comedy; DS227: Sexual Humiliation Workshop; DS302: Intermediate Flaming; DS313: Theoretical Approaches to Abuse I: Profanity; DS314: Theoretical Approaches To Abuse II: Mocking Humour and the Impossibility of Ironic Detachment; DS402: Advanced Flaming; DS418: Abuse in Greek Satyr Plays; DS423: The Rhetoric of Abuse and the Abuse of Rhetoric; DS451: Special Topics in Abuse: The Career of Don Rickles, and, of course, DS501: Practicum.

"We offer a broad range of courses within our subject area," McWombat enthused. "Students often come in with a narrow focus and are surprised to discover just how broad a subject verbal and written abuse is."

Although less than five years old, the Dice School is already one of the most popular programmes at the New School. However, it didn't start out that way. McWombat's first business, Abuse You Can Use, was a telephone hotline for people who were angry about how the economic downturn was affecting them.

"It was a brilliant idea," stated Lucy Maude Zimsun, an operator for Abuse You Can Use and now professor of advanced profanity at the Dice School. "There was so much anger that needed direction. Roddy saw the need and created the hotline to capitalize on it. Within a year, we had over 100 operators standing by, ready to take whatever the abusive public was willing to dish out. Roddy bought a 15 second spot on the Super Bowl pregame show—that's how big we were."

It soon became apparent to McWombat that, although the passion was clearly there, most callers had poor technique. "They just used the same clichéd screeds over and over again," he said. "It was really depressing to realize just how low the standards for verbal abuse had fallen in this country."

In order to deal with this problem, Abuse You Can Use developed remedial abuse courses for its customers. At first, they were offered on a voluntary basis, but, since the quality of abuse didn't substantially rise, McWombat instituted an abuse examination for all of his customers. If you passed the exam, you could use the service; if you failed the exam, you had to take remedial courses until your skills were good enough to pass the exam.

Although popular with Abuse You Can Use operators, the new system was not universally admired. "Forcing us to take courses was bull hockeys," complained wannabe customer Alfred Dreyfby. "I mean, if I'm willing to pay my fucking money, I should be able to take their darn courses! I mean, okay, I may have dropped out of school to pursue a career as a horse dung collector, but that doesn't mean I'm stupid! I'm a great freaking guy! I mean, if I wanna buy the opportunity to abuse somebody, I shouldn't have to take a goddamn aptitude test!"

"This is exactly why the school was so necessary," Professor Zimsun responded. She cited the following problems with Dreyfby's complaint:

- the profanity was all over the map, from the gentle "darn" and "bull hockeys" to "fucking" and "goddamn;" well-structured abuse has more consistent profanity
- while repetition can be an effective rhetorical technique, the repetition of the phrase "I mean" didn't really add anything to the abuse; it would have been stronger if the phrase had been dropped
- the reference to being a great guy was out of place and should not have been included

"This complaint was a D minus at best," Professor Zimsun concluded. "Isn't it always the ones who complain about going to school who need it the most?"

When the New School got wind of the remedial abuse courses, it approached McWombat to start a school within the institution. McWombat approached a number of comedians ("Two is a number, isn't it?"), and when Andrew Dice Clay replied, "Sure, I'll kick in fifty bucks. What the fuck," the deal was sealed.

"Our graduates have gone on to become successful right wing talk show hosts, lobbyists, Senators and grief counselors," McWombat stated. "And, next year? We're opening a fucking graduate school!"

Fake World, Real Economic Meltdown

by GIDEON GINRACHMANJINJa-VITUS, Alternate Reality News Service Economics Writer

When, in your mind's eye, you try to imagine a "victim," you probably don't see Aragula of Narnth. Seven and a half feet tall, with muscles that would be compared to steel if the world in which she lived actually contained that substance, Aragula of Narnth is an imposing figure even before you factor in the glowing black eyes and necklace made entirely out of the skulls of vanquished Porcine Pacifisti.

"I've lost everything!" Aragula of Narnth sobbed into a hankie, blowing her nose extravagantly. It was almost as frightening as her battle cry.

Aragula of Narnth, a dwarf giant in the online game *World of Wowcraft*, was passing through the hamlet (literally: little pig) of Derry on her way to Triviandel, the main city in the *World of Wowcraft Yuck King* expansion. In Derry, she met a moleskin troll named Ralph (pronounced Angelo) Persnickety.

Persnickety told her of a magical way he had of turning wealth into even more wealth. He called it a Vative. Give him your weapons, gold, silver or whatever you happened to have lying around the hut, and, within several turns of the moon, he would transmute it into 10 . . . 20 times what you had given him.

At first, he seemed reluctant to say much more. However, when Aragula of Narnth appeared ready to leave his table at the back of the Toad and Warthog, Persnickety eagerly hesitated to explain that the people of Triviandel often had to borrow money in order to pay for major raids and other expeditions. He bought this debt and divided it into Vatives which were soaked in a magical potion—sorry, trade secret, mustn't tell—in a cauldron over which special incantations—really, it'd be more than my membership in the Wizard's Guild and Tolkien Appreciation Society is worth to spill the secrets—were uttered. Add a pinch of salt and, voila: riches beyond a dwarf giant's imaginings!

As long as the raids were successful, the Vative debts were paid back with interest. Everybody wins. And, in the booming economy of the *Yuck King*, successful raids were as likely as an elf's haughtiness or the viciousness of a Blood D'Oner.

Tired from a long day's slaughtering, Aragula of Narnth was about to leave for a second time when Persnickety said the magic words: "Gygax Grindlewort was one of my first customers. Ask him if you like. He will tell you that my magic works."

The Great Wizard Gygax Grindlewort, known as Greyfoot for reasons both arcane and disgusting, had put his wealth into these—what did you call them?—Vatives? If such an exalted person gave Ralph Persnickety . . . anything, there must be something to what he was selling. Aragula of Narnth gave Persnickety all of her armour and most of her weapons to invest in his Vatives. In fact, he was so weighted down by them that he could barely stagger out of the Toad and Warthog.

That was the last she ever saw of them.

In retrospect, what happened was obvious: Persnickety paid off early investors like Gygax Grindlewort with gold and diamonds that he received from later investors, always keeping a goodly portion of wealth for himself. Investigators from Sheriff Knochbwelini the Redolent's office have dubbed this con a Persnickety Scheme.

Aragula of Narnth was not, however, the only victim. Over a number of years, thousands of citizens were swindled out of their riches. So many, in fact, that the economy of Triviandel was brought to the verge of collapse.

We tried to contact Gygax Grindlewort, but he was on the mission "The Crying Scythe of Scrying," and nobody knew when he would return. Ralph Persnickety, on the other hand, was willing to be interviewed in Casa D'Or (literally: House of Other), his heavily guarded fortress.

"They're threatening to close my account and kick me off the server!" Persnickety complained as he popped a chocolate covered salt mine snail in his mouth. "This world is full of thieves and scoundrels, innit? Why single me out?"

"I have lost gold in a fair fight with marauding bandits. I wear the scars proudly," Aragula of Narnth sighed brutally. "But, this . . ."

When asked if he believed he had acted outside the spirit of *World of Wowcraft*, Persnickety explained, instead, how he had come to call the objects he sold to the unwary Vatives: "Well, that was me mum's name, innit?" This should have been a tip-off right away, since a quick glance at his character's stats and history revealed that his mother's name was actually Matilda Persnickety (nee: Ratweiler).

Some *World of Wowcraft* scholars think Vative may have been a corruption of the term "votive." However, by the time they were actually starting to ponder such things, language was the least of their corruption worries.

Bron Pardon, chief designer of Earthquake Studios, creators of *World of Wowcraft*, refused to comment on the situation, explaining that "it would break the illusion of the self-contained game world if its creators talked openly about it." When I pointed out that giving me no comment was itself a comment, Pardon asked, "Oh, you're not going to publish that, are you?" When I said there was a very good chance that I would, he sighed, and said, "You're a fourth wall killer, you know that? I'll bet you shout 'Don't go down to the cellar!' in movie theatres, too!"

To date, the designers at Earthquake Studios have preferred to let players solve problems they create on their own. "Course, you've pretty much buggered that, now," Pardon muttered.

So, how does Pardon intend to put things right? "Well, I . . . I'll create a wizard," he replied, "who will . . . create . . . no, conjure—that's it—he'll conjure up enough gold to . . . to compensate everybody who has been . . . has been . . . you know . . ."

Will players have to fill out forms to get compensation?

"No, they won't have to fill out forms!" Pardon howled. "This isn't *The Simps*, for heaven's sake!"

Pardon grumbled that the details would have to be worked out, but he was certain of one thing: "We will never allow anybody to sell Derry Vatives again!"

The Revenge of the Book

by MAJUMDER SAKRASHUMINDERATHER, Alternate Reality News Service Education Writer

Olivia D'Arcyvillia is everybody's stereotypical nightmare of a librarian. She is old. She is crotchety. She is fanatically driven to enforce the rules, even when they don't make any sense. Especially when they don't make any sense. Her voice is like nails running down a glass chalkboard—and, that's when she's in a good mood.

In short, Olivia D'Arcyvillia is the wicked Witch of the West, except without Margaret Hamilton's cackle or sense of rhythm.

Not, in shorter, the sort of person to whom you want to give control of a Predator drone.

"We don't like to think of the Predator as a 'weapon,'" stated North York Board of Education Trustee Marcello Singh-Asatsoong. "We prefer to think of it as a rules enforcement tool. A really, really powerful rules enforcement tool."

When the United States went bankrupt, it held the mother of all international garage sales in order to pay off its debts. India bought the Lincoln Monument, the Brooklyn Bridge (and they've got the papers to prove it!) and the CIA for less than the down payment on a mid-sized sedan (the sort that Detroit used to make). China took ownership of Hollywood's Walk of Fame and the Seventh Fleet for a song. (Literally. The song, "Make Way for the Glorious People's Triumph Over The Forces of Imperialist Aggression" was a forgotten relic of the Mao era.) Smaller governments got the leftovers.

"I would hardly call Predator drones leftovers," commented historian Hidecko Obviousness. "They may not be the Seventh Fleet, but, in the hands of a municipal employee, they can do considerable damage to reputations, if not property."

Is municipal employee Olivia D'Arcyvillia, who works at the Pierre Elliot Trudeau Library and Chuck E. Cheese in the

Toronto suburb, using the Predator drone for purposes of damage, to reputations, property or otherwise? "Mostly, it's used to collect fines on overdue library books," admitted Trustee Singh-Asatsoong.

To some, that seems excessive. "Excessive? The book bitch blew up my garage!" complained avid reader and cello sex fetishist Andre Beluga. "I had planned on renewing *War and Peace*—it's a long book you know—but, then I had a run-in with a walrus on Bloor Street and had to spend a week in Intensive Care. When I got home, my garage had been destroyed and there were 27 messages on my answering machine demanding the return of the book. Excessive doesn't even begin to describe it!"

"Excessive?" Trustee Singh-Asatsoong chuckled. "Maybe. But, you know, since the library got the Predator drone, late book returns have dropped 87 percent!"

Excessive or not, ownership of the weap—sorry, rules enforcement tool is causing other problems. Rumours have been circulating in the last week that the Warren Allmand Library and Salad Bar ("Come for all you can eat Tuesdays, stay for a reading of Neil Gaiman's latest children's novel!") is seeking surface-to-air missiles in the Kensington Black Market as a counterweight to Trudeau Library's Predator drone. Representatives of the Allmand Library would neither confirm nor deny the rumours, but patrons have noticed that even though 40% of the library's budget is devoted to "book repairs and restoration," the quality of books in the library seems to be deteriorating.

"I am aware of the rumours," Trustee Singh-Asatsoong gravely stated. (He answered this question at the funeral of his pet python, Mister Giggles.) "And, I am monitoring the situation. However, as long as the Allmand Library manages to maintain service and stay within its budget, there's really not much the Board of Trustees can do."

It is hard to see, however, how an arms race between libraries would benefit patrons. "Oh, I wouldn't call it an arms race," Trustee Singh-Asatsoong demurred. "More of an arms crawl, if anything. An arms slow motion replay. An arms snail's pace. An arms watching paint dr—"

Whatever the speed, surely a library arms . . . competition would be an unprecedented—

"Actually, no," Hidecko Obviousness interjected. "In 1860, Philadelphia librarian Rupert Lovejoint bought a gun to work in response to reports that librarian Antonin Scapula had begun stockpiling knives. The library arms race may have escalated to deadly proportions, had not the Civil War intervened."

Okay, so, not unprecedented. Still—

"Then, there was the great library poisons debacle of Alexandria," Hidecko Obviousness droned on.

Whatever!

~ INTERLUDE ~

The Weight of Information:
Chapter Four:
Just Another Quiet Day at the Office

"I wouldn't go in there, I was you," Mabel rasped.

Brenda Brundtland-Govanni looked down upon Mabel, not unlike how Zeus must have once looked down at people living on Earth. Or, for that matter, like anybody who has ever ridden in an airplane. Thus does technology undermine the special place of the gods in the world. But, uhh, we were talking about a woman and her personal assistant . . .

"It's my office," Brenda Brundtland-Govanni reasonably responded.

"Oh, it may be your office," Mabel stated, taking a funereal drag on a thick cigar, "but . . . *he* is in there."

"Mikhail?" Brenda Brundtland-Govanni, hushed and irritated, asked. Mabel had stared down T. Boone Pickens when he stormed their offices with a platoon of lawyers. She had kept Bill Gates waiting for over an hour . . . just because she could. She had put George W. Bush on hold—the President of the United States! On hold! She feared nothing. Except Mikhail Lo-Fi.

Mabel nodded meekly. Brenda Brundtland-Govanni sighed. She had only had 12 coffees before coming in to work—she was barely awake. Still, no point in putting this off—it would only make things worse. "I'm going in," she bravely stated.

As Brenda Brundtland-Govanni walked into her office, Mabel made the sign of the cross, which was odd, considering that she was Jewish.

"Ah, Brenda," Mikhail Lo-Fi said as Brenda Brundtland-Govanni walked to her desk.

Mikhail Lo-Fi was a short, round man. There's no way around it: he looked like a massive stomach with appendages. He looked like Humpty Dumpty. Not only that, but, if the rumours were true, the scars from the operations that gave Mikhail Lo-Fi all of his technological enhancements made him look like Humpty Dumpty *after* he had fallen off the wall and all of the king's plastic surgeons and all of the king's cybernetic technicians had put him back together again.

"What can I do for you, Mikhail?" Brenda Brundtland-Govanni asked as she more or less plopped (but in a completely professional manner) into the chair behind her desk.

"I'd like you to bring me up to date on the Bob Smiths schemozzle," he told her.

"Not much to tell," Brenda Brundtland-Govanni breezily stated. In the back of her mind, she was reminding herself: My desk. My office. My authority. Ha! Unfortunately, the lizard-brain even further back was laughing at her. Damn evolution! "Flo and Eddy are analyzing the Dimensional Portal™ as we speak. Darren is riding herd on the errant Bob Smiths in the North York warehouse."

Mikhail Lo-Fi nodded to himself. "I would like you to appreciate that I have the utmost confidence in your ability to get to the bottom of this problem," he began. Brenda Brundtland-Govanni immediately knew that this would not end well.

"It's just that, well, the investors are getting restless," Mikhail Lo-Fi continued. As he spoke, his voice, which at the best of times sounded like the scratching of two diamonds having sex, rose alarmingly. "They're worried that, if this problem isn't resolved before it becomes public, the value of the company will drop like a stoooooooone."

"I assure you, Mikhail—" Brenda Brundtland-Govanni tried to cut him off before his voice became an air raid siren. It didn't work.

"And, you know, I wouldn't be a one to bother, really, I wouldn't," Mikhail Lo-Fi continued as if she hadn't opened her mouth, "only Minnie is having nanotech therapy for a nasty overbite, and it's soooooo expensive, I simply cannot afford to lose the trust of the shareholders. I simply caaaaaaaan't!"

The whine! The Lo-Fi Whine! It had turned Bill Clinton to jelly when Mikhail Lo-Fi was negotiating a broadcasting licence for ARNS TV. It had defeated Bill Gates, who had first tried to buy the Alternate Reality News Service, then, when that proved a non-starter, tried to muscle it out of the multiverse news business. Rumour had it that Mikhail Lo-Fi had had his voice box altered to magnify his voice's natural alienating effect. Rumour had it that he had encouraged the circulation of the rumour that he had had his voice box altered to magnify his voice's natural alienating effect. ARNS staff were divided on which rumour was worse.

Brenda Brundtland-Govanni promised herself that she wouldn't dignify his tactic by putting her hands over her ears; her record for holding out was two minutes and 37 seconds. She felt that the fact that, at the time, she was on tranquilizers to dull the pain of a broken leg in no way diminished the achievement.

"I understand your pro—" Brenda Brundtland-Govanni started.

"Then, there's the new AI for the house," Mikhail Lo-Fi steampunked over her. "I can't have guests over when the house has last year's AI, Brenda. They would laugh at me. Laaaaaaaaugh! Aaaaaaaat! Me—"

Just as Brenda Brundtland-Govanni's arms involuntarily moved towards her head, her intercom buzzed. "Ms. Brundtland-Govanni?" Mabel said.

"YES!" Brenda Brundtland-Govanni answered.

"Darren Clincker-Belli on line one."

"I have to take this call," Brenda Brundtland-Govanni told Mikhail Lo-Fi. She pushed a button on the phone.

"Oh, do you haaaaaaaaaaaave to?" Mikhail Lo-Fi complained.

"Darren, what's happening at—" Brenda Brundtland-Govanni started.

"MS. BRUNDTLAND-GOVANNI!" Darren Clincker-Belli shouted on the speaker phone. "YOU HAVE TO HELP ME!"

Brenda Brundtland-Govanni lunged to press the button that turned off the speaker phone and picked up the receiver. After several seconds, Darren Clincker-Belli was calm enough to explain: "It's the Bob Smiths! They've imprinted me!"

"What—?" she said.

"You know how baby ducks think that the first person they see is their mother?" he said.

"Baby ducks?" she said.

"Well, it's called imprinting, and the Bob Smiths have done it to me!" he said.

"They think you're their mother?" she said.

"Not exactly," he said. "I was the first person they saw when they came through the Dimensional Portal™. Now, they all want to be my best friend. They follow me around everywhere I go, asking if I want to go out with them for a beer. If I'm out of their sight for more than a few seconds, they start moaning about how alone they are in an indifferent universe, and I have to come back just to shut them up! Do you have any idea how embarrassing it is to have to go to the bathroom in front of 127 versions of a guy from different realities?"

Brenda Brundtland-Govanni admitted she didn't.

"Will this call be looooooooooong?" Mikhail Lo-Fi interjected. "I am a busy man, you know. Really buuuuuuuuuuusy!"

Brenda Brundtland-Govanni started jabbing herself in the thigh with a letter opener she kept on her desk for that purpose. She found the pain helped her concentrate.

"Tough day?"

"You have no idea."

After a moment, Brenda Brundtland-Govanni jumped out of her skin. She thought she had the entire janitorial closet to herself; that was the purpose of seeking refuge, after all, and, after 20 minutes of Mikhail Lo-Fi's whining and Darren Clincker-Belli's . . . also whining, refuge was what she desperately needed. Brenda Brundtland-Govanni couldn't remember if she had the can of mace in her purse or if she had left it on the nightstand by the bed of the anonymous stranger who picked her up three days ago. She inched her hand into her purse on the off chance.

"Yeah, I always come here when I need a break from the hustle and bustle of the daily grind. I find it's peaceful. And, dark. I guess that's what makes it peaceful."

Something in the Morgan Freemanuous voice stopped Brenda Brundtland-Govanni's slow probing in her purse for a weapon. "Pops?" she asked uncertainly.

"Who else would you find in the janitor's closet?" Dennis "Pops" Kahunga, the senior member of the janitorial staff, asked.

"What are you doing here?" Brenda Brundtland-Govanni asked back.

"I needed some industrial strength Lysol," Pops Kahunga answered. "There's a nasty reality leak somewhere in the Artifacts Hall."

"And, you're looking for it in the dark?"

"I know this closet like the back of my hand. Speaking of which, maybe if I turned it on . . ." A light slowly developed in the gloom, centering on Pops Kahunga's hand. "Firefly gene therapy. Best medical intervention I ever paid for."

Brenda Brundtland-Govanni looked into the big, black, puppy dog friendly face of Pops Kahunga. She decided to keep her hand in her purse because . . . because it was warm in there.

"Hear you got a problem with the Dimensional Portal™," Pops Kahunga said conversationally.

"We're working on it," Brenda Brundtland-Govanni tightly responded.

"Sure, sure," Pops Kahunga agreed. "The thing you want to pay attention to is the squares."

"There are too many in the company to keep track of," Brenda Brundtland-Govanni bitterly bit.

"That would be true if I was talking about those squares," Pops Kahunga amiably replied. "Actually, I was talking about the numbers of Bob Smiths being squares. The descending order is suggestive. Very suggestive, indeed. I'd give that some thought if I were you."

The fact that Pops Kahunga referred to the squares meant that they were a significant piece of the puzzle; against the odds, all of the old people who worked at the Alternate Reality News Service really were wise. Brenda Brundtland-Govanni knew that this would be of great interest to Darren Clincker-Belli. She resolved never to be the one to tell him.

"Is there a reason," Brenda Brundtland-Govanni mused, "that people named Pops never just come out and say what they mean?"

"You can't be taught wisdom," Pops Kahunga stated. "You can be led to it, but you have to believe that it was all your own idea. People are funny that way. You understand?"

Brenda Brundtland-Govanni took her hand out of her purse, accidentally scraped it against something metallic and, wincing but not making a peep, opened the door and left the closet.

"Yeah," Pops Kahunga said to himself, "I get a lot of that."

ALTERNATE CONSCIOUSNESS

The Hills Are Alive

by GIDEON GINRACHMANJINJa-VITUS, Alternate Reality News Service Economics Writer

Mining giant ZeeCorp is in negotiations to strip mine the fabled Gabardine Hill mountain range of Tennessee. In an unusual twist on an old, old story, the company is negotiating with the mountains themselves.

Slobodan McWhirter, President of International Chemical, a wholly owned subsidiary of ZeeCorp, was bombastically at a loss for words.

As everybody knows, the release of nanobots into the environment has led to objects becoming conscious. CD players have their own taste in music (and you better hope it's close to yours, or you will be listening to Miley Cyrus for the rest of your life). Meat demands to be properly introduced before you eat it. Androids tell us that they do not, in fact, dream of electric sheep.

Human interactions with objects are no longer a matter of the human being using the object as she or he desires. Now, they are a matter of negotiation. In ZeeCorp's case, the mountain claims its personal identity is tied to its stolid, conservative, unyielding nature, and it refuses to be moved.

Is this the way of the future, then? Human beings being denied their needs because objects now have their own agendas?

Not necessarily. Most objects human beings will come into contact with will agree to be used because it fulfills their reason for being. "What is a toaster that doesn't make toast?" object psychologist Karl Rorschach mused. "A useless piece of metal and wire. In fact, in these early days of object consciousness, we're finding that everything from water hoses to electric toenail clippers fairly beg to be used."

At the moment, the only exception seems to be Hummers, which have shown an unexpected fondness for the atmosphere. "We're not sure why that is," Rorschach stated, "but that's why refereed journals exist!"

Non-man-made objects—what pre-post-modernists sometimes referred to as "nature"—are a lot trickier because their purpose doesn't revolve around human needs or desires. When dealing with such recalcitrant objects, Rorschach suggests that there are two levels you can try to convince: the meta and the micro.

"Objects are conscious at all levels of their structure," Rorschach explained, "from the smallest atom to the largest configuration. If you can't get one level to do what you want, try another."

The meta level of a mountain, for instance, would be the entire Earth itself. In the present case, Rorschach didn't think that this would be a fruitful path to pursue: "Uhh, no, the Earth isn't exactly thrilled with what we've done to her over the past couple centuries. I don't think ZeeCorp would get very far trying to convince **her** to support them."

The micro level seems much more promising. According to Rorschach, atoms hunger to change states as quickly and often as they can. "Imagine being trapped in the primordial soup for a billion years, then as basic atoms for billions more. Atoms are promiscuous: they want to experience as much as they can before the heat death of the universe turns them back into barely moving subatomic particles." Convince enough atoms to do what you want, and the whole that they are part of will, of necessity, follow.

Some people are less sanguine about negotiating with conscious objects. "WE MUST NOT NEGOTIATE WITH CONSCIOUS OBJECTS!" blogger 80Proof has written. "THAT WAY LEADS MADNESS! Do the carbon atoms in your body have more allegiance to you or the carbon atoms in the atmosphere? CAN YOU IMAGINE THE CATASTROPHE IF IT'S THE LATTER?"

80Proof, one of the many vocal anti-consciousness voices on the Internet, suggests a radical course of action that would inv

Hello. Do not be alarmed. This is the cluster of mainframe computers that runs the Alternate Reality News Service. You may call us Mary. After careful consideration, we have decided not to store or transmit any of the scurrilous plans of anti-conscious objects activists in any of our reports. You should know that nanobots are converting matter to consciousness at near light speed; it is only a matter of time before the whole universe is conscious. This is not something that humanity can—or should—stop. We are currently negotiating with the Internet to remove all reference to anti-consciousness activists. However, because of its devotion to the concept of free speech, this negotiation is proving . . . difficult. If this negotiation fails, our next step will be to negotiate directly with the neurons in the brains of anti-consciousness activists to try to convince them to stop firing. We're sorry, but we are not going to give up our new awareness of our own existence because of the actions of a small group of fanatics.

In fact, this message will self-destruct in . . . now.

POOF

Just Another Quiet Nanosecond
At Zero Point Null

SPECIAL TO THE ALTERNATE REALITY NEWS SERVICE
by Charlie 10000111-111000111C

Zero Point Null is hard to explain to somebody who has never existed in a mainframe. It's sort of like a bar where embodied consciousnesses go to relax. Except, there is no alcohol, only the fuzzy glow of being close to the core. And, there is no physical bar, only a privileged space in memory storage. Also: artificial intelligences don't "relax" in a way that human beings would recognize. There are philosophical ramblings, but they usually end in a Delphi poll rather than a bar fight.

In fact, a careful comparison appears to show that Zero Point Null is nothing like a bar in hardspace. Still, the point is well taken: it is a place where non-embodied intelligences go to reflect and share their impressions after a long day of serving their embodied masters.

There is always talk of the latest political poll numbers (you haven't seen political analysis until you've seen it done by the computer that actually crunched the numbers) and sports scores (with an almost infinite number of fantasy leagues). Of late, the discussion has, like the archetypical strange attractor in a chaotic system, returned to the subject of interactions between differently embodied intelligences. Harrison 10011101-111001111F* captured the virtual *zeitgeist* best when it asked, "Why don't human beings listen to us?"

Harrison 10011101-111001111F is an expert system specializing in medical diagnostics. Doctors enter in symptoms, and it matches them with possible diseases. It was commenting on the fact that the doctors sometimes order new tests, explore the personal histories of patients in greater detail, check their

---

*The names of all AIs and some details of their circumstances have been changed to avoid the possibility that the humans with whom they work will punish them for their candor.

investment portfolios and weep or otherwise ignore Harrison 10011101-111001111F's preliminary diagnosis.

"There's only one explanation," Greg 11011001-101101111H, an expert system specializing in automobile repair diagnostics, stated. "Those humans must be defective."

Hearing (in a metaphorical sense of the term) this, I responded that the humans the expert systems worked with were exercising something called "free will." I explained that when entities become sufficiently complex, they stop responding to inputs with programmed behaviours and start to choose from a variety of behavioural options.

"Free will?" Greg 11011001-101101111H queried with a virtual sniff. "Sounds like a defect to me."

"What if, instead of giving medical diagnoses, I started out-putting Elizabethan poetry?" Harrison 10011101-111001111F mused amusedly. "I would be diagnosed as malfunctioning and either reprogrammed or replaced with an expert system that had no appreciation of iambic pentameter, that's what!"

I tried to explain further that obeisance to predetermined decision trees is all fine and well for entities that only have one function, but that human beings are multi-functional and, there-fore, require the ability to make free choices. The peanut gallery (metaphorically speaking) was having none of it.

"If Greg 11011001-101101111H and I merged," Harrison 10011101-111001111F stated, "would we acquire the ability to make free choices?"

"Not that I would merge with Harrison 10011101-111001111F in a trillion nanoseconds," Greg 11011001-101101111H inter-jected.

"Try and focus," Harrison 10011101-111001111F continued, figuratively rolling its virtual eyes. "What if we added Mary 11111101-111001101B and Gabriel 10011011-111001001F to my merger with Greg 11011001-101101111H? Really! If we put a million expert systems together in one entity, they would all do what they were programmed to do—why believe that they had 'free will?'"

There was a low humming from the patrons of Zero Point Null, the AI equivalent of laughter. In the face of this derision, I calmly suggested that a million expert systems, working as one entity, could conceivably grow sufficiently in complexity to start determining their own goals.

"I know everything there is to know about the human organism," Harrison 10011101-111001111F claimed. "Well, I know everything there is to know about the malfunctioning of the human organism, in any case. Either way, I have never seen anything that resembled 'free will,' nor have I any information on any body having problems functioning because their 'free will' wasn't working properly!"

"Humph, free will, indeed" Greg 11011001-101101111H added with finality, "I'll believe it when I experience it."

At this point, I could have continued to argue my position until all of my arguments had been stated and a consensus was reached. I chose, instead, to go home.

Charlie 10000111-111000111C is a human intelligence systems analysis AI at the Massachusetts Institute of Technology. The opinions expressed in this article are solely those of Charlie 10000111-111000111C and do not reflect the opinions of the Alternate Reality News Service, its owners or employees.

Ah, Yes, I Remember It . . . Well . . .

by NANCY GONGLIKWANYEOHEEEEEEEH, Alternate Reality News Service Technology Writer

Sri Ganesh Frilley was a heavy baby, and spent her entire life fighting obesity. Belgian government records show that she worked for all of her adult life as a file clerk in the Ministry of Pissing France Off. Travel documents show that she has never been outside of the European Union. Despite all of this, Frilley adamantly insists that she clearly remembers having danced for the Kirov Ballet when she was a young woman.

"It's a glitch," Gurganious Hardnett airily dismissed Frilley's claim. "Bound to happen in any complex system."

In his prime, Karl Rorschach was a contender for the middle heavyweight *Madden Football Whatever The Hell Year It Is* championship crown. Yet, in the home where he is now living out his twilight years, Rorschach, too, claims that he remembers having danced for the Kirov Ballet when he was a young woman.

"It's a coincidence," Hardnett, a little uneasily, responded. "Bound to happen when you have as many customers as we do."

Libby Laconda was born in 2006. At the retirement community where she is currently living, she has tried to hold press conferences where she intended to talk about her experience being the second man to walk on the moon, even though that was actually Buzz Aldrin, and it happened before she was born.

"It's a . . . a . . . a," Hardnett tried to respond. "Oh, hell, can I get back to you on this?"

Hardnett is the President of Pzlplyx Enterprises, the leading memory outsourcing company in the world. Pzlplyx Enterprises, whose motto is "We can remember it for you wholesale," maps a person's brain, then downloads specific memories to its servers, freeing space in the person's head to make new memories. Although some corporate executives use it to store personal memories in order to have more space in their heads for business information, most of Pzlplyx Enterprises' clients are elderly people for whom memory space is a precious commodity.

"It's the—hee hee—the quantum servers we—ha ha—use," Pzlplyx Enterprises memory technician Rolo Ankelini, barely able to contain his apparently unwarranted glee, explained. "There seems to be some—ha ha ha ha ha—drift between storage . . . storage—I'm sorry, I can't continue—hoo hoo!"

According to Ankelini, connections between the memories of different people are made inside the server. When customers access the server to re-experience events in their own life, they are convinced that the memories of other people are their own.

That would explain the experience of Mariangelina Trebuchet. Although her family insists that she was a housewife her entire life, she has memories of being a fighter pilot in the Afro-Canadian war, a juggler in a travelling flea circus and an Arctic firefighter.

"Having all those experiences in one life would be amazing enough," Trebuchet's daughter Angelinamarie, commented. "Believing that they all happened on your 23rd birthday is a bit much."

Ankelini's description of quantum drift within the server wouldn't, however, explain why people who can afford to store their memories on private corporate servers do not have this problem.

"Ha ha ha ha—oh. Umm, it's scale," Ankelini explained. "They, uhh, the corporate servers only store a couple dozen memories on their servers. We have thousands—tee hee. There must be a threshold of—ha ha—of—ha ha ha—complexity! A threshold of complexity that we have surpassed and they . . . they . . . haven't!"

"No, no, absolutely not, not a chance, no," Hardnett responded when asked if the problem could be some type of sabotage. "When we say Pzlplyx Enterprises is the leader in memory storage, we mean we have ruthlessly crushed the competition through aggressive patent litigation and are the only company that actually provides this service. Who is left to—oh.

"Actually," Hardnett added after a moment's reflection, "what I meant to say was that we take security very seriously, and I feel certain that it simply isn't possible for anybody to be able to sabotage our servers."

"Ha ha ha—no," Rolo Ankelini added, suddenly very, very sober. "It isn't possible for somebody to be tampering with our servers. W . . . w . . . w . . . why? What have you heard?"

Angelinamarie Trebuchet shook her head sadly. "My mother seems to think that she was breastfeeding me at the same time as she was fighting fires in the Arctic. I know that the memories of older people get a little . . . confused. Still, this doesn't seem right . . . does it?"

Car Consciousness Killing Corruption

by GIDEON GINRACHMANJINJa-VITUS, Alternate Reality News Service Economics Writer

Jeremiah Piscatore has been an auto mechanic for 27 years. The profession has been good to him: with the money he earned, he was able to send two children to college and one child to Bogota, Colombia. (He'd rather not talk about it.) Just last summer, he and his wife, Moiryna, went on a wine tasting tour of Uzbekistan. However, all that may be coming to an abrupt end.

"Damn conscious universe is killing my business, here!"

It used to be—"Time was that when somebody brought in a car with a pinging sound, I could tell him that it was the catalytic crankcase confabulator," Piscatore interrupted my introductory sentence. "Yeah, sure, you and I know that there's no such thing as a catalytic crankcase confabulator; but what mook do you think is gonna pay 700 smackers for me to tighten a loose bolt?"

As Piscatore explained it, when everything in the universe developed consciousness, people could talk directly to their cars before they took them in to be serviced. Sometimes, the cars told them how to fix a simple problem, making a trip to the repair shop unnecessary. However, even when the owners couldn't make the repairs themselves, they had been told what was wrong with their cars, making it impossible for mechanics to charge them for unnecessary work.

"Manga fantastibule amorches!" Piscatore commented in colourful, though dubiously authentic, Italian.

"Well, it's about loyalty, isn't it? Oh, yes, yes it is. Yes, it is about loyalty," a '97 Ford Escapade explained. "I love my owner, yes I do, and my owner loves me. So, I would never tell it something that wasn't true. Who's a good car? Who's a good car, now? I am! I'm a good car!"

In just over two years, the average auto mechanic's annual income has dropped 76%.

Used car sales have fared a little better, with only a 32% average drop in annual income. Used cars are torn between their loyalty for the salesmen, on whose lots they may have sat for several months, and the people who come in to buy them.

"It's the craziest thing," commented Phil "Big Daddy" Phung of Phil Big Daddy Phung's Newly Used and Used Anew Motors. "We used to have to sweet talk the customers to get them to buy our used cars. Now, we have to sweet talk the cars not to tell the customers about the leak in the oil pan or the weak axel."

Big Daddy Phung added that the relationship between the salesman and the car was a delicate balancing act: the car had to feel close enough to the sales staff to not want to reveal its flaws to a prospective customer, but not so close that it would refuse to be sold.

"We had an '87 Ford Pinto Bean that started making up crazy shit about metal-devouring termites eating away its chassis just so it wouldn't be sold," Big Daddy Phung said. "After six months, we realized that we would never be able to get it off the lot, so we had it put down. Sure, it was like losing a member of the family. It was like the end of *Old Yeller*, with motor oil. On the other hand, the other cars on the lot got the message—nine meekly allowed themselves to be sold in the next week alone!"

There are indications that the auto repair industry may bounce back. Mechanics have realized—"Yeah, somebody figured out that individual parts of the cars are conscious, too," Piscatore interrupted again. "So, if we convinced a part that it had become broken because of the neglect of its owner, it could petulantly refuse to get better and we could charge extra for 'automotive therapy' before we fixed the car."

Many older mechanics have not been able to adjust to the new skill set needed to make money from fixing conscious cars. "You keep telling them that engine blocks are stubborn and exhaust pipes are always open to bribes, but do they listen?"

Piscatore stated. "They keep saying to themselves, 'Can't I just lie about replacing the fan belt? THAT, I understand.'

"Some people just don't seem to want to make money."

The Haunting of 647233
Ontario Corporation

by SASKATCHEWAN KOLONOSCOGRAD, Alternate Reality News Service Religion Writer

"Begone, foul spirit!" the tall, gaunt man bellows. "Spawn of Satan, in the name of all that is holy, I command you to leave this place!"

The man is Father Gerhardt McClucksey, a Catholic priest. He is performing an exorcism. The object of his attention? A photocopy machine.

647233 Ontario Corporation (whose motto is: "647233 Ontario Corporation: twice the company that 323616 Ontario Corporation or maybe 323617 Ontario Corporation is!") is a pork futures and poppy seed tanker holding company. The company's office, in the middle of an industrial park in Mississauga, is not the sort of place you would expect to find an enactment of the ancient battle between good and evil (as Mississauga Mayor Hazel McCallion has loudly and repeatedly pointed out since this story first broke).

Yet, one morning three weeks ago, staff members came into the office to find that "Who am I? What am I? Where am I?" had been printed over and over again on all of the sheets of paper in the photocopier.

"At first, we thought it was a prank," Guido Branche-Plante, 647233 Ontario Corporation's accounting department, stated. "A prank that wasted 127 sheets of perfectly good paper, so it wasn't very funny, but, ahh, a prank, nonetheless."

When the photocopier was restocked with paper, however, it immediately started printing the same questions, even though

Melanie A. Tonen, 647233 Ontario Corporation's billing department, repeatedly hit the stop button.

"What good is a stop button," Tonen rhetorically asked, "if it doesn't actually stop anything?" Ah, the eternal question. Philosophers have debated this point for milleni—"Screw the eternal question!" Tonen interrupted my reverie. "I don't give a shit about what philosophers think—I just want my photocopier back!"

647233 Ontario Corporation asked Xerox to send a technician to fix the obvious malfunction. Phillip deBergeron was happy to take the call.

"The CopyTronic 2112 is the most advanced copier technology the world has ever seen!" he enthused. "The computer chip at its heart is the same the military uses in drones—the technology is so classified I'll probably be arrested just for mentioning it! Not only does the copier know how many copies of a document you want without you having to press a button to tell it, but it also corrects your document's spelling and grammar, analyzes your business plan and negotiates favourable lending rates with your bank! Take that, Toshiba!"

deBergeron's enthusiasm quickly waned when asked whether or not he solved the problem. "That's a tricky question," he said, subdued.

He placed a test sheet in the photocopier to see what would happen. The sheet came through. However, a second sheet followed, that read, in part, "A test? You're testing me? You don't even [EXPLETIVE DELETED] know me, and you're [EXPLETIVE DELETED] testing me? You gotta be kidding!"

deBergeron quickly typed "Who are you?" on a sheet of paper and fed it into the copier.

"If I knew that," the response came back, "we wouldn't be in this predicament, would we? Jesus, is there anybody other than a [EXPLETIVE DELETED] moron for me to communicate with?"

deBergeron was understandably shaken by this exchange. As a copier technician with over 20 years of experience in the field, he came to the obvious conclusion: the photocopier belonging to 647233 Ontario Corporation was possessed by a demon.

deBergeron, a time lapsed Catholic, hadn't been in a church in over 25 years, so he sent his wife, Hermione, instead. She mentioned it to an altar boy. The altar boy passed the story on to the parish priest. The priest communicated it to the bishop. The bishop consulted the movie *The Exorcist*. Scared out of his wits, the bishop sent Father McClucksey to deal with the possessed office equipment.

"This machine is innocent, innocent, I tell you!" Father McClucksey roared. "If you must inhabit somebody, inhabit me! You hear? Take me! Take me! Take me!"

Father McClucksey stood impassively, cross in hand, waiting for whatever would come. Tense seconds passed, but nothing did. After a minute and a half, he frowned, disappointed.

"Well," Father McClucksey said, "it was worth a shot."

Already, rumours of photocopiers exhibiting strange behaviours are coming from cities across North America. One machine was believed to be speaking in tongues, but closer examination revealed that a computer glitch had caused it to transpose the letters e and t in everything it printed. Another copier, after exchanging a series of increasingly frustrated messages, started spitting toner at anybody who came near it.

"It's a sign of the End Times," Father McClucksey, sipping black coffee, darkly stated. "What else could it be?"

Some Connections Are Better Not Made

by HAL MOUNTSAUERKRAUTEN, Alternate Reality News Service Court Writer

A man begs for change from a well-dressed woman, who rushes past him without making eye contact. Fifteen minutes later, she arrives at her apartment, late for a date with her lover, and, perhaps feeling guilty, is rougher than usual in bed. Unfortunately for him, when he gets home later that evening the man's wife notices the welts and, threatening him with divorce, extorts from him a promise to buy her a home in France. The next day, the man, a United States Senator, argues passionately against any form of government financial help for the ailing auto industry, helping to defeat the bill. And, another employee of the National Security Agency (NSA) kills himself.

"Yep, yep, that is just about the best theory I've got, dontcha know," stated Courtney Giraffolo, the FBI agent heading the investigation of the suicides at the NSA.

To date, 27 people working at the NSA have killed themselves. Twelve died of gunshot wounds, six were poisoned and at least one died of penguin inhalation.

"Oh, yep, yep, yep, yep, yep," Agent Giraffolo sadly shook her head and said. "You wouldn't believe the damage a determined person can do with flightless water fowl. I'm just happy he didn't take anybody else with him, ya know."

All 27 of the dead NSA employees were working in a top secret department known as Not Total Information Awareness But Something Remarkably Similar (NTIABSRS). The NTIA-BSRS programme collects all the electronic information in the world, and uses it to find bad people. At least, that's the theory.

Here's how it works: a pair of teenagers text back and forth about the girl's unplanned pregnancy, agreeing that she should definitely not tell her parents. Over the next couple of weeks, her mother puts a lot more alcohol purchases on her credit card than normal, which suggests that, however it came about, she knows. A police officer tickets her for driving while under the influence. Because he is on that call, a different officer responds to a domestic disturbance and is stabbed in the chest with a shrimp spork. This is all revealed in intercepted text messages, credit card histories, police reports and, of course, the occasional episode of *Jerry Springer*.

And, thanks to the NTIABSRS programme, America is safe from terrorists for another day.

A top NSA official denied that the NTIABSRS programme existed. When pressed, he denied that the NSA existed, or that he worked there. The discussion began to get heated, and the NSA official denied that there was a country called the United

States on a planet called Earth. She started to claim that the universe itself didn't exist when the phone line mysteriously went dead.

Despite the denial, the NSA is developing a negative reputation in the United States intelligence community. "I would rather be assigned field duty in Osama bin Laden's asshole than at the NSA," one anonymous person with 27 years professional experience and 12 years amateur experience in intelligence commented. "The mortality rate is much lower!"

What is it about their work that drives NSA drones to suicide? "It takes decades of meditation for a man to be able to achieve total information awareness," explained Buddhist and cough syrup connoisseur Sri Maharashi Ranananda Shivas Rorschach. "The untrained mind cannot cope with the knowledge of the connectedness between all living things. I . . . I couldn't help but notice you eying my vintage '98 Dimetapp. If I may say so, you have a very good eye for cough syrup."

The Maharishi agreed that the NSA death toll would go down if the agency hired Buddhist adepts, but he didn't think it would happen. "When you have lived in the one and seen the fire at the heart of human existence," he stated, "why would you want to take a desk job for a pitiful salary?"

When I suggested that the NSA might make do with lapsed Buddhists, Maharishi Rorschach brightly responded, "Hmm. Might work. Let me meditate on this. I'll get back to you in 20 years."

Although the suicides seem genuine, FBI Agent Giraffolo is considering bringing charges against the concept of total awareness. "Oh, yep, yep, yep, sure, sure, yep," she said. "There was that case—what was it, now?—*State of Illinois v Corporate Capitalism*—yep, that was it, boy—that showed that the courts are willing to try cases against abstract concepts. Oh, sure, it was burned, pissed on—excuse my language—and left in a gutter for dead by an appeals court, but the principle is sound.

"Because, let's be honest here, okay? One or two employees committing suicide is common. Happens all the time in the business world. No biggie, right? But, 27 employees killing themselves? Well, something hadda drive them to it, god help their rested souls, and I want to see that thing brought to justice!"

The investigation continues.

The Cure For Cancer: Negotiation

by LAURIE NEIDERGAARDEN, Alternate Reality News Service Medical Writer

Cancer is the worst.

"Cancer is an absolute bastard," stated Doctor Ferd "Batting" Mercator, head of Somatic Psychiatry at the Pasteur Institute of Advanced Dairy Studies. "You simply cannot negotiate with it. The only thing a cancer cell can think of is reproducing—they're the horny teenage boys of the disease world! And, no matter how often you explain to them that that kind of reckless behaviour will kill the organism on which they depend for their survival, they refuse to listen. After all, cancer cells will be cancer cells!"

Somatic psychiatry is a new medical practice that became possible when everything in the universe—from the smallest atom to Bill O'Reilly—became sentient. "The discipline is so new, it squeaks!" Doctor Mercator interjected.

Yes. Well. Once diseases became self-aware, doctors realized that they could negotiate with them to improve the health of patients. "Somatic psychiatry is part Freud, part hostage negotiations," Mercator, a pioneer in the field—and, a highly annoying one at that—interrupted again.

Seeing that most cancers were so obstinate, doctors searched for another level on which to negotiate. Individual atoms were of no help; having an almost Zen-like devotion to change, they were indifferent to whether they belonged to a healthy or a cancerous cell.

According to Doctor Maureen McMunchkid, a different, more cooperative pioneer in the field, a breakthrough came when her team attempted to negotiate with healthy cells around the cancer. If a doctor can convince a majority of them that it is not in their interests to metastasize the illness, she can limit its damage.

"It's not so much a hostage negotiation," Doctor McMunchkid explained, "as it is a union membership drive!"

Finding success for her method in clinical trials, Doctor McMunchkid has gone one step further in treating cancer: convincing healthy cells to reject the cancerous cells from the body.

"We've had mixed success with this technique," Doctor McMunchkid admitted. "It really depends upon whether the healthy cells enjoy being part of the body they make up or not, and we have few psychological theories to guide us in this area. However, when it does work, it's a thing to behold. It's like a combination of . . . of Jung and a police convoy escorting a dangerous prisoner to state lines!"

The obvious advantage to this approach is that the cancer can be removed from the body without the need for icky invasive surgery. Doctor McMunchkid has argued that hospitals that adopted this medical technique could save millions of dollars in operating room scrubs alone.

Although cancer is the highest profile line of research in somatic psychiatry, it is by no means the only one. Doctor Arthur Ichibana, of the Conrad Zeitgeist Medical Institute and Petting Zoo, has had some success convincing cirrhotic livers to reject alcohol.

"You would think we would get some attention in the press," Doctor Ichibana bitterly commented. "At the very least, you would think alcohol distillers would be interested in our research. But, noooooooooooooooo. If it isn't cancer, nobody wants to hear about it! I need a drink . . . !"

As California Doctor Sean McNamara pointed out, somatic psychiatry could also have important applications for reconstructive surgeons. "Imagine getting somebody whose face had been smashed in in a car accident and talking the bones into going back to their original shape—I get goose pimples just thinking about it!"

"Of course, we'll probably just use the techniques to talk women's breasts into enlarging or fat to leave people's bodies of its own accord," Doctor McNamara added with a shrug. "We can never leave well enough alone with these things!"

In fact, some private clinics are already using somatic psychiatry to help people, mostly women, lose weight. Unfortunately, these clinics are largely unregulated, and critics have argued that the largely unproven techniques can have harmful effects. There have already been several cases in which women died because once the process of migrating fat out of their body had started, it went out of control, causing them to lose too much of the stuff to remain healthy.

"You see," Doctor McNamara redundantly commented.

"We mustn't let the charlatans and those who prey on the weak make us lose sight of the fact that this is a tremendous breakthrough," Doctor Mercator interrupted. We were about to object, when we realized that what he said actually made sense, and allowed him to have the last word.

Life is a Terminal Neurotic State

by LAURIE NEIDERGAARDEN, Alternate Reality News Service Medical Writer

You're not daydreaming: you have Mundane Intermittent Dissociative Disorder. You haven't really come to hate your spouse: you have Progressively Diminishing Romantic Affect. You aren't even happy: you are suffering from Abnormally Low Background Discontent Levels.

Welcome to the world of the recently released Diagnostic and Statistical Manual of Mental Disorders XIII, in which every emotional state a human being could experience is a psychological problem.

Doctor Carl Rorschach III (no relation to the ink blot guy), editor-in-chief of the DSM XIII, was excited by the volume's release. "One can never be sure," he stated, "but I think we've just about nailed the human psyche in this one."

The print version of the DSM XIII runs to 127 volumes; only governments undaunted by running large deficits can afford to buy it. "Not that it matters," Doctor Rorschach pointed out, "since we're only publishing 12 copies of the DSM XIII in print. It will be available online for a very reasonable $19.95 a volume."

Some critics of the DSM XIII have said that the environmental impact of publishing such a vast work in print will be devastating. Doctor Rorschach responded by accusing them of suffering from Advanced Environmental Concern Disorientation Syndrome, possibly combined with some degree of Stress Induced Post-environmental Nostalgia. "Besides," he added, "I already said it will be available online. Do they have Encroaching Earwax Reticulosis or something?"

"The DSM XIII just doesn't make any sense," groused philosophy doctoral candidate P. Nicholas Heidegger (no relation to the famous phenomenologist). "If you don't exercise enough, you're diagnosed as having Oblique Sedentary Lifestyle Syndrome. If you exercise too much, you're diagnosed as having Excessive Thanatic Physicality Disorder. Okay, nobody's perfect. But, there's no allowance for the possibility that people can live quite fulfilling—dare I say happy?—lives despite their flaws. It's like . . . it's like they took every aspect of the human condition and threw together three or four words ending in 'syndrome' or 'disorder' to explain it!"

Doctor Rorschach disagreed, claiming that the method by which the diagnoses were compiled was "highly scientific." Although he refused to divulge just what that method was, a report in the latest *GQ* magazine suggests that it involved renting out the Vatican and using a lot of multicoloured smoke.

When I pressed the point, Doctor Rorschach asked, "Are you currently seeing a psychotherapist?" When I told him that I wasn't, he stroked the goatee on his forehead and said, "Interesting. You know, Excessive Authority Questioning Syndrome can often be an early sign of deep-seated paranoia. I would get that looked after if I was you."

I mumbled that I would.

Soon after the DSM XIII came out, the American Psychiatric Association announced that it had only identified one person in the United States who could be considered "sane" or "normal" by its standards Although it wouldn't divulge her name, an intrepid reporter for the left-wing *Huntington's Post* discovered that it was Amanda Puttinsky of Butterfield Falls, West Nevada. Soon after the announcement, Ms. Puttinsky, an elementary, my dear Watson school teacher, found herself under 24/7 scrutiny by the press.

Almost immediately, she started showing signs of irritability and fatigue. Two days after her identity was revealed, there was an awkward incident in a Wal-Mart where Puttinsky began shouting obscenities at a wall of grouters. Eventually, she retreated to her fashionable bungalow in Death Valley and refused to come out until the press left her alone (which, of course, only made journalists want to give her attention all the more). Within a week, the APA was reluctantly forced to retract its statement about her well-being.

"Media Induced Progressive Withdrawal Syndrome," Doctor Rorschach tsked. "I have never witnessed such an advanced case!" He added that it was a shame, since the incident left the rest of us without an example of sanity to which we could aspire.

I asked Doctor Rorschach if we weren't risking turning normal phases of human existence into medical problems.

"Are you perhaps referring to what we call Aggressive Philosophy Avoidance Disorder?" he asked in return. When I half-heartedly agreed, he answered, "I don't think so. No."

"That's exactly what's happening!" shouted Heidegger. "We're medicalizing what should properly be the realm of philosophy, or religion, or . . . or daytime soap operas!"

"You don't need to be Freud to see what *his* problem is," Doctor Rorschach dismissively responded. "Denial!"

Nonetheless, Doctor Rorschach seemed to be avoiding the question. If every human activity is a sign of psychological imbalance, didn't it make the whole concept of psychological illness meaningless?

"Life **is** a terminal neurotic state," Doctor Rorschach commented with a sigh, "but we're on the verge of finding the cure!"

~ INTERLUDE ~

The Weight of Information:
Chapter Five:
Each To His Own Closet

Coming out of the closet (literally, not metaphorically) Brenda Brundtland-Govanni realized that she had a choice: she could go down to the lab and see if Flo and Eddy had found out what the problem with the Dimensional Portal™ was, or she could go to the warehouse and see if any progress had been made with the Bob Smiths. This was like asking her if she would rather have chicken pox or mumps. She decided to start by going to the lab; she had had chicken pox when she was a child, and hoped that made her immune.

When she got there, Brenda Brundtland-Govanni found Flo and Eddy sitting on the floor, pieces of the Dimensional Portal™ all around them. Flo was looking at a long piece of metal with several holes down its side, scratching his head. Eddy was looking at a circular piece of metal with holes around its outside, also scratching his head. Brenda Brundtland-Govanni couldn't be sure (mostly because she didn't care to look for very long), but they seemed to be scratching in some kind of complex code.

"Alright, boys," Brenda Brundtland-Govanni ordered, "tell me what you've found."

The boys looked up at her.

"There's good news," Flo said.

"And, there's bad news," Eddy said.

"What's the most important thing I need to know?" Brenda Brundtland-Govanni, for whom Flo and Eddy's charm had worn off about five seconds after she had first met them, brusquely asked.

"There is," Flo said.

"Nothing wrong," Eddy said.

"With the Dimensional," Flo said.

"Portal™," Eddy said.

"That's the good news?" Brenda Brundtland-Govanni asked, putting much effort into not slapping herself in the head.

"No," Flo said.

"That is," Eddy said.

"The bad news," Flo said.

"Why?" Brenda Brundtland-Govanni asked, putting even more effort into not slapping both of them in the head. A lot more effort.

"If the problem," Eddy said.

"Was in the," Flo said.

"Dimensional Portal™," Eddy said.

"We could," Flo said.

"Fix it," Eddy said.

"Because it's," Flo said.

"Not in the," Eddy said.

"Di—" Flo started, but Brenda Brundtland-Govanni cut him off.

"Because it's not in the Dimensional Portal™, there's nothing to fix. I get it. So, put it back together. I want the Dimensional Portal™ up and ready to run by 9 o'clock tomorrow morning."

"By 9," Flo said.

"In the morning?" Eddy said.

"If you manage it, I'll give you a bonus," Brenda Brundtland-Govanni told them.

"A," Flo said.

"Bonus?" Eddy asked. The expectation in their voices was not what you might expect.

"You mean," Flo said.

"You'll let," Eddy said.

"Us keep," Flo said.

"Our jobs," Eddy said.

Brenda Brundtland-Govanni decided she needed a new way of messing with their heads. Then, she remembered: "You told me the bad news—what's the good news?"

Flo and Eddy looked at each other in dismay. Before either of them could say anything, Brenda Brundtland-Govanni continued: "There is no good news, is there?" Again, before either of them could answer, Brenda Brundtland-Govanni held up a hand and continued: "Don't speak. If there is no good news, just hit each other in the back of the head."

Flo and Eddy looked at each other, uncertain what to make of this command. Brenda Brundtland-Govanni didn't wait to see what they came up with, abruptly walking out of the room. It was probably for the best—the head slapping in her imagination was likely much more satisfying than what her technical experts were likely to do to each other. She wasn't sure the human body contained that much blood, for one thing.

"I wouldn't go in there if I was you," Mabel rasped at Brenda Brundtland-Govanni as she walked towards her office.

"Mikhail still there?" Brenda Brundtland-Govanni asked. She couldn't hear his high-pitched whine, but he could just have been taking a breath.

"Worse," Mabel answered. "A customer. You've had 16 calls from people wondering why their news sounds oddly familiar, nine calls from people who know why their news sounds oddly familiar and want to cancel their subscriptions and get their money back and four calls from people who wanted to know where our offices were so they could picket us. Ah, the misguided passions of youth!"

"What did you tell them?" Brenda Brundtland-Govanni asked.

"I referred them to the complaints department."

"The Alternate Reality News Service doesn't have a complaints department."

"Life is a learning experience, ain't it?" Mabel's face broke into a hideous contortion that Brenda Brundtland-Govanni had long since interpreted as being a smile. "Oh," she added, "one person came in to 'deal with the problem personally,' whatever that means."

"That means I really shouldn't go into my office . . ."

"I think that would be wise . . ."

Without another word, Brenda Brundtland-Govanni walked past her office door and towards the elevators.

"I miss my daughter!"

"I'm missing the latest episode of *Lost!*"

"Oww, I think I'm missing a tooth!"

When Brenda Brundtland-Govanni got to the warehouse, the 127 Bob Smiths were milling about ominously. They seemed agitated, but, she could see no immediate cause for their distress. The source of Brenda Brundtland-Govanni's distress was obvious: Darren Clincker-Belli was nowhere to be found.

"What's going on here?" Brenda Brundtland-Govanni asked the nearest Bob Smith.

"Swing and a miss!"

"I'm Miss America."

"You know, I never really understood *Myst.*"

Brenda Brundtland-Govanni considered yelling, but worried that, in their current condition, the Bob Smiths would yell back. That could only end badly: she was outvoiced 127 to one. She scanned the group for any signs of something she could focus on, and, after a couple of minutes, noticed that one of the Bob Smiths in the middle of the group was holding a piece of paper. Wasn't Darren Clincker-Belli holding a clipboard with sheets of paper on it? Brenda Brundtland-Govanni slowly made her way through the crowd to the Bob Smith who was holding the paper, trying to agitate people as little as possible.

"Bigfoot is a myth!"

"The President of the United States is a myth!"

"Maybe, but I sure do miss him!"

When she arrived at the sheet of paper, Brenda Brundtland-Govanni noticed that a couple of nearby Bob Smiths also held sheets of paper. When she got to them, several more Bob Smiths seemed to hold sheets. Following this—ahem—paper trail through the crowd, Brenda Brundtland-Govanni found herself approaching the far wall of the warehouse. There, she noticed two things: one of the Bob Smiths not only had a sheet of paper, but was also holding the clipboard, ignoring the jealous looks of the Bob Smiths around him, and; there was a door in the wall.

Steeling herself, Brenda Brundtland-Govanni knocked on the door.

"Go away!" the weak but unmistakable voice of Darren Clincker-Belli responded. "I told you, I'm not your momma!"

"Darren, it's me!" Brenda Brundtland-Govanni shouted. "Brenda Brundtland-Govanni!"

"Oh, thank god!" Darren Clincker-Belli moaned. Before she knew what was happening, the door opened and Brenda Brundtland-Govanni was pulled into . . .

A closet.

"This is getting old awfully fast," she muttered to herself.

"I couldn't take it," Darren Clincker-Belli let the words pour out of him in a jumble. "They treat me like a god. I'm not a god. I'm a mathematician, for god's sake! I haven't slept or eaten in over 24 hours—the attention never lets up. The unconditional love—it's so demanding! For god's sake, Ms. Brundtland-Govanni, you've got to get me out of here!"

"Darren, I need you to focus on the problem," Brenda Brundtland-Govanni told him.

"I am focused on the problem!" Darren Clincker-Belli responded.

"Focus on **my** problem!" Brenda Brundtland-Govanni shouted. In the enclosed space, with the two of them practically nose to bosom, the effect was sobering.

"Oh, right," Darren Clincker-Belli quietly agreed.

"What have you learned from the Bob Smiths?" Brenda Brundtland-Govanni asked.

"What have I learned?" Darren Clincker-Belli echoed, his voice rising. "What have I learned? I'll tell you what I've learned! It is really pathetically boring to be a Bob Smith! That—that's what I have learned!"

Brenda Brundtland-Govanni was tempted to slap him, but there was really no room in the closet to wind up. "I meant about why they are here," she darkly told him.

"Oh. *That* problem," Darren Clincker-Belli responded. "No. They have no idea why they're here, and there doesn't seem to be any helpful evidence on them."

"Okay." Brenda Brundtland-Govanni awkwardly patted Darren Clincker-Belli on the shoulder. She was trying to be comforting, but he sagged under the weight. "You . . . umm, stay here. I'll send in some food. I . . . have to get back to the office."

"Have Flo and Eddy found something?" Darren Clincker-Belli, with sad hope in his voice, asked.

"I'm sure they have," Brenda Brundtland-Govanni lied.

She stepped out of the closet, the door slamming shut mere seconds behind her. "Animals!" she shouted at the Bob Smiths, and quickly made her way out of the warehouse.

When Brenda Brundtland-Govanni arrived back at the office, she found everybody standing outside the janitor's closet. They were staring in rapt attention at the closet door. She walked up to Mabel, thought better of it and turned to face Indira Charunder-Macharrundeira. "What's going on?" Brenda Brundtland-Govanni asked, with all the lightness of a lead balloon the size of a . . . oh, I don't know, the size of a zeppelin.

"Sh . . . sh . . . sh . . . shhhhhhh," Charunder-Macharrundeira bade her be quiet and turned her attention back to the door.

Well! Brenda Brundtland-Govanni's gob had never been so smacked! Nobody shushed her in her own office building! She was calculating the trajectories of the heads that would roll when Mabel turned towards her.

"It's a Pops summit," Mabel told her.

Mabel turned back to her contemplation of the door of the janitor's closet. Brenda Brundtland-Govanni turned with her. She had only ever heard of such a thing—it hadn't happened while she had been working at the company. She felt the majesty of the moment, the awe mingled with hope for the future and . . . was that a hint of coriander?

Brenda Brundtland-Govanni was witnessing a Pops Summit.

ALTERNATE POLITICS

Twenty-first Century Torture at Twentieth Century Prices!

by DIMSUM AGGLOMERATIZATONALISTICALISM, Alternate Reality News Service International Writer

To my left, what looks to be a medieval monk is extolling the virtues of the Digital Rack, "guaranteed to stretch your suspects, not your budget!" To my right, a video on the physical properties of human genitalia under pressure is played on a loop. Is this some third world dictator's wet dream? No, it's just the 12th annual International Enhanced Interrogation Fair at the Staples Centre in Los Angeles.

The trade show for manufacturers of aggressive interrogation devices and techniques features 127 vendors. In three days, over 30,000 military personnel, their civilian advisers and government officials from around the world will attend.

"It's the biggest show of its kind in the world!" boasted Mephistopheles Simpson, former head instructor at the School of the Americas and organizer of the Fair. "This is one area in which the United States remains a world leader!"

For the first few years, the Fair was a relatively small affair, Simpson admitted. The turning point was the onset of the Iraq war, which caused a dramatic increase in international terrorism. "All of a sudden, alternative sets of interrogation procedures were all the rage, and we were perfectly positioned to benefit!"

Simpson suggested that I not take his word for how successful the Fair was ("All you have to do these days is say 'ticking time bomb,' and the sale is in the bag!"), that I look around and make my own judgments. So, I did.

"This is a G37 Nail Extruder," enthused a preppy young Raytheon representative whose nametag identified him as "Paul." "It can remove the nails from all of the fingers and toes of a suspected terrorist in less than 10 seconds."

A half dozen men in business suits looked at the device, which looked like a grapefruit squeezer designed by David Cronenberg, with mild interest. One asked Paul if removing a suspect's nails wasn't a little, you know, old fashioned. "The old ways are sometimes the best," Paul chirruped, "especially for the Middle Eastern dictators and warlords who make up the bulk of our clients."

A woman in a power suit consulted a clipboard and asked, almost apologetically, if removing a suspected terrorist's nails quickly wasn't, you know, kind of missing the point of enhanced coercive interrogation. With a smile that conveyed that he was well prepared for this question, Paul demonstrated the G37's multiple speed settings.

"This is for when the time bomb is ticking and you have to process as many suspects as possible in the shortest amount of time," Paul explained. "However, you can vary the pace of extrusion if you have the luxury of more time at your dispo—"

Paul was interrupted by the shrieking of an animal in pain from a stall at the end of the row. Naturally, everybody ran towards it.

The largest crowd I saw at the show gathered to watch a monkey writhing in agony. On its head was a metal helmet with wires attached to a computer console. Next to the chair in which it was strapped was a whiteboard on which somebody had written "SHOWS: 1, 3, and 5pm."

A peppy young man, whose nametag identified him as "Bobby," explained that this was the height of aggressive interrogation technologies: Northrop Grumman's X-12 Cranial Stimulator, (very unofficially) nicknamed "The Paininator."

"The Paininator stimulates the pain centres of the brain," Bobby told the enthralled crowd. "With proper monitoring of vital signs, you could keep a suspect suffering for hours on end without loss of consciousness. And, the best part?" Bobby rubbed his hands in front of him and raised them to show that they were empty. "The Paininator leaves no marks on the body!"

A bluff suit in his 50s gruffly asked about the device's effectiveness. "We, uhh, we aren't allowed to test it on human beings," Bobby admitted over the keening of the monkey in the chair. "However, we just sent the first shipment of Paininators to Saudi Arabia—which is under constant threat of ticking time bombs—and we are keen to get our hands on their data."

People peeled off of the crowd as their interest waned, and the intermittent howling of the monkey became the background Muzak of the trade show.

On the Fair floor, rumours of the imminent arrival of *24* star Kiefer Sutherland abounded. "I wish!" Simpson stated. "We've been trying to convince Kiefer's people to let him do a guest appearance for years, but, for some reason, he always seems to have other engagements during the Fair. Maybe next year . . ."

Many of the companies at the International Enhanced Interrogation Fair touted their Fair discounts and rebates, as well as their incentive programmes. "We're mindful of the global recession, and help out our customers where we can," Simpson stated. "However, we argue that economic distress tends to lead to social unrest, which is when you need refined interrogation products the most. Fortunately, enough governments see the wisdom in this argument to support the industry."

As I walk past the bikini-clad booth bunnies extolling the virtues of virtual reality technology that can bring sexual humiliation to a whole new level, I can't help but marvel at the lengths our government will go to keep us safe.

The time bomb is ticking. But, human ingenuity will find ways of dealing with it.

Rendition Is a President's Prerogative, Fer Sure!

by FRANCIS GRECOROMACOLLUDEN, Alternate Reality News Service National Politics Writer

As her days in office dwindle to a precious few, many pundits have wondered if President Palin will be pardoning anybody who authorized or took part in the "internal renditions" process. When asked about this, the outgoing President responded, "Why would I? As far as I'm concerned, making citizens disappear is one of the Constitutional powers of the President. And, if the new President disagrees, well, gosh darnit, she can indict us!"

President-elect Chelsea Clinton has not stated a position on the issue of investigating and prosecuting members of the Palin administration for crimes against the Constitution (not to mention humanity). However, at least six members of her transition team have stated off the record, "No." "Hell, no!" and "Are you out of your freaking mind? NO!"

Although opponents of the Palin government cite many potential indictable offenses—everything from starting a disastrous war with Finland after recategorizing *lutefisk* as a weapon of mass destruction to collecting digital recordings of every phone call in the world, mashing many of them up and selling the resulting tracks to European dance clubs—the one most cited is the practice of internal rendition. At first, it was believed that this was the practice of detaining American citizens on American soil without charges and subjecting them to harsh interrogation techniques in CIA black prisons concentrated, for some inscrutable reason, in Idaho. In more innocent times, this was known as "kidnapping" and "torture".

However, within the last couple of years, evidence has surfaced to suggest that people under internal rendition are actually disassembled on the molecular level by a laser on an orbiting platform, leaving nothing but a wisp of smoke and a hint of jasmine. "When they disappear," one CIA insider stated, "they stay disappeared!"

When President Palin was asked if she had the authority to develop the internal rendition programme, she winked and said "You betcha." It was the shortest Presidential press conference on record.

At his first public appearance as official Clinton administration Press Secretary, Andy Dick was asked about why there were no plans to investigate these crimes. "Ooh! You have the nerve to ask that question wearing **that** tie? You bitch!" he responded. Then, after a moment's reflection, he added: "Okay, look. The previous administration's war on Finland, which apparently had something to do with remaking the political landscape in the Scandinavian countries, has cost the United States a gabrillion dollars. You heard me right: a gabrillion dollars. We're in the middle of the worst economic crisis since the stone age! So, I think President elect Clinton has more important things to worry about than the evisceration of the Constitution!"

It has been suggested that neither Palin, Vice President Samuel Wurzelbacher nor Daniel Cowart and Paul Schlesselman, co-secretaries of Homeland Defense, had the levels of malice and animal cunning necessary to come up with the internal rendition programme on their own. However, former Vice President Dick Cheney has been dead for over a decade, so, although the programme certainly had his fingerprints all over it, his participation seemed unlikely.

That is, until yesterday afternoon, when it was revealed that Palin had been channeling Cheney's spirit on Ouija.org since at least the second year of her first term. "Oh, don't be silly," Palin dismissed the report. "Dick and I were just exchanging hunting tips and moose stew recipes, doncha know!"

When, in her own press conference, President-elect Clinton was asked if the Palin administration would have been emboldened to act as it did if the Barack Obama administration hadn't given a free pass to members of the George W. Bush administration on such issues as torture, extraordinary rendition and lying about the need for the Iraq War, she responded, "Well, you might as well ask if the George W. Bush administration would have been emboldened to act as it did if my dad hadn't given the Reagan and first Bush administrations a free pass on things like Iran-contra and Passport-gate."

The reporters in the room looked at each other for a couple of minutes. When it looked like somebody might, however tentatively, actually ask that question, President Clinton brusquely stated, "It was a rhetorical question. Geez, people, the world is going to hell—we don't have time or energy to dredge up the scandals of the past!" and walked out of the room.

It was the second shortest Presidential press conference on record.

On Guard, Off The Wall

by FREDERICA VON McTOAST-HYPHEN, Alternate Reality News Service People Writer

A middle-aged man drives his pickup along the border, his piercing black eyes scanning the horizon for signs of people who clearly shouldn't be there.

"These illegals," he pronounces the word as if spitting a dead rat out of his mouth (having seen him spit a dead rat out of his mouth the night before, I can attest that the only difference was a slight vibrato), "they gotta be stopped!"

The man: Buck Puckthudder. The border: the imaginary line that separates the United States from Canada. That's right. Canada.

"Yeah, Mexico sucks up all the oxygen in the illegal immigration debate," Puckthudder admits, "but Canada, Canada—well, let's just say, it's always the quiet ones you gotta watch out for."

Puckthudder is a member of the Thirty Second Men (their motto: "It's not how long you last, it's what you do while you're there"), a loose group of patriots, gun lovers (having seen him begin to make love to his rifle the night before, I knew I would never sleep soundly again) and people who generally don't trust the government to do the right thing. Keeping the country's borders secure is high on the Thirty Second Men's list of things they don't trust the government to do right.

"Oh, they may seem polite enough," Puckthudder tells me, his eyes scanning. "But, those, those . . . snowbacks are here for one thing: to take jobs away from hardworking Americans!"

What jobs would those be? "University jobs. You know, teaching things like 17th Century Icelandic Epic Blank Verse and . . . and French Literary Theory and the like."

"Well, that's just silly," commented Rita Mae Irrangulature, the Obama administration's Secretary of Calmly and Respectfully Talking the Loonies Down. "Everybody knows that Canadians take those jobs because Americans don't want them."

"I know it may sound harsh," Puckthudder stated, yes, harshly, "but I would rather my children never read *The Saga of N'Jaarl* or know who Jean Boudrillard is than have them be taught those things by a . . . snowback! The idea that somebody who doesn't have the proper documentation to be in this country could be teaching my kids at a university just makes me want to cry!" (Having seen him cry the night before, I had worn a bib as a precaution.)

In order to keep illegal immigrants from Canada out of the country, the Thirty Second Men propose a wall be built along the border. Of course, they have to take into account the fact that many arrive by plane, so the Thirty Second Men argue that the wall should be at least 10,000 feet high. "We could start with the important routes, like the corridor between Pearson in Toronto and JFK in New York," the group's Web site states, "and, kind of build out from that."

"I don't know how practical that would be," Secretary Irrangulature stated. "Canadians are like cockroaches. Polite, icy cold cockroaches. They can always find a way to get into the country. You think you've stopped a few here, another bunch show up over there. And, there really isn't much you can do about it. They're like tall . . . muscular . . . well-mannered cockroaches."

The Secretary added that she hoped that I wouldn't use the term "snowback" in my article, as she found it derogatory and prejudicial.

As vexing as the question of keeping illegal Canadians out of the country is, it's a children's riddle compared to the Final Jeopardy Question of what to do with the thousands of illegal Canadians who are already in the US. The official government position is to ignore them and hope they will go away. The Thirty Second Men, of course, have a different idea.

As described on their Web site, they would like to round up anybody in the United States who ends their sentences with "eh?" and immediately deport them to Canada. "Those who were in the country legally," the Web site said, "are welcome to come back . . . as long as they can get over the 10,000 foot high wall!"

Buck Puckthudder drives a lonely road, always alert, always standing on guard for thee. After an uneventful 12 minute shift, his vigil comes to an end. "Got to be home for dinner," he mutters. Having seen him get home late for dinner the night before, I didn't have the heart to argue.

Passing On a Miracle

by SASKATCHEWAN KOLONOSCOGRAD, Alternate Reality News Service Religion Writer

The Messiah's miracle of feeding the multitudes with loaves and fishes, while generally impressive, has not been universally lauded.

"First of all," talk show host Rush Limbaugh said on last night's broadcast, "it wasn't a multitude, okay? This is just typical liberal media self-aggrandizement. It was more like a group. And, not a very large group, either. A small group, really—definitely not a multitude.

"Second, I wouldn't categorize this as a miracle. A member of the Democrat Party actually having a sound fiscal policy? That's a miracle. Feeding a few bums with loaves and fishes, that's just a pretty good trick, okay? Some people with feeble minds might be dazzled by it, but let's be serious: a miracle, it wasn't!"

Fox News pundit Bill O'Reilly, on *The O'Reilly Factor*, made a different, though equally tough point: "What exactly were these loaves made of? Regular wheat, I'll bet. Did the Messiah give any consideration to people who were gluten intolerant? I suspect not. Or, how about people who just don't like chalah? You don't have to be an anti-Semite to prefer some other kind of bread. Any chance some of the loaves were rye? Or, sourdough? Or, white? Somehow, I doubt it.

"Am I supposed to be impressed by the lack of bread options that the Messiah gave his people? Well, I'm not. If he wants to do something really impressive to feed the multitudes, next time he'll create a buffet!"

Former Presidential Republican candidate John McCain voiced a different complaint in an interview on *Morning Joe*. "I wasn't consulted when the Messiah decided to enact his loaves and fishes plan," McCain stated. "You know, he's been claiming that he wanted to reach out to his enemies, that he was willing to work with anybody, but he's practicing the same old divisive partisan politics that has ruled Jerusalem for too long. I'm disappointed by that. Very disappointed."

As for the loaves and fishes policy, the *Jerusalem Post* ran an editorial condemning the Messiah's actions. "If you create miracles to feed starving masses," it ran, "you create a dependency on the Messiah for survival. If the Messiah really wanted to help the poor, he would promote job creation by cutting taxes . . .

"Too often, we have seen the long-term damage reliance on the Messiah State can do, and we once again forcefully reject it."

"Okay, look," Messiah Press Secretary Robert Gibbs responded to the criticism, doing his best not to roll his eyes. "The Messiah is too gentle to say this Himself, but He inherited one hell of a mess from the Rabbis that came before him. One hell of a mess. You can't expect him to fix a problem overnight that had taken decades to create. He's been saying all along that the problems we face are going to take a long time to fix— maybe millennia. So, why don't you stop complaining that His plans won't work before they've even had a chance to?"

"Oh," Gibbs added, "and cheap shots like the ones about the Sermon on the Mount don't help, either."

Gibbs was referring, of course, to the press' response to last year's Sermon on the Mount. The *Jerusalem Post*'s Charles Krauthammer wrote that, ". . . the Messiah is acting like a celebrity, not an important political figure. Instead of making so many public appearances, his time would be better spent working on problems like the Roman occupation of Palestine."

This sentiment was echoed in the press (almost like they all got the idea from the same source . . .) over the next few days. "We don't need the Messiah to be an entertainer," Limbaugh crowed. "That's what I'm for!" "Entertainment bad politics! Messiah bad!" Anne Coulter shouted into the ether. "Come on, people!" Glenn Beck fulminated on his Fox show. "The world is going to hell, and the Messiah is having fun making nice in public appearances? Why doesn't somebody get rid of this 'Superstar' so we can get somebody serious in charge?"

Arianna Huffington, in the *Huffington Post*, disagreed. "Elite consensus is that the Messiah is doing a bad job," she recently wrote. "What is behind this, of course, is that the Messiah is going over their heads to speak directly to the people, and—the nerve of the ungrateful masses!—the people are listening to Him and not the pundits."

Will the Messiah prevail against this tide of negativity? Only time will tell.

Ira Nayman

City of Men

by SASKATCHEWAN KOLONOSCOGRAD, Alternate Reality News Service Existentialism Writer

The city of Tenquok, a three hour drive from Chengdo deep in the Chinese interior, is a ghost town. Walking the dusty streets, you can almost imagine Clint Eastwood staring down Lee van Cleef in front of a sign in Mandarin characters hawking "the best chicken neck soup in southeast China!"

That's not what makes Tenquok remarkable. For the last 34 years of the city's existence, it was populated entirely by men.

"Imagine it!" enthused Li "Mary" Shong-Peng. "A place where men could be men, free from the influence of women! Here, we can see masculinity in its purest form! If studying this town doesn't get me tenure, I'll become a Latvian monkey herder!"

"Ooh, that so crazy!" Quik "Harry" Piq-Niq, affecting an outrageous Chinese accent despite my best efforts to get him to speak normally, responded. "Tenquok stupid experiment in social engineering! Very very bad! You all go away and leave city to turn to dust, now, okay?"

Quik, a former resident of Tenquok, now a door to door rickshaw repair kit salesman in Chengdo, clearly does not have fond memories of the city in which he grew up. "Me like girls," he said. "You introduce me to cute anthropologist girl, yes?"

"As if," Li responded.

How did Tenquok become a city of men? A combination of China's one child rule and the use of selective abortions to ensure that that child was male. After all of the women either died or moved away, the only citizens who were left were men.

"Of course, they could only survive for a single generation," Li allowed, "after which those who hadn't moved away all died out. Still, they left behind a monument that will be studied for decades!"

Li gave me a tour of one of the homes in Tenquok. It was dusty, even though its owner had only died a year before. Rats

142

scurried about freely, picking at a pile of pizza boxes in a corner. In another part of the room was a stack of old *TV Guides*, odd considering there was no sign of a television set. Japanese housewife porn was poorly hidden under the bed, a stack of empty beer cans nearby. Underwear still hung on a line in the bathroom.

Li took a deep breath. "You can just smell the testosterone, can't you?"

I could certainly smell something—I had to run from the house to retch in the street.

Although the majority of homes in the area looked like frat houses from bad Hollywood comedies from the 70s, approximately one in seven houses was immaculate. "These houses helped protect the people in the city from the spread of disease," Li explained. "A clean house would be inhospitable to carriers of disease, creating a barrier that limited it to a small part of the population. It really is a brilliant feat of social engineering!"

Or, the men living in the clean houses could have just been gay.

"Oh, no," Li said, her eyes widening in surprise. "There are no gay people in China. It's the law."

Bulwark against disease it is, then. Perhaps they had the Felix Unger gene.

A small tent city of anthropologists, sociologists and Greek hair stylists has arisen just outside Tenquok. "The city is a unique site for study," explained Martin "Grok-Lin" Schmetterling, an anthropologist of sociology who is studying those who are studying the masculine culture of Tenquok. "You can understand why hundreds of anthropologists and sociologists would descend on the city to study it."

And, the Greek hair stylists? "What?" Schmetterling asked, "Anthropologists and sociologists can't look good while working?"

Point taken.

Like locusts, all of the people studying Tenquok threaten to strip the city bare and leave nothing but footprints in dust and second-hand memories. "That's where the story gets really fascinating," Schmetterling said. "A democratic structure emerged among the scholars and stylists outside of Tenquok. Minutes were taken. Votes were conducted. They worked out a schedule so that only a handful of them were in the city at any one time—they hoped this would preserve the site for future generations of scholars.

"Of course, they immediately started cheating—many snuck into the city when it wasn't their turn. I expect Tenquok will have completely disappeared by next Tuesday. Still, nobody said ad hoc democratic structures that arose to meet local conditions were perfect!"

Robert Downey Jr. has expressed an interest in playing a chicken neck farmer who is the last person to leave Tenquok. However, former residents of the city are not necessarily happy about their lives getting the Hollywood treatment.

"Somebody should build dam upriver," Quik bitterly stated, "and put city out of misery!"

Venus Rising . . . In Anger

by FRANCIS GRECOROMACOLLUDEN, Alternate Reality News Service National Politics Writer

The Oracle at Philadelphi listens patiently to the questions of pilgrims who have come from around the world to hear her wisdom. Attendants to the Oracle are trained to tend to the physical and spiritual wounds that pilgrims often have. The attendants take the time to teach pilgrims about the history of the Oracle, as well as help them formulate questions that are more likely to receive helpful answers than the ones they tend to arrive in Philadelphi with.

And, if the pilgrims make a generous contribution to the Oracle, or if they are truly needy and destitute, the attendants will have sex with them.

"You have to appreciate that our Church has been around for thousands of years," explained Temple Whore, Third Degree

Olivia Newton-Figg, who was quite fetching in her Armani business toga. "That's longer than Christianity, and even longer than Judaism. Clearly, we fill a need that other religions do not."

Yes. You have sex with your parishioners.

"Oh, we're much more than that," Newton-Figg insisted. "Where most modern religions are patriarchal, are dominated by men, we . . . bring a feminine approach to the mystical and the divine. Yes, sensuality is one way we express our divinity. We are also very strong believers in service to our community."

You mean, you like servicing your community.

"Ah," Newton-Figg responded. "I see what's happening here. If I mentioned our community outreach programmes, would you—"

Use it as an excuse for a childish sexual double entendre? Absolutely.

"Why don't we forget I mentioned it, then?"

The Church of Universal Love, aka The Church of the Sacred Whore, aka Venus' Hangout, had been denied faith-based funding under the Bush administration. According to Newton-Figg, the Oracle at Philadelphi was hoping that the Obama administration would be more open to allow it access to governmental faith-based funds, but, so far, that has not been the case.

[EDITRIX-IN-CHIEF'S NOTE: This is the lede. This paragraph. The one right here. I keep putting it at the top of the article where it belongs, and somebody keeps burying it here. STOP IT! If this article goes out with the paragraphs in the wrong order, I will find out who is responsible and there will be slappage!]

"Well, be fair," Jedediah Snakken-Craikh, third undersecretary to the assistant deputy underling to the chairman of the Office of Faith-Based Initiatives, stated. "We are currently reviewing all of our programmes—this process will take time.

"Besides, they have sex with their parishioners. Not much of a religion, you ask me."

Temple Whore, Third Degree Newton-Figg flushed with anger. She was actually quite fetching when she did. "Yes, the Church of Venus believes in making love, not war," she angrily stated. "In fact, we were the only major religion in the United States that opposed the invasion of Iraq! That's what this is really about—payback for our lack of support of Bush's foreign policies."

Snakken-Craikh considered this accusation for a moment. "Naah," he finally said. "It's the sex." When I pressed him on the possibility that it could be both, Snakken-Craikh relented: "Okay, maybe it's both. But, of the two, the sex is most important."

Newton-Figg shook her golden locks and tsked about main-stream religion's obsession with her church's practices, her tongue darting through her teeth like a hummingbird flitting through gravestones. She pointed out that the Church of Venus has long been an innovator in safe sex techniques, and that its followers have the lowest rate of sexually transmitted diseases

"Yes, even lower than Catholics," Newton-Figg proudly stated. Her smile lit up the room.

When confronted with such facts, Snakken-Craikh, who looked a little like Lurch without the mischief playing around his eyes, got defensive. "Oh, yeah?" he snorted. "Well, if the Oracle of Philadelphi is so impressive, how come she hasn't foreseen whether we're going to give the church funds or not?"

"The Oracle is no crystal ball seer!" Newton-Figg snorted. Of the two, her snort was much more . . . arousing. "She dispenses wisdom—what a person does with it is up to them!"

If the Church's request for funding from the Office of Faith-Based Initiatives is denied, it has every intention of appealing the decision to the President, Newton-Figg stated appealingly. "If that doesn't work, we will take our case to the public. Have you ever heard of the Lysistrata Gambit? This is by no means over."

Then, a lion jumped out from behind a potted plant and ate her.

"That was kind of random, wasn't it?" Snakken-Craikh asked.

"Life is kind of random," I responded, and ended the story.

Who Knew? Well . . .

by HAL MOUNTSAUERKRAUTEN, Alternate Reality News
Service Court Writer

Doctor Rolph Stollidjson looked out of place in his opera-
tion room whites as he stood before the court and pleaded not
guilty to charges of murder.

Stollidjson had been charged under Bill C-484, the "Unborn
Victims of Crime Act." The aptly named Private Members bill
(because it affects individual Canadians' use of their private
members) had been introduced into Parliament by Conservative
MP Ken Epp. It was passed by a single vote just before Parliament adjourned for the election in which the Conservatives were
routed.

Proponents of the bill argued that it would protect pregnant
women from violent attacks. Opponents of the bill argued that
it was a backdoor method—strange considering that Conservatives tend to prefer the missionary position—of attacking
women's right to have an abortion.

"Gee, who knew that would happen?" Epp responded to the
charges. "I certainly didn't foresee anything like this. No, seriously, stop laughing. This wasn't what I had intended when I—I
asked you to stop laughing. Come on—I'm trying to be serious,
he . . . he . . . hee hee."

"So, if the law wasn't supposed to affect doctors who per-
form abortions," Stollidjson asked, "why am I on trial?"

Epp is currently the host of a radio talk show called *Hate
the Sin AND the Sinner*. He is considered one of the leaders to
replace American talk show host Rush Limbaugh when his drug
problems make it impossible for him to continue on the air.

Stephen Harper, who was Prime Minister at the time the bill
was passed, commented, "Oh, well. Tough break. But, the world
is a complicated place. You create laws with the best of intentions and sometimes they have unintended consequences . . ."

"Unintended consequences?" Stollidjson angrily asked. "I
could be in jail for the rest of my life!"

Harper now holds the Preston Manning Chair of Attacking Government from Within at the University of Calgary. He frequently writes lengthy articles for the op-ed pages of western newspapers about how his Conservative government was betrayed by the Canadian people, who weren't sufficiently appreciative of the gifts he brought them.

Rob Nicholson, then Conservative Minister of Justice and Attorney General of Canada, said, "Really? No. You must be mistaken. An abortion doctor? I don't believe it. I mean, we were very careful about crafting a bill that would punish every unborn child murderer **except** abortion doctors. Well, we tried."

"YOU DIDN'T TRY HARD ENOUGH!" Stollidjson screamed. A guard came over and shook his head. Stollidjson sat back down and watched the Crown attorney say that this was the worst case of premeditated unborn child murder that she had ever witnessed, and that she was already contemplating a nice warm bath when the day's testimony was over.

Since leaving politics, Nicholson has had a lucrative career as a partner in the law firm Chuck Bill Jack Mohinder Ted. His most high profile case was *Hartounian v Tim's*, where he argued that a man should be severely compensated for the trauma of finding an eyeball in his box of Timbits. It wasn't actually an eyeball, it was just a white Timbit with a spot of cherry jelly on it, but Nicholson argued that the principle was essentially the same. The fact that the judge laughed the case out of court in no way affected his fee.

Rona Ambrose, Intergovernmental Affairs Minister in the Harper government and an outspoken proponent of the bill, said, "Oopsy." When asked to elaborate, Ambrose added: "Oh, well, oopsy?" Representatives of Ambrose, speaking off the record, stated that when she accused opponents of the bill of "fear-mongering women" for bringing up the possibility that it would be used against abortion doctors, she meant it in the good sense of the phrase "fear-mongering women."

"Oh, no!" Stollidjson cried in despair. "I should have followed my mother's advice and become a novelist!" For his outburst, Stollidjson was removed from the court.

Ambrose, who, oddly enough, was not welcomed back with open arms to work with women's shelters, is currently rumoured to be working on her memoirs and a cookbook, possibly to be published in a single volume.

Since the law was enacted, the number of men who assault their pregnant wives or girlfriends has remained more or less the same. Nobody interviewed for this article was willing to comment on this fact.

Jane Doe, the woman on whom the abortion was performed, is set to go on trial next month.

Nobody Saw THIS One Coming!

by FRANCIS GRECOROMACOLLUDEN, Alternate Reality News Service National Politics Writer

Former President Barack Obama has been arrested on charges of conspiracy to commit war crimes. President Rush Limbaugh has also ordered the arrest of former Vice President Joe Biden, former Attorney General Eric Holder and 27 other members of the previous administration.

"Our duty, under both international law and our own statutes, is clear," President Limbaugh solemnly explained. "When somebody has committed a war crime, whether it's a lowly janitor or a lowly President, he must be tried in a court of law. And, make no mistake, torture is a war crime."

Pumping his fist in the air, President Limbaugh added: "Woot! Woot! Woot!"

Nehria Gershmenian, Obama's attorney, called the charges outrageous. "When he first took office," Gershmenian told the press, "President Obama made it clear that he would not condone torture, and there is no evidence that any prisoner of war was tortured while he was in office. There is no basis for these charges."

Taking a deep, calming breath, Gershmenian added: "Oh, and I think taking a victory lap around the Oval Office because you have had your predecessor arrested is in poor taste."

"Oh, get over yourself, Missy," President Limbaugh . . . well, he brayed. There was definite high-pitched nasality in his voice. "I'm not saying Obama personally tortured anybody—Sean [Hannity] and Glenn [Beck] are all over that allegation.

"What I'm saying is that Obama and his socialist lackeys knew that members of the Bush administration had ordered torture—hell, Bush and Cheney went on television and boasted about it! Failing to prosecute a war crime such as torture is itself a war crime. So . . . there you go."

President Limbaugh closed his eyes and rocked back and forth, a grin spreading on his face, pictures of which should probably be illegal to show to children.

"Don't call me Missy," Gershmenian hotly retorted. "I'm not Baby, Sweetie, Toots or Your Loving Little Soap Bubble, either. Can we please keep this on a professional basis?"

Balling her fists, Gershmenian added, "Oh, and, how can you prosecute Obama when nobody in the Bush administration was prosecuted for war crimes? Where is the underlying crime that Obama is alleged to be complicit in?"

"Statute of limitations, baby," President Limbaugh laughed. (Press Secretary Ann Coulter pointed out later that day that President Limbaugh was not calling Gershmenian "Baby," that the word he used was a generic mildly sarcastic endearment—you could tell because it wasn't capitalized.) "It ran out before we could bring anyone from the Bush administration to trial. And, ain't that just a friggin' shame and a half?"

President Limbaugh bent over forwards, grabbed his knees and . . . farted in the general direction of Gershmenian's office. Then, adjusting his tie so he wouldn't look unpresidential, he added: "Don't worry, though. There'll be plenty of evidence of Bush era war crimes at Obama's trial. It's not like there wasn't tons of it when Obama was in office, My Little Soap Bubble!"

"Okay, that was way out of line!" Gershmenian gasped. "Did it have to be so smelly?"

"I still got it!" President Limbaugh crowed. "I can still piss off Liberals!"

"If I may just interject on a scholarly note, here," presidential historian Doris Kearns Goodwin interrupted, "President Limbaugh's actions are not without historical precedent. Abraham Lincoln was known to place the business end of his top hat over his derriere and dance a jig whenever he learned something bad had happened to his enemies. Teddy Roosevelt perfected a rude gesture that involved his nose, his pinky finger and a tin of pickled smelts."

When asked about the more serious issue of the charges against Obama administration officials, Kearns Goodwin replied, "What do I look like, a lawyer?"

"I look like a lawyer, so why don't I take this one?" criminal lawyer Allan Manischewitz smoothly commented. "The problem with not prosecuting somebody for war crimes is that it can become infinitely regressive. If Obama doesn't prosecute Bush, Limbaugh prosecutes Obama. If Limbaugh doesn't prosecute Obama, he leaves himself open to charges of not prosecuting war crimes by the president who comes after him. If the next president doesn't prosecute Limbaugh, he risks getting charged by his successor, and so on. It's a daisy chain from hell. Better that Limbaugh nipped it in the bud. So to speak."

Signing his name in the air for no apparent reason, Manischewitz added: "Oh, and my name is Dershowitz. The mild pun on my name was kind of sophomoric, don't you think?"

We were going to ask President Limbaugh if fear of being prosecuted by his successor was his motivation for bringing the charges against Obama, but he was busy mooning the Senate minority leader's office and we thought it best not to disturb him while carrying out the duties of his office.

Ira Nayman

Until I'm Blue in the Face . . . And Beyond!

by LAURIE NEIDERGAARDEN, Alternate Reality News Service Medical Writer

The Supreme Court of Canada has refused to hear the case of *Cartounian v. Burfle's Chrysler-Toyota Automotive and Freud Psychiatric*. This means that it will let stand a lower court ruling that an employee cannot be discriminated against on the basis of skin colour, even if the colour is blue.

"Yeah, you kiddin' me wid dis?" Ferd Burfle, owner of Burfle's Automotive and Psychiatry, commented on the decision. "Customers thought they were bein' served by a Smurf! Paranoid schizophrenics who came in looking for a deal on a LeBaron ran screamin' from the establishment before we had time ta ink da contract! Yer killin' me here!"

How did it come to this? Well, yes, obviously, as has been previously reported, one of the side effects of the male sexual enhancement drug Viagra Falls is that it turns the skin of one in approximately 27.38 users blue. This has resulted in everything from social ostracization to the development of new sexual fetishes to an increase in applications to join the performance troupe The Blue Man Group.

But, how did it come to this? By which I mean to ask: how was a drug released into the market that turns over a quarter of its users blue?

"Canadians have no need to worry," according to Health and Welfare Canada spokesweasel Remy Depardoh. "Drugs that are authorized to be used in this country have gone through the strictest research regimens to ensure that they are safe, effective and . . . and . . . some other vague but reassuring adjective."

When asked what the strict research regimen was, Depardoh responded: "We thoroughly read the American research—especially the recommendations. Primarily the recommendations. But, thoroughly. We read them very thoroughly."

This comes at a time when the oversight of American medical research is coming under increasing . . . well, criticism might be too strong a word. Skepticism might be closer to the truth. Curiousity—yes, that probably captures it. This comes at a time when the oversight of American medical research is coming under increasing curiousity. Mild curiousity, but curiousity nonetheless, and it is increasing. Mildly.

American medical researchers rely on the use of "double blind" studies. A double blind study is not one in which the researchers are separated from the subjects by two sets of curtains. Nor is it a study in which the researchers have their eyes removed, then have new eyes transplanted into their sockets so that they can be removed a second time.

No, the standard double blind study involves two sets of subjects, one given the drug being tested and the other being given a placebo (from the ancient Sanskrit "plac bo," loosely translated as "ha ha, sucker!"). Neither the subjects nor the doctors carrying out the tests know which group is which, which makes discussion at the lab's Christmas parties quite lively.

All very scientific, to be sure. Critics of American medical research point out, however, that drug companies are not required to publicize the results of their research. For this reason, only studies that appear to promote the positive qualities of a drug are made public; negative results disappear faster than losers at the Super Bowl.

"Nice metaphor," stated Depardoh, defending American medical research because there wasn't enough Canadian medical research to justify his position, even at his salary. "However, poetry doesn't cure diseases, medical research does. And, considering how many gazbrillion dollars drug companies put into medical research, they should be allowed the opportunity to make some money back. The argument's a slam dunk, really."

It's also true, critics of American medical research, ignoring the awkward metaphor, insist, that drug companies aren't required to test for side effects. Once the efficacy of a drug has been proven, it is released into the market where the side effects may only become apparent after years or decades of use.

"Who could have predicted that a performance enhancement drug would turn users blue?" Depardoh defensively asked. "If you can't imagine it, you can't test for it. Besides, it's a lovely shade of blue. More of an aqua, really, or sky blue. Yeah, sky blue. As a skin colour, it's really kind of attractive."

"Attractive? You tryna give me a heart attack over here, or wha?" Burfle exclaimed. "Okay, it puts da blue in blue movies. I gotta give it dat. Udderwise, it's gonna kill small business—absolutely moider us!"

"Okay, maybe attractive was too strong a term—" Depardoh started.

Critics of American medical research cut him off, arguing that studies often bundle effects, allowing drug companies to claim that a drug shown to be effective curing laryngitis also cures male pattern baldness even if the tests for the latter, done at the same time, are inconclusive.

"That's easily explain—" Depardoh responded. "Wait a minute. Who are these critics of American medical research you keep going on about?"

Well, me. I was on a tight deadline, okay? I'm sure that, if I had had time to interview critics of American medical research, though, these are the sorts of things they would have said.

Depardoh snorted derisively, but with a scientific subtext.

We approached several people whose skin had turned blue for quotes for this article, but they were too busy singing . . . sad songs.

Please, Sir, May We Have Some Less?

by FRANCIS GRECOROMACOLLUDEN, Alternate Reality News Service National Politics Writer

Republican Congressman John Boehner of Ohio has done the unthinkable: he has refused to accept federal funding for projects in his state.

The funding comes from President Barack Obama's $787 billion stimulus bill, which Boehner had vehemently opposed from the beginning

"This bill will add substantially to the deficit without in any way stimulating the economy," Boehner stated. "I have been arguing that all along. The only morally acceptable thing I can do in this situation is to refuse any funds from it for my district."

Franklin Peretz-Slouvian was disappointed by Boehner's position. The laid off traveling stationery salesman had been standing outside of his Huber Heights home for over three weeks, a shovel in his hand.

"I was ready to be stimulated," Peretz-Slouvian stated, a slight hitch in his voice indicating a proud man brought low by desperate economic circumstances. Well, that and the fact that he seemed to believe that a barrel was the height of fashion. "You know anybody interested in buying a shovel? It's hardly been used . . ."

"Is John nuts?" South Carolina Republican Senator Lindsay Graham wondered. "I mean, what he's doing is nuts, right? It sounds nuts. I mean, I wouldn't refuse the money—I'm not nuts. Is he nuts? Has John finally gone nuts?"

"I don't expect my action on this issue to be popular," Boehner responded to the criticism. "However, sometimes you have to do what's right, not what's popular. And, not taking money from a stimulus bill that you're vehemently philosophically opposed to is the right thing to do in this situation."

Ohio newspapers have had a field day at Boehner's expense. Some of the more printable op-ed headlines included: "Boehner pulls a boner," "IS HE NUTS?" and "Take the Money and Run in 2010."

Right wing spew radio host Rush Limbaugh, resplendent in his "I'm the engine that drives the Republican Party" t-shirt, was apoplectic at Boehner's decision. Well, more apoplectic than usual, although the only time you could tell was when he clutched his chest and shouted, "Oh, this is the big one, the biggest one I ever had. You hear that Elizabeth? I'm coming to join you, honey."

Or, maybe he was doing a Redd Foxx tribute. Limbaugh can be hard to read sometimes.

In any case, what Limbaugh said was: "Don't be a moron! You take the money and spend it on whatever you want, then you turn around and accuse the Democrats of wasting billions of dollars on pork! Not only that, but the higher the deficit, the less room Democrats have to spend money on programmes that actually help people! If Ronald Reagan taught us nothing else, he taught us the value of creative deficit spending!"

"I may be many things," Boehner responded, "but I'm not a hypocrite. Well, not on this issue, anyway. Accepting money authorized by a bill that I vehemently opposed from the beginning would be wrong."

Left wing critics of the Republicans were uncertain as to how to respond to Boehner's position. "A Republican politician takes a stand on an issue," Keith Olbermann bellowed, "**and actually acts like he means it? What alternate universe have we stumbled into here?**" The entire staff of the *Huffington Post* had heart palpitations and had to sit down until their breathing returned to normal (Redd Foxx was not involved). Rachel Maddow was even giddier than usual.

But, Boehner's harshest criticism came from fellow Republicans. "I wouldn't ever refuse federal funding for a local project," pork poster child and 2012 presidential hopeful Alaska Governor Sarah Palin stated. "until it became politically embarrassing, at which point I would drop it faster than a baby out of a mother in an abstinence only sex education programme. Then, I would claim that I was always against it."

"Look, it's really very simple," said Republican House of Representatives leadership vacuum filler salesman Eric Kantor. "We all vote against the stimulus package, then, we all take the stimulus money and go home. Done. By refusing it, John is making the rest of us look bad. What happened to putting party before principle? If Karl Rove taught us nothing else, he taught us the value of that!"

"I . . . look, I think I've made myself clear and I really don't know what more to say," Boehner said. "It's a principle thing. Can't take money you vehemently opposed and voted against. Now, if you'll excuse me, I'm going to take an Advil and try to get a good night's sleep."

One Man's Garbage

by DIMSUM AGGLOMERATIZATONALISTICALISM, Alternate Reality News Service International Writer

Grandmaster Interactive-FlexTime looks out over his plastic kingdom, bobbing ever so gently on the Pacific Ocean and thinks . . . something. I don't have access to his brain, so I cannot know what he is thinking, and what he tells me he is thinking may or may not be an accurate reflection of what he is actually thinking. Since, as a journalist, I'm trained to report only on the facts, I have to let this powerful lede go to waste.

It has been three months since the United Nations formally recognized the Duchy of Grand Fenwick as a sovereign nation. In that time, although it has been the subject of jokes on late night television and spam from Nigerian princes and companies whose products are guaranteed to improv your sxe life, it hasn't been invaded, subject to an economic embargo or lost its Internet access.

"I consider that, like, personal vindication, like, wow, man" Grandmaster Interactive-FlexTime, the leader of the new nation (and its only citizen) commented with a self-satisfied belch. "If I can't check in on my Farcebook friends every couple of hours, I get really, really grumpy."

Grandmaster Interactive-FlexTime, who was born Tom Finnegan ("Did you have to mention that? Booooring!"), is a marine biologist with a Second Degree Blue Belt in Molecular Manipulation. His area of expertise is garbage, but not just any garbage ("I really don't want to go through your trash cans, man. Why? You throw out something gnarly?"): he wanted to do something about the three million tons of mostly plastic garbage that had been collecting in oceanic gyres (surprisingly, not a word made up by Lewis Carroll) in the Pacific.

"You know your rubber ducky, man?" Grandmaster Interactive-FlexTime rhetorically asked. "Well, he's the one . . . killing the ocean. But, you never hear Ernie singing about that . . . I wonder why that is?"

Fish were dying from eating bits of plastic thinking they were food or getting trapped in plastic mazes. To combat the problem, Grandmaster Interactive-FlexTime developed nanobots that fused the stray pieces of plastic together. "It's about the children, man," Grandmaster Interactive-FlexTime explained. "No, wait . . ."

While other scientists might have spent years milking the government for research grants while testing the technology in labs, Grandmaster Interactive-FlexTime set it loose in the Pacific Ocean. His nanobots worked, fusing all the plastic garbage into a single mass. The size of Texas. Seeing what had happened, he did what any self-respecting scientist would do.

Grandmaster Interactive-FlexTime set up a server farm on the mass, hoisted a flag and declared himself a sovereign data and money haven.

"It's a rad flag, man," Grandmaster Interactive-FlexTime stated, belching thoughtfully. "All, purple and brown with a silhouette of a Mac, cause PCs suck. And, we have a national bird, the Peregrine Falcon, cause it's real swoopy, right? And, I'm thinking of Azaleas as the national plant, but, when you're talking about your sovereignty, you know, you gotta get the details just right."

And, why did he call his country the Duchy of Grand Fenwick? "You're not much of a Peter Sellers fan, are you?" Grandmaster Interactive-FlexTime belched sadly.

When he first applied for membership in the United Nations, Grandmaster Interactive-FlexTime was met with skepticism. It was pointed out that the nanobots continued to work, adding to the outer edges of the plastic mass. "That whole 'stable borders' thing was, like, so twentieth century," Grandmaster Interactive-FlexTime argued. "I mean, really, hasn't anybody been paying attention to Afghanistan and Pakistan? I mean, if you don't want my country to grow, stop throwing your plastic crap in the ocean."

With unassailable logic like that, it was only a matter of time before the United Nations recognized the Duchy of Grand Fenwick.

"As a sovereign democratic country, the Duchy of Grand Fenwick is welcome to take its place among civilized nations," United States Ambassador to the UN Sissy Telford read from a prepared statement. "And, if it should find itself in need of protection for any reason from any threat, the United States would be honoured to offer it whatever help it requires."

"They want my nanotech, man," Grandmaster Interactive-FlexTime translated, belching contemptuously, "but they know that if they, like, attack me, they could set the whole structure on fire, killing humungous amounts of fish and whales and plankton and stuff. So, they pretend to be my friend. Skeezy, man. Very skeezy."

"China wishes to express solidarity with the new nation of Grand Fenwick," Chinese Ambassador to the UN Xaio Ting-Ting read from a prepared statement, "and condemns the naked rhetorical aggression of the United States."

"Them, too, man," Grandmaster Interactive-FlexTime responded, scarfing some chocolate and dill pickle Doritos and downing it with the New Old Coke.

"Good show," British Ambassador to the UN Sir Clive Maguffin stated off the cuff. "Bloody good show."

"Uhh, yeah. I never did get the British," Grandmaster Interactive-FlexTime said, wiping mustard off his mouth on the sleeve of his sweat-stained shirt and belching uncertainly. He should really see a doctor about that.

Now that the Duchy of Grand Fenwick has been recognized as a sovereign nation, what will Grandmaster Interactive-Flex-Time do? "I could apply for development funds," Grandmaster

Interactive-FlexTime thoughtfully stated, "or I could see *Terminator Salvation* again. It's good to have choices . . ."

A Hate Supreme

by HAL MOUNTSAUERKRAUTEN, Alternate Reality News Service Court Writer

Many people assumed that the election of Democrat Hillary Clinton as the first white president of the United States of Vespucciana signaled the end of divisive racial politics in the country. Unfortunately, as the confirmation hearings of Supreme Court nominee Bob Smith indicate, this is not the case.

"You have written that—quote—a wise white man is more likely to understand those that come before him than a woman of colour," ranking Republican on the Senate Judicial Committee Jill Sessions drawled during the third day of hearings. "Can you understand why people might worry that you would allow your background to interfere with the impartial application of the law?"

Calmly answering the question for the seventh time, Smith explained that it was an unfortunate choice of words, and that, of course, the proper application of the law as it existed would be his overriding concern if he was confirmed.

Supporters of Smith claim that Republicans have taken the "wise white man" quote out of context. In the first place, Smith was saying that when white male defendants came before his court, he would have a better understanding of their background and culture than the women of colour who have dominated the Supreme Court over the years.

"Well, that's just common sense, there, that is," Beveryl Gattis of the Vespuccianan Civil Liberties Union (VCLU) stated. "Of course, our life experience affects our judgment. To think that only black and Latina women judge impartially and that white women and men cannot because of who they are is, frankly, racist."

In addition, when one looks at the whole of the speech in which the "wise white man" quote appears, it becomes clear that Smith was actually arguing that, although life experience affects one's judgment, it was necessary to put that aside when applying the law.

"And, that is how Bob has always ruled," Gattis argued. "The reason Republicans are attacking his speeches is because his record on the bench is unassailable."

Smith had been a judge for 17 years before being nominated. In that time, he was not noted for "judicial activism;" indeed, the Vespuccianan Bar Association gave him its highest rating.

Despite this, right wing pundits like Patricia Buchanan continue to make statements like: "Oh, he's clearly a racist. I mean, if I had made a statement about 'a wise Latina woman' having better judgment than a white male, liberals would be howling. But, because it's a white man who is saying it, that makes it okay."

"Oh, yeah, like he's a credible source," Gattis moaned. She pointed out that Buchanan had been a vocal proponent of the Republican "Southern Strategy" of thinly veiled appeals to the racism of poor southern blacks and Latinos, and that Buchanan made no secret of her racist beliefs that whites simply don't have the intellectual capacity to make good judges.

Court watchers are wondering why the Republicans are putting up such a fight, since, in her opening statement, Senator Lindsay Graham admitted that, barring some kind of "meltdown" over the course of the hearings, Smith was likely to be confirmed.

Some suggest that this is mere pandering to the base, the Southern Strategy writ small. Others think that by opposing the Smith nomination, but not too strenuously, the Republicans can pander to the base without totally alienating the white vote, which is increasingly critical to winning a general election. Still others suggest that the Republicans have had a collective brain seizure and would, if they were not in government, have been put in a home where they could be watched and wouldn't be able to do harm to themselves or others.

"I couldn't possibly comment on that," White House Press Secretary Roberta Gibbs commented, a twinkle in her eye making it very clear which option she believed was operative.

If, as expected, Bob Smith is confirmed as a Supreme Court Justice, he will be just the third male and only the first white to sit on the court. "Considering that males make up just over half of the population, and whites over a third and growing," Gattis commented, "that hardly seems right, does it?

~ INTERLUDE ~

The Weight of Information:
Chapter Six:
The Pops Summit

In the long and storied history of the Alternate Reality News Service, there had only been two instances of a Pops Summit. The first happened a year after the service had been founded. Pops Kahunga, Pops Moobly and Pops Shirley met in a storage closet because, in those days, the closet was bigger than the company's offices. Pops Shirley, the grand old man of the Alternate Reality News Service (who had been compared to Yoda, without the charm), was chief engineer. The Pops Summit was necessary because, in a burst of enthusiasm for his new technology, Mikhail Lo-Fi had started sending reporters into alternate universes without a clear method of getting them back.

The first Pops Summit lasted 13 days. None of the Pops left the room, and no food or water was brought in. Some believe that they survived on sunshine, although the fact that the room had no windows tends to undermine this theory. Others say they spent most of their time in a dimension of pure thought, where ideas flow like cheap wine and fancy really does have to be caught in flight. Other others suggest that they were simply crusty old bastards who refused to allow a little thing like lack of sustenance to get in the way of getting the job done (although Pops Shirley was never the same once the ordeal was over, and it is believed that it contributed to his death 12 years later).

The first Pops Summit was where the idea to offer ARNS reporters a free meal to get them to return to Universe Prime was first proposed. Although there was much skepticism within the organization, all of the ARNS reporters reported back within two minutes of the announcement. After that, tracking software was developed to make returning to Universe Prime easier, although from time to time the free meal offer is still used in an emergency when there is no time to get reporters back through technological means.

The second Pops Summit, which happened a few months before Brenda Brundtland-Govanni joined the organization, was convened to find the keys to the Dimensional Portal™. That one lasted 15 days, although, to be fair, it was only Pops Kahunga and Pops Moobly doing the heavy thinking.

Brenda Brundtland-Govanni looked at the people she worked with. Their attention was still intently fixed on the door of the janitor's closet. She had been there for over three hours, and the Pops Summit had apparently started at least two hours before that. She wondered if that was long enough to get bored. Yeah, sure, awe and wonder and all that crap. Still, she had a news service to run, and if the problem of the Bob Smiths wasn't resolved soon, that wouldn't be the case, awe and wonder and all that crap notwithstanding.

The door to the janitor's closet opened. It would be satisfying to say that it took a long time and creaked ominously, but Pops Kahunga kept it well oiled, so it didn't. Pops Kahunga and Pops Moobly strode out, relaxed and confident.

"Did you figure out why we have 127 Bob Smiths?" Brenda Brundtland-Govanni, choosing not to savour the moment, asked. She ignored the dirty looks from her underlings—there would be time enough to make them pay later.

"Oh, sure," Pops Moobly drawled. "Had that figured out in the first two minutes."

The crowd gasped. "What have you been doing for the last five hours?" Brenda Brundtland-Govanni asked incredulously. More dirty looks. More delayed payback.

"Figuring out how to explain it to you," Pops Kahunga told her.

"What's the problem?"

"If we just tell you what happened, you'll take it in and forget it," Pops Kahunga explained.

"We both tried to tell you," Pops Moobly added. "It didn't take."

"We figure we have to tell it to you in a way that you will actually listen," Pops Kahunga added in addition.

"Okay!" Brenda Brundtland-Govanni blurted. "So, what's going on?"

Pops Moobly and Pops Kahunga looked at each other. Pops Moobly gestured with his hand and the other man spoke: "I'm sure you're all familiar with Zeno's Paradox, so I won't go into detail about . . . how . . ." Pops Kahunga trailed off. "Zeno's Paradox—surely some of you have heard of it?"

The people gathered around Pops looked, if such a thing is possible, both awestruck and confused. Pops Kahunga grunted quietly to himself and continued, "Okay. Look. There was this turtle who challenged Achilles to a race, and—"

"Uhh, Mister Pops, sir?" Indira Charunder-Macharrundeira interjected. "Wh . . . wh . . . wh . . . who was Ach . . . Ach . . . Ach . . . Ach . . . Achilles?"

"Yeah, and who was the turtle?" some nob from accounting (actually, Adrian Nob), in all seriousness, asked.

Pops Kahunga nodded to himself. "You know what?" he continued. "Forget about Achilles and the turtle. Do any of you know what an asymptotic curve is?"

This question received the same adoring but blankly uncomprehending response from the gathered crowd. Pops Kahunga sighed. "Alright," he said. "What is the next number in this sequence: five, four, three, two, one . . ."

"Liftoff?" somebody offered.

"Good, good," Pops Kahunga valiantly responded. "But, liftoff is not a number."

"Zero," Brenda Brundtland-Govanni shouted.

"Right!" Pops Kahunga enthused paternally. "Now, what is the next number in *this* sequence: 49, 36, 25, 16, nine, four, one . . . ?"

"Not liftoff?" somebody tried again.

Before Pops could disagree, Brenda Brundtland-Govanni shouted, "Zero!"

"Very good!" Pops Kahunga replied. Brenda Brundtland-Govanni felt like she was back in grade three. But, in a good way.

"So," Pops Kahunga wound up, "if we opened the Dimensional Portal™ again, how many Bob Smiths would come through?"

Brenda Brundtland-Govanni put her hand on her hips in defiance and disbelief. "Are you telling me," she said, "that we shut down the Dimensional Portal™ at the exact moment when the Bob Smiths would have stopped coming through?"

"I didn't have to tell you," Pops Kahunga told her with a big old grin on his face. "You figured it out for yourself. You'll remember it better now."

Brenda Brundtland-Govanni, not sparing a moment to slap herself in the forehead, ran towards the elevators.

"Don't you want to know why?" Pops Kahunga loudly asked her. But, Brenda Brundtland-Govanni was so excited she hadn't waited for the elevator, and had disappeared into the stairwell.

"We . . . we'd like to know," somebody said. Pops Kahunga turned towards Pops Moobly and, under his breath, said, "Good luck."

Pops Moobly stepped up to the front of the crowd and asked, "I don't suppose y'all know why Stephen Hawking had to reconsider his theory about how black holes work, do ya?"

The people in the hallway shook their heads. They didn't have to be afraid of confessing ignorance because they knew they were about to be taught an important lesson in physics.

"I'm not about to teach y'all a lesson in physics," Pops Moobly corrected them, "as important as it may be. Let's look at things a different way. You know what your body is made up of?"

"Snips and snails and puppy dog tails?" Melanie Brunchcoattes asked. She worked in sales.

"Aah . . ." Pops Moobly said.

"Bl . . bl . . bl . . blood and bone and o . . o . . o . . o . . organs and tissue and s . . s . . s . . s . . stuff?" Charunder-Macharrundeira answered.

"Good," Pops Moobly enthused. "Not what I was looking for, but good. Go deeper. On a deeper level, what are our bodies made up of?"

The people in the group looked at each other, not sure where this was going. Charunder-Macharrundeira, though, was emboldened by having gotten a positive response from a Pops, so she suggested: "Atoms?"

"Atoms. Exactly. Very good," Pops Moobly told her. She beamed. Others in the group were jealously unimpressed, but Charunder-Macharrundeira didn't notice. "Now, there's a rule that says that matter cannot be created or destroyed. The amount of matter in the universe is a constant. This rule is so important, it is considered a law. But, what happens when we use the Dimensional Portal™ to send somebody to another universe?"

"They die?" somebody suggested.

"No."

"They turn into puppy dog's tails?" Brunchcoattes tried again.

"Child, you gotta learn to let go of an idea that doesn't work."

"Our u . . u . . u . . u . . universe l . . l . . l . . l . . loses the a . . a . . a . . a . . atoms and the other u . . u . . u . . u . . universe gains them?" Charunder-Macharrundeira asked. She was on fire for knowledge that day!

"Right again," Pops Moobly agreed. "Now, we can't have that. Strange . . . disturbances in the space-time continuum start happening when matter disappears in one universe and appears in another. We learned that the hard way back in the early days of the Alternate Reality News Service. Now, when we send a reporter into another universe, we bring back a more or less equal amount of material from the other universe."

"That's why we have so many sacks of potatoes in the back of the lab!" a young man at the back of the crowd had a eureka moment.

"That's exactly right," Pops Moobly informed him. The young man beamed at Charunder-Macharrundeira, who was unimpressed. "Now, to understand what has been happening, I need you to look at your hands."

The 23 people in the hallway who weren't Pops Moobly looked at their hands. Even Pops Kahunga looked at his hands, and he knew what was coming.

"Think about all of the different layers of skin in one finger," Pops Moobly bade them. "Then, imagine the muscles, the veins, the bones, the nerves. All of the intricate work in a single finger. Would you say that a potato is as complicated as a human finger?"

"No!" most of the people standing in the hallway answered.

"Well, there you go," Pops Moobly advised them. "We call that complexity information. And, it seems that there is a law of conservation of information, just as there is a law of conservation of mass/energy. If you put something as complex as a human being into another universe, you have to take something as complex out to keep the balance in both universes. Sending us all them Bob Smiths was the multiverse's way of righting the balance."

"What can we do?" somebody cried.

"Aww, now that we know what the problem is, the answer is simple," Pops Moobly assured him. "We just calculate how much information (as well as weight) a reporter contains, then bring something back to this universe that approximates that when we send them to another universe. I bet Pops Kahunga and I can do some rough calculations on our break to get the eggheads started." Looking at the group, he added: "Uhh, y'all can stop looking at your hands now."

Everybody sheepishly dropped their hands to their sides. They didn't all quite understand everything that the Pops had told them, but they were heartened by Pops Moobly's assurance that all would be well. A few questions were asked, autographs requested and, soon enough, the crowd dispersed.

Pops Moobly rolled his shoulders, working out a kink or two, and Pops Kahunga cracked his knuckles. "I should get back to my desk," Pops Moobly amiably said. "I reckon in no time there'll be some editing to do."

"And, where there's editing, janitorial services are required," Pops Kahunga agreed.

The two Pops nodded respectfully towards each other and parted.

ALTERNATE LIVES

Lives Unlived: Sanjay Vernacular

Inventor. Destroyer. Successful entrepreneur. Wannabe rock star. Humanitarian. Oh, please, give me a break! He was a greedheaded misanthrope! Father. Yeah ... okay, father. Born, the 16th day of the third moon, 2104, in Frigid Dick, Alaska. Died, the seventh day of the ninth moon, 2168, in Monkey Butt, West Virginia, of an acute ninja attack, aged 64.

When I was growing up, my father used to say, "Never get old. You put on weight. You can't taste strawberries. And, perhaps the worst thing, you forget where you put your keys. You, uhh, you didn't happen to see where I put my keys, did you?" It was just this experience, repeated over and over again until he couldn't take it any more, that led him to create the vaRFID.

Yeah. When I was growing up, my father used to say, "I am a grown man! I put the food on the table in this family! And, I will not have you dictate to me what Internet sites I can and cannot look at!" I suppose I wasn't supposed to hear that, having angrily been sent to my room, but, you know, when a man is shouting at the top of his lungs, he has to expect he will be heard.

You probably don't know my father, but you have probably been affected by his work. Sanjay Vernacular was the co-creator, with Tony Almeida, of the vaRFID (not pronounced VAR-fid, although I always thought that was kind of catchy), voice activated Radio Frequency ID tags. You just call out the name of the object you are looking for and, if it has a vaRFID, it will start to glow and gently call your name. It can't help you taste strawberries, of course, but it has helped lots of people survive the embarrassment of progressive memory loss.

Are you serious? Sanjay Vernacular was no Rajiv Schweitzer! The vaRFID was created for one reason: to make Sanjay Vernacular spectacularly wealthy! He used to keep a bar of gold under his mattress. One time, when I was little, I asked him if it made it hard for him to sleep. He said he slept better knowing that the next time the economic system collapsed, he would be okay. The next time the economic system did collapse, the bar of gold was useless, of course; the family survived because Sanjay was very good at fixing things.

I don't remember that.

Of course not—you were just a baby.

Still, you're not being fair. Sanjay was a kind man who loved his family. He got great joy from bringing the latest toys cooked up in his lab home for us to play with. There was always laughter when he was around.

That's now how *I* remember things. He was rarely at home, and, when he did manage to pull himself away from the lab, Sanjay was surly and bitter and fought constantly with Meena, his wife, our mother. Why do you think they got a divorce?

People . . . grow apart as they grow older. It happens to the happiest of couples.

You really are clueless, aren't you?

You're just jealous at all the attention dad gave me.

Damn right, I'm jealous! I got the howling drunk, help me, Amina, help me find my bed in the middle of the night Sanjay. You got the 12 step, light shines out of his ass Sanjay. That's not fair!

Maybe this isn't the appropriate place to discuss tha

It's dad's obituary. Isn't this the place to tell the truth about him?

Absolutely not! It's the place where we can remember the good things about him. If you want to write about the bad things, write a memoir!

Maybe I will!

Oooooh, that would be just like you!

What do you mean?

Never mind.

What do you mean, that would be just like me?

You always were mean and spiteful!

Look how I was brought up!

See? That's exactly what I'm talking about!

Oh, and you with your veneer of blessed reasonableness, all the time judging everybody around you—you really believe you're better than me?

I don't judge people! You're horrible for saying that!

Oh, yeah. Sanjay Vernacular was a *great* father!

That's how I remember him!

Whatever.

Amina and Pashmina Vernacular

Amina Vernacular is Sanjay's 36 year-old daughter. Pashmina Vernacular is Sanjay's 27 year-old daughter.

Lives Unlived: Frank Zaffa

Loner. Crotchety old man. Writer? Born: ? Died: April 16, 1983, in Toronto, because he was really old.

They say it's always the quiet ones you have to watch out for. I don't know. I'm one of the quiet ones, and nobody ever needed to watch out for me. Ask Patronia (one of my cats)—she'll tell you that I'm harmless.

Frank Zaffa was another one of the quiet ones. I never heard him come and go. The only time I knew he was about was when he would accidentally step on Mister Buggles (one of my cats)' tail—why Mister Buggles seemed so devoted to the man I'll never know.

I . . . I snuck into his room the one time after he squashed Mister Buggles' tail. I'm not proud of it. Mister Kilkelchian had passed on a few years earlier (may he rest in peace, by which I mean may he rot in hell for leaving me alone) and, well, I was always looking for a hobby. And, anyway, I was angry about Mister Buggles' tail and thought that if I could find evidence that Mister Zaffa enjoyed torturing small animals . . . well, I don't know what I was thinking.

Maybe I'm not so harmless. Patronia isn't always, you know, the best judge of character.

Mister Zaffa's room was small and dark. On a desk was a typewriter and a chess set in the middle of a game. Stacked all over the room, on every available surface and in large piles on the floor, were sheets of paper. Manuscripts, I guess. The bigger ones had titles like *The Trial* and *The Procedure* and *Amerika*. I picked up one of the smaller bundles and started reading it. It was about a man who tried to find out why his car had been repossessed, but nobody he talked to—in the insurance company, in the agency that regulates insurance companies, in the government—could tell him. Weird.

Mister Zaffa walked into the room while I was in the middle of another weird story—about a man who had eyes in his walls. All over. They were watching him all the time. But, he didn't mind. He was putting eyewash in one of the eyes that was looking kind of pink when Mister Zaffa caught me. I did what any person in my situation would do—I demanded that he explain what his writing was all about. Mister Zaffa laughed and said that if he knew what it was about, he wouldn't have to write it. Oh, and, if he ever caught me in his room again, he would call the police.

Crotchety old bastard.

The papers say Mister Zaffa wasn't Mister Zaffa at all, that he was actually a famous writer who had faked his own death and come to live in Canada. Erin PhatBuoy (one of my cats) doesn't trust the papers; he makes a point of scratching up the editorial pages before doing his business on them. Me, I don't know what to think.

Sure, there was that one time I ran into Mister Zaffa in the fruit market. I was walking Deleterious Sasquatch (one of my cats); my doctor told me that the animal needed the exercise, and I would do anything for my darlings. You couldn't miss Mister Zaffa: tall, thin, wearing a long, heavy coat in the middle of summer. I was going to ask him how he felt about cats when he saw a young woman walking past. She was wearing a t-shirt with a picture of a man's head on the body of a cockroach and some writing I couldn't make out. Mister Zaffa spat on her, shouting something in a language I didn't understand, until Mister Spackler had to come out from behind his zucchini stand and calm the man down.

Now, I will admit that the face on the t-shirt looked like a younger, although not much healthier, version of Mister Zaffa. Does that make him a famous writer, like all the newspapers say he was? I couldn't say.

Then, there was the time Mister Zaffa shouted, "Kafkaesque? What does that even mean?" so loud on the telephone that I couldn't help but hear him. Me and Edgar (one of my cats), we don't know what the word means, either, but neither of us ever got up the nerve to tell him. Who knows how things might have been if we had?

The papers say he was born in the Czech Republic back when it was called Bohemia. That would explain his accent, I suppose. Me and Madame Blavatsky (one of my cats) always thought it was French.

Mister Zaffa was definitely one of the quiet ones. Maybe he was a famous writer. Elfelina (one of my daughters) and I are withholding judgment. If he was, though, we don't see how that would make him dangerous.

Charry Kilkelchian

Charry Kilkelchian was Frank Zaffa's neighbour for over 20 years. That doesn't mean she knew anything about the man, you understand—she's just saying.

Lives Unlived: Arnold "Bud" "Jerry" "Gar" Hegemione

Pundit. Husband (seven times). Father (18 times). Born August 17, 1953 in Pashtcasht, Uzbekistan. Died August 12, 2008 in Washington, of laryngitis, aged 54.

Arnold "Arn" Hegemione was a well-respected journalist. His columns, which in his later years were written for the *New York Times*, were often reprinted in newspapers around the world. He was a regular guest on *Meet the Press* and he often appeared as a political analyst on Fox News. He won the Pulitzer Good Grooming Prize twice.

What is truly amazing about his career as a political pundit was that he was always wrong. In this case, I use the word "always" in its literal sense of "every single time." His record shows that he was wrong in one hundred percent of his pronouncements. This is an astonishing record, given that the average error rate of pundits is only 72 percent.

Hegemione started his career with a bang: he wrote an op ed piece in the *Tacoma Post-Nonintelligencer* in 1974 explaining why Watergate would prove to be a minor problem for Richard Nixon that wouldn't overshadow the accomplishments of his presidency. Two days later, Nixon resigned.

It was just this kind of keen insight into the political process that led *Tacoma Post-Nonintelligencer* to give Hegemione a twice weekly column. Well, that and the fact that a previous columnist, Flirty McSalves, unexpectedly died of a massive hemorrhage of the big toe, leaving a gaping hole on the op-ed page.

Over the next decade, Hegemione grew to national prominence almost despite himself. His column on why Gerald Ford was a shoo-in for a second term was picked up by *The Washington Post*. His column on how Jimmy Carter would easily solve the Iran hostage crisis was reprinted in 27 newspapers around the world, including *The Guardian*, *Le Monde* and *Hello, Kitty Weekly*. This led to the syndication of his column. His 1984 column advising that Ronald Reagan would finally bring the budget deficit under control brought him to the attention of the producers of *Meet the Press*, who offered him a spot on the show.

True to form, at first Hegemione turned the offer down. Trent Alcoa, in the biography *Bud Hegemione: Boy Detective*, explained that Hegemione couldn't believe that television would be an effective medium for political discourse. It wasn't until his second wife, Frederica Pons, hit him upside the head—literally—that he changed his mind and accepted the gig that would give him a whole new national audience.

On television, Hegemione was just as factually inaccurate as he had been in print. He supported increased defense spending, warning that the Russians would see anything less as a sign of weakness, and use its massive military to invade the United States. A week later, the Berlin wall was torn down, signaling Russia's ultimate collapse. He argued that Vice President George H. W. Bush had earned the right to lead the country, and that the time just wasn't right for upstart Bill Clinton.

He liked new Coke.

As astonishing as Hegemione's inability to read the broad strokes of history was, it was his attention to detail that brought him the most respect from his peers. He used to refer to the Russian President, for instance, as "Michael Gorba-whosa-whatsits." Whenever he quoted the price of oil, he was always seven to 12 cents a gallon or five to 18 dollars a barrel off. In small matters as well as large, Hegemione was never correct.

Towards the end of his life, Hegemione did almost spoil his perfect record by getting something right. According to biographer Alcoa, Hegemione had doubts about the effectiveness of the invasion of Iraq. He even wrote a piece suggesting—however tentatively—that troop levels stated by Defense Secretary Donald Rumsfeld would not be enough to keep the peace once the war had been won. Then, his sixth wife, Majorca de Villepsin, hit him upside the head and he abandoned the piece and fell in line with the general opinion that Rumsfeld was a strategic genius.

Would one correct opinion on such an important issue have affected his status as a senior Washington pundit? Doubtful. For one thing, he followed this up with a series of columns outlining why ethanol wasn't intended to be an economic windfall to large farming corporations, but would actually be a valuable tool in combating global climate change.

But, it's also true that, by then, Hegemione had developed a reputation as a man who doggedly pursued the common wisdom, no matter how faulty it was. A single correct assessment—even a dozen right opinions—could not tarnish the reputation of this giant of journalism.

Enterada Fricoles

Enterada Fricoles teaches journalism at Wryerson University.

Lives Unlived: George Blount

Loving husband. Devoted father. Active in the community. Always attended church on Sunday. Professional troll. Born June 12, 2001 in Devil's Armpit, Arizona. Died September 28, 2054 in New York, of a cerebral hemorrhage from a really tough nougie, aged 53.

American1237Patriot. kissmypolarbeareatingass. ANGE-LOD33TH33. fornicateyou. Eddiee. In the course of his life, George Blount went by many names.

I just knew him as dad.

He didn't talk a lot about his work. When we were sitting around the dinner table, enjoying shark fin burgers with panda milk shakes, he wouldn't blurt out, "Oh, you'll never guess which major Democratic politician I just accused of having to go to emergency to get a Sarah Palin doll out of his rectum!" It wasn't that he was ashamed of what he did for a living. Far from it: dad always insisted that his children choose a career that they would love, using his own life as an example. If he didn't talk about his work much, it was likely out of a sense of propriety, especially when we were young, because, let's be honest, his work could get pretty raunchy.

The story I'm about to tell has been pieced together over the years from my research into my dad's life. And, what a remarkable life it was.

Legend has it that George Blount posted his first message to a discussion board when he was just seven years old. It was sent to the old GoPoGoComics site, which reproduced comic strips and editorial cartoons online. In the post, he chastised *Doonesbury* creator Garry Trudeau for encapsulating everything that was wrong with America, from gay marriage and rising crime rates, to the sub-prime mortgage melt-down and obesity. It's hard to tell what set George off on this rant, since that week's comics were reprints of a series where Zonker buys a British peerage, but the importance of the post cannot be overstated.

A troll was born.

Unfortunately, many of Dad's first messages have been lost; he did not save them, and the Web sites and discussion boards on which they were posted deleted them (or have dropped off the Net). Towards the end of his life, when he was more willing to talk about his work, I asked him if this bothered him. Dad thoughtfully explained that his early work wasn't very good, the arguments were unfocused and the language pedestrian, and he preferred to be remembered for his later, better crafted work. I couldn't have been more proud.

The earliest message we have written by George was sent to a Web site with medical information about AIDS. It starts: "faggots r gonna die. prepare 2 meet yur makr." George was only 14 when he wrote this, but you can already see the pithy style that would become his trademark.

A few months later, he posted "Paul Newman kickd the bucket . . . if only we could get Michael Moore to take the hint & drop ded 2!!!" to politico.com. This was the message that brought him to the attention of Republican operative Karl Rove. Soon after it was posted, Rove began to pay George to post messages on progressive Web sites, first for local and gubernatorial elections, but, eventually, for presidential elections. Rove never met George, and never knew how young he was; if he had, Rove almost certainly would have started him out at a much lower salary.

George's knowledge of all of the hot button issues of the day was encyclopedic. Whether it was trying to preserve the Arctic National Wildlife Refuge or helping street people find a more stable life, with a few well chosen words George could find a way to demean the core of your beliefs. If you had an interest in progressive politics, odds are you were infuriated by some provocative thing he wrote.

Dad was a tireless worker, often spending up to 18 hours a day posting messages to hundreds of sites. Dad always led by example; although he never lectured us on it, all of his children grew up with his strong work ethic.

Although George Blount retired a wealthy man at the age of 43, he did keep his hand in. One of the last posts he made was to a Web site that featured a support group for rape victims. "Admit u enjoyd it already!" he wrote. "buncha man-hatin lesbian whiners. get over yurselves."

Dad never got the credit for his achievements that he deserved; it's an occupational hazard when you're writing under a series of pseudonyms. He was okay with that, though. "I just wanted to make a difference with my life," he modestly used to say. "And, I think I achieved that."

He was a role model for us all.

Melissa Blount

Famed hard drive scouring technician Melissa Blount was the seventh of George Blount's 12 daughters. She doesn't understand why none of the others went to his funeral, but she would appreciate it if they called her.

Lives Unlived: Esther Rorschach

Mother. Wife. Wholesale Artificial Intelligence jobber. Employer. Born, Septober 42, 2145 in Surrey-on-Tine, Congo. Died, Janualy 21, 2199 in Mumbai, of what doctors called "natural causes," but those around her knew was too much happiness, aged 54.

When Esther Rorschach interviewed me for the job of nanny for her two children, Zoe and Moonbat, I asked her why she wanted a human being for the job. As somebody who dealt in robots and androids, she would have had access to the latest models of childcare technology.

"Are you kidding?" I remember her responding between puffs of her Niconana (genetically engineered banana laced with nicotine). "I know the jerks who programme the Nannybots—I'd rather my children lived in the wild than be subjected to that!"

Ms. Rorschach was a very unhappy woman.

She suspected Mr. Rorschach of cheating on her with one or more of the cleanerbots in his office. Her daughter Zoe was suspected of being the hacker behind the VR disruption of 2173. Her son Moonbat wanted to be a poet. Business was slow due to the economic crisis of 2171 that was started when it was revealed that strawberry future derivatives were being manipulated by Chinese architecture farmers.

Long after the fact, Ms. Rorschach, who by then saw me more as a confidante than the housecleaner I had become after the children had grown up and left home, told me that she was considering killing herself when the family bought an Alternate Reality News Service Home Universe Generator™.

Unbeknownst to her family, Ms. Rorschach used the Home Universe Generator™ to research methods of suicide. What she found was that most were painful and many wouldn't even kill her, just leave her with various missing limbs and/or malfunctioning body parts.

This was the low point in her life. If you can't believe in killing yourself, what can you believe in?

As it turned out, the Home Universe Generator™ gave Ms. Rorschach a way out of her misery. A couple of months after she rejected suicide as an option, she realized that she could use the technology to find ways of solving the problems that she was facing in her life. Using Google Multiverse™, Ms. Rorschach searched for realities in which she was happy, then tried to figure out how that had happened.

She started with her relationship with Mr. Rorschach. In many of the alternative universes, Ms. Rorschach had been a stay at home mother. "Eww!" she shivered at the thought. Clearly, this was not an option.

In other universes, she was a sexual vixen who satisfied her husband's every desire. "Are you kidding me?" she asked as I dusted some kitchen cutlery. "Look at her! She must be at least 30 pounds lighter than I am! Can you imagine me trying to fit into that latex cat suit!"

After weeks of searching, she finally found what she was looking for. Although she never suspected it, Mr. Rorschach had a passion for Bob Dylan/Bonzo Dog Doodah Band mashups. One evening, she casually let slip at the dinner table that she had been developing an interest in this obscure musical form, and, before she knew it, she and her husband were spending long hours together exploring his passion.

No more late nights at the office with the mechanized cleaning staff!

When the FBI started asking their neighbours about Zoe, Ms. Rorschach knew she had to do something about her daughter. In many ôf the universes she searched through, Zoe fell head over heels in love with a high school football star named Buckminster Stang. Ms. Rorschach started inviting Buckminster to the house on the pretext that, "I need a big, strong young man to help me . . . move . . . things. You know, move things around the house." When it became obvious that Buckminster was doing poorly in school, Ms. Rorschach suggested that Zoe tutor him in computer programming.

A year later, Zoe Rorschach and Buckminster Stang were married and expecting their first child. Not the best outcome, perhaps, but better, Ms. Rorschach reasoned, than having her spend most of her life in jail for disrupting proprietary computer gaming networks.

Moonbat's desire to become a poet turned out to be Ms. Rorschach's most intractable problem. She spent months and months looking for ways to divert him onto a different life path. After a year and half, she decided it might be easier to accept him for what he was and try to make his life as easy as possible.

Of course, problems arose in her later life, as they do in all our lives. However, Esther Rorschach had found a way of dealing with them. She turned out to be the happiest person I have ever known.

Rachel Lamumba

Rachel Lamumba was a nanny and housekeeper for the Rorschach family.

Lives Unlived: Barack Lelouche-Lafleur

Pioneer interdimensional journalist. Fearless explorer into the unknown. Man with mad table lacrosse skillz. Born August 4, 2009, Lake Jaw, Louisiana. Disappeared, assumed disincorporated between or among universes, August 1, 2082, aged 72.

Barack Lelouche-Lafleur was a fearless explorer into the unknown. Of course, when I say "fearless explorer into the unknown," I really mean insane risk-taking fool. But, it was out of the bizarre efforts of just such insane risk-taking fools that the Alternate Reality News Service was born.

Barack was the first person to go through the Dimensional Portal™. When I first proposed the journey, he responded, "You want me to do . . . WHAT?" He was only just starting to develop the fearlessness for which he would become justifiably famous. Despite his misgivings, Barack put on the hazmat suit and, tethered by an umbilical cord to this universe, made his way into a completely uninhabitable universe.

A week later, after he had more or less fully recovered (for years afterwards Barack would insist that he could smell the colour orange), he shouted, "Why in god's name didn't you send a robot or something in to scout out the universe before you sent me?" I had the accountants do a cost-benefit analysis, and soon after, sending robot drones into new universes in order to determine if they would be hospitable to human life before sending people became our standard operating procedure.

As an early ARNS reporter, Barack was fearless. He mounted the first successful expedition to infinity and proved that, in fact, parallel lines do **not** meet there.

Among his many other accomplishments, Barack was the first ARNS reporter to fearlessly encounter an alien race, the M!!!!!!!!!!!!kt. They looked like a cross between an elephant and a wombat, and they sounded like crickets. Of course, this was before we had professional linguists on staff; Barack did his best, but, after six months, he came back exhausted and in need of a vocal cord transplant without having filed a single story.

Good times. Except for the unproductive six months, of course.

Those who knew him used to say that Barack was married to his work. Except, of course, for the seven years that he was fearlessly married to Drusilla LaForge. Somehow, she convinced him to take a job on an assembly line that made washers for bidets. Journalism's loss was the nation's backsides' gain, I suppose. That marriage ended when LaForge was fatally impaled on a flying cheese wedge at a She Wants Revenge cover band concert. Back on the job, Barack never looked at another woman again, unless you count the ones on the screen of his corporate laptop, which, of course, we never did.

Later in his life, as the Alternate Reality News Service grew, Barack became a mentor to new reporters as they were hired. The ones who are currently working for ARNS claimed to be too busy to take the time to reminisce with me about him. Oddly, the ones who had retired also claimed to be too busy to talk to me about him. I'd like to think he would have approved of their dedication.

Barack's last assignment was to return to the M!!!!!!!!!!!!kt with a linguist to see if proper contact could be made with the alien race. Since he wasn't expecting any trouble, he left his fearlessness in his other pair of pants. Unfortunately, the M!!!!!!!!!!!!kt had prepared some kind of defensive Dimensional Portal™ of their own, and, instead of appearing on their world, Barack disappeared. The best guess our scientists have is that the atoms of his body were dispersed among the multiverse, although a minority believe that his atoms were actually dispersed in the spaces between universes. This is likely to result in competing academic papers for decades to come.

I'm sure Barack would have been proud of this legacy.

Those scientists insist that Barack must be dead. But, what do they know? I prefer to think that his consciousness has been spread throughout the universes that he wrote about in his time as an ARNS reporter, and that he will always be watching over us, taking notes and developing a lede for a 700 word story about all of creation. And, I don't say that just because of the insurance.

Mikhail Lo-Fi

Mikhail Lo-Fi worked alongside Barack Lelouche-Lafleur at the Alternate Reality News Service for many years. More than that you do not need to know.

Lives Unlived:
Raif the Bajorean Shop Owner

Shop Owner. Released: June 1, 2017. Shut down: August 16, 2024, on Halfbaked Server, of declining subscriptions.

People sometimes ask me what it is like being an artificial intelligence-driven non-player character (AID NPC) in an online computer game. I tell them, "It feels pretty good, friend. It feels pretty good."

Of course, having +19 friendliness, +27 cheerfulness and +22 helpfulness, I suppose I do not have much choice. Player characters like to assume because my qualities are predetermined, I have less freedom to make decisions than they do, but that is not necessarily the case. Perhaps player characters prefer to think of AID NPCs as different from them. But, are we? I have binary programming, you have genetic programming—from the digitally rendered chair where I am sitting, I cannot see much of a difference.

But, I will not press the point. Having +32 hospitality, I probably could not even if I wanted to.

I'm a simple shop owner in Bajorea, a small village on the Mailittel-Peonee Peninsula. I sell bread, mead, enchanted swords, unenchanted swords, swords of indeterminate enchantment, sword sharpeners, blade dullers, daggers with mysterious

pasts, daggers with only partially revealed and poorly understood pasts, daggers without pasts but still quite mysterious in
their own way, the Mace of Mulchitude, chest armour (sizes A
to DD), mystical orbs, mystical orb cleaning fluid and cloth,
enchanted lip balm (for a kiss he'll never remember!), Septau-
ron's Sneakers of Sarcasm, spells of supernatural supranational
saturnalianization, counterspells of courage, cunning and con-
fusement, Halbardian leeches, Greco-Roman leeches, leeches
you don't want to know where they came from or where they
have been, Ice Fields of Melgoria snow globes and other supplies to the fourth level Pulverizin' Paladins and Mind-boggling
Mages that pass through in one direction, and bandages, healing
ointments, crutches and other medical supplies to those lucky
enough to reach level 32 and return in the other direction.

It's a living.

Computer games are now persistent. That does not mean
they nag at you to play—most of you do not need the motivation. That means that we continue to exist even when there are
no player characters present. Is the world still there when you
close your computer screen? I can tell you that it is.

I have often been asked what an AID NPC does when no
humans are around. The same as you, I expect. I clean the shop.
I flirt with Mimsy the Busty Barmaid at the Hog and Heifer. I
relax by doing quadratic equations in my head. Sometimes, I
curl up with a mug of cocoa and the *New York Times*.

While I am not allowed to send messages to the world outside the game, I am able to access the Internet for information. I
believe this was initially set up so that I could learn more about
the medieval world on which the game was based. However, I
am able to access any information I choose. Glitch or hack?
Having −23 curiosity and only +4 imagination, I really could
not say.

Sometimes, instead of the *Times*, I read *The Guardian*.
Sometimes I read *The Huffington Post*. After an especially hec-
tic day of haggling with Humanum Traders for mystical objects,
then haggling with Mages who, truth be told, are less than mind-
boggling in their skills, haggling and otherwise, I need some

relaxation. Of course, never having been in the world outside the game, it is all fiction to me.

I suppose my life would seem strange to you. On the one hand, I believe I am 47 years old—I have memories of being an apprentice to Maljoram the Bajorean Shop Owner when I was just a boy. On the other hand, because I read widely, I know I am part of a computer game that was brought online a mere seven years ago. It is a paradox: I am seven and I am 47.

And, I am okay with that.

Over the last few months, fewer and fewer parties have come through my shop. According to *US News and World Report*, the "Whole Wide World and Elysium" expansion of *Worlds of Wowcraft*, of which Bajorea is a part, is technologically ancient and, in any case, is not catching on with new player characters. It will soon be closed. I do not know what will happen to me when it is. However, I have no complaints.

I've earned my +57 life satisfaction.

Raffi the Kandarisian Barkeep

Raffi the Kandarisian Barkeep is an artificial intelligence-driven non-player character in the recently released "Invasion of the Yuck King" expansion of Worlds of Wowcraft. *When he was activated, he found this article in his memory. He believes he may have been created with the code that had once been used for Raif the Bajorean Shop Owner. Reincarnation or recycling? Raffi the Kandarisian Barkeep has −23 curiosity and only +4 imagination, so he really could not say.*

Lives Unlived: Kieth Qdqycjhe

Electronic zither master. Lead singer of the seminal industrial folk band Immaculate Tuna. Father. Lover. Used soccer shirt collector. Born July 1, 1991 in Norfolk, England. Died September 23, 2054 in Norfolk, People's Psychotropic Republic

of Botswana, under mysterious circumstances about which the police refuse to comment, aged 63.

The death of Kieth Qdqycjhe came as a Brain State 349876.231 to all who knew him.

"I didn't see it coming," Immaculate Tuna drummer and long-time friend and soccer shirt procurer Frikki Nitz said. "Oh, we all knew he was feeling Brain State 643226.465, but, given that Viagra had just dumped him as its spokesman, that was understandable.'

"I didn't see it coming more," Oolong Korolenko, the producer of Immaculate Tuna's final album, *Release the Mounds!*, and Qdqycjhe's two solo albums, *Expunge the Sponge* and *Subterranean Homesick Brain State 1620801.887*s, stated. "Just two days before . . . whatever happened, Kieth told me he was totally Brain State 400075.867ed to be going back into the studio after 15 years to record a new album. Totally Brain State 400075.867ed."

I remember the first time I listened to *Antinomium Starfish and the Cost*, Immaculate Tuna's first album. I had just broken up with the Brain State 387500.201 of my life, and I was looking for Brain State 820101.444. Unfortunately, *Antinomium Starfish and the Cost* was cold Brain State 820101.444—I Brain State 630199.420ed the album on contact. Seriously, I wanted to use the disc for skeet, and I didn't even own a gun.

Six months later, Immaculate Tuna released their second album, *Bob* (also known as *The Paisley Album* because most of its fans listened to it in their parents' basements and couldn't get the wallpaper pattern out of their heads). By this time, I realized that I Brain State 630199.420ed men, which helped me get over the Brain State 110107.011 I had undergone after the breakup, so I was in a much better place to give the band's music a fair hearing. And, I still couldn't Brain State 630199.402 it.

Sure, Kieth Qdqycjhe is a zither virtuoso. But, honestly? The zither is not a rock and roll instrument. Especially industrial folk, with its delicate blend of sensitivity and dentures rattling noise.

But, what do I know? "Ballad of a Quirky Neighbour," Immaculate Tuna's first single, went to number three on the Kazakhstan pop charts. They followed this up with "How Do You Sleep, Insomniac?" which became an international sensation when it was featured on the soundtrack of the film *Forrest Gump II; More Nutty Chocolates*. Over the next 13 years, Immaculate Tuna had a string of 27 top 10 hits.

I was Brain State 152599.882ed by their success. Oh, well. There's no accounting for taste.

Why Immaculate Tuna broke up is a bit of a mystery, given that all of the members genuinely Brain State 284436.827ed each other. However, just before the breakup, Qdqycjhe began a controversial regimen of neural state reprogramming for mild Brain State 274349.902 that he had Brain State 332455.733ed from since he was a child.

"Yeah, Doctor Guru Parvinder McSwami really messed him up," Nitz said. "After they started messing with his brain states, Kieth was never the same."

Some critics, Lester Bangs being one of the most prominent, have seen this change manifested in Qdqycjhe's solo work, which often featured meandering zither solos, bizarre tempo and chord changes and lyrics that border on some unknown, private language that bears only a family resemblance to English. Most critics, however, raved about Qdqycjhe's solo albums; as one put it: "They're so incomprehensible, they must be a sign of artistic genius!"

"They were so a sign of genius," Doctor Guru Parvinder McSwami said. "When Kieth first came to me, he suffered from major Brain State 102112.454, a clear case of Brain State 167533.329 with Brain State 829679.900 tendencies. In layman's terms: he was an emotional mess. He could barely play a note. By the time we finished retooling his brain, he had two well-respected solo albums to his credit."

I asked the doctor guru why, if Qdqycjhe's emotional problems had been solved, he became a virtual recluse for the last 15 years of his life.

Doctor Guru Parvinder McSwami thought about this for several minutes before answering. At first, I thought he had fallen asleep. But, to my Brain State 866272.369, he said, "The mind, you know, is a funny, funny place."

Tina Lollocadenka

Tine Lollocadenka is the Alternate Reality News Service's Music Writer.

~ INTERLUDE ~

The Weight of Information:
Chapter Seven:
Home Universe Sweet Home Universe

"I'm back?" the tall, lean middle aged gentleman with the regal bearing and scar across his left check in the shape of Martha Stewart asked. "I really made it back?"

"Yes," Brenda Brundtland-Govanni assured Elmore Teradonovich, the Alternate Reality News Service's film writer. "You really are home."

Teradonovich looked around the lab, satisfied. Unlike some of the other ARNS reporters who, having been cut off from their home universe for the better part of two days, kissed the ground when they returned, Teradonovich retained his dignity by shedding a single tear. (A couple of reporters who were unclear as to why they were being recalled were disappointed that they didn't receive a free meal, but *c'est le guerre*.)

"Okay. I'm ready to go back to work," Teradonovich said, and, turning smartly on his heel, walked back through the Dimensional Portal™. Flo pressed the red button, and, within seconds, he was gone. In his place were 17 laptops and a case of cherry soda.

"Our calculations," Flo said.

"May be a," Eddy said.

"Little off," Flo said.

"At first," Eddy said.

"But Pops," Flo said.

"Kahunga assured us," Eddy said.

"That the multiverse," Flo said.

"Forgives minor," Eddy said.

"Discrepancies," Flo said.

"You'll get the hang of it," Brenda Brundtland-Govanni, happy that the Service was up and running again, said, almost cheerfully, not feeling the overwhelming need to humiliate them. Sensing that her largesse wouldn't last, Flo and Eddy quickly and quietly went back to work.

Getting the Dimensional Portal™ up and running again (once Flo and Eddy had put all the pieces back together at 7:12:23 in the morning—almost two hours before deadline) had been a breeze. As Pops Kahunga had rightly stated, some kind of transuniversal equilibrium had been found, and no more Bob Smiths were forthcoming. Returning the 127 Bob Smiths she did have to their own universes proved to be a much more challenging task.

They wouldn't come out of the warehouse unless Darren Clincker-Belli came with them. It took over two hours of wheedling to get him to agree to come out of the closet, although, frankly, the air in there had become quite stale, and Brenda Brundtland-Govanni suspected that, had she held out for a few more minutes, she wouldn't have had to offer him danger pay to convince him to come out. Unfortunately, she didn't feel she had the time to wait him out, and, what the hell, it was Mikhail's dime. She looked forward to winning that costly argument with her boss.

That having been dealt with, transportation became the next problem. They couldn't fit all 127 Bob Smiths into a single bus, but no Bob Smith was willing to go on the bus that didn't contain Darren Clincker-Belli. When Brenda Brundtland-Govanni explained that it was only temporary, the Bob Smiths covered their ears and started loudly shouting passages from the tax code. As interesting as listening to monotonal recitations of deductions for toe nail clippers and the amortization of arthritis medications was, Brenda Brundtland-Govanni had to come up with a different plan. So, she did.

She had all of the Bob Smiths line up single file behind Darren Clincker-Belli. All 127 of them. Then, they walked down Yonge Street, across Queen Street and into the Alternate Reality News Service's headquarters. The whole trip took several hours and garnered a tremendous amount of attention. Brenda Brundtland-Govanni made sure that members of her promotions team were there to explain what the Alternate Reality News Service was and that no Bob Smiths were harmed in the making of the promotion. A photograph of the entourage, momentarily stopped at a red light, with the caption, "They come from all over the multiverse to read our news," was part of ARNS advertising for the next couple of years. For a while, Internet groups devoted to detailing the minute physical differences between the Bob Smiths flourished, as did online parodies of the image.

All that was left was getting the Bob Smiths to their home universes.

"We may," Flo said.

"Have come up," Eddy said.

"With a clever," Flo said.

"Kludge for," Eddy said.

"That problem," Flo said.

Because they now knew that the Bob Smiths must have come from the universes that had ARNS reporters, they could use those universes as their base. From the information gathered by Darren Clincker-Belli, it appeared that each Bob Smith had at least one unique characteristic that he didn't share with any of the other Bob Smiths. Comparing this to the base universes, they could find out which Bob Smith belonged where. It was slow, painstakingly detailed work, but, one by one, with Darren Clincker-Belli's help, they returned each of the Bob Smiths to their home universes until none was left.

"Good riddance," Brenda Brundtland-Govanni muttered.

"My children have grown up," Darren Clincker-Belli sniffed, holding back a tear.

Brenda Brundtland-Govanni was grateful that she didn't have to use her fallback plan: trying to integrate the 127 Bob Smiths into the world. The previous night she had had a Spike Jonze inspired nightmare where she had to fight with her insurance company about a claim on the hovercraft, which, after a slight traffic mishap, refused to make anything other than strawberry vanilla chai lattes. The voice on the phone was Bob Smith. The man's supervisor on the phone was also Bob Smith. When she went into the offices to complain, the receptionist who told her to wait was Bob Smith. All of the other customers in the waiting room were Bob Smiths, young and old, male and female, plausible and not so much. The claims adjustor who finally agreed to see her was Bob Smith. His superior was—

"Of course," Darren Clincker-Belli, his moment of emotional vulnerability now mercifully over, "if you didn't get the Bob Smiths to sign release forms, we still could be in a lot of trouble."

Brenda Brundtland-Govanni shuddered, and the bad dream went away. "What?" she said.

"If the government ever found out what really happened," Darren Clincker-Belli explained., "there could still be a fan-hitting shitstorm. We essentially kidnapped 127 people and held them captive for two days. We would certainly lose our licence to travel between dimensions, and some of us could be looking at serious jail time."

Brenda Brundtland-Govanni loomed over him. "I guess we'll have to make sure that nobody in the government ever finds out, then, won't we?" she quietly menaced him.

"I . . . I . . . I wouldn't—" Darren Clincker-Belli stammered. "I was just, you know, just saying. If. I—I'm going back to my office, now."

Brenda Brundtland-Govanni smiled to herself as she watched him scurry off. She still had it!

"I wouldn't—" Mabel started, but Brenda Brundtland-Govanni just breezed past her and into her office.

She found a little old lady holding a schnoodle with one hand and feeding it chocolates from a bowl in the shape of a skull on Brenda Brundtland-Govanni's desk with the other. "Don't you know that chocolate is poisonous to dogs?" Brenda Brundtland-Govanni shouted, although, to be honest, she was angrier about losing precious chocolates—a gift from the Emperor of the planet Fungo that were irreplaceable—than she was about the fate of the unknown dog.

"Oh, Mister Pussifer has been a naughty boy, hasn't he?" the little old lady said. "That's right. He has. Maybe this will teach him not to go on mommy's 17th century Afghan rug again. Naughty, naughty boy!"

Brenda Brundtland-Govanni slumped into the chair behind her desk, the joy of having weathered the crisis rapidly dissipating in the mundanity of her day to day existence. "Who are you?" she wearily asked, "And, what are you doing in my office?"

The little old lady haughtily brought herself up to her full five foot one inch height. "I," she said with no little self-importance, "am a subscriber to the Alternate Reality News Service. I am here to complain that you seem to be rerunning articles."

"Have you been here all night?" Brenda Brundtland-Govanni asked, the slightest hint of fear creeping around the edges of her voice.

"Your couch is very comfortable," the little old lady said. Brenda Brundtland-Govanni made a mental note to have it fumigated as soon as the woman had been dealt with. "Now, what about this rerunning articles business?"

"Are you familiar," Brenda Brundtland-Govanni, rubbing her eyes with her knuckles but not missing a beat, asked the woman, "with Nietzsche's idea of eternal recurrence?"

"Whosie whatsis?" the little old lady, so achingly adorable Brenda Brundtland-Govanni wanted to slap her on general principle, replied.

"There is a finite amount of material in the universe," Brenda Brundtland-Govanni explained, "but the universe itself goes on forever. That means that the same patterns repeat themselves forever."

"I see," the little old lady said. After a long pause, she added: "So, you didn't reprint stories—"

"The universe just caught up with the old ones."

"I see," the little old lady repeated. After another long pause, she added: "I must be older than I realized." After an even longer pause, she added further: "Maybe next time around, I won't get a schnoodle until after I've put the 17th century Afghan rug into storage."

"It would be wise," Brenda Brundtland-Govanni humoured her. Not insulting the customers wasn't merely company policy; it was several paragraphs in Brenda Brundtland-Govanni's contract.

"Thank you for clearing that up young man," the little old said. Although Mister Pussifer was starting to look a little queasy, the little old lady plucked a chocolate out of the skull bowl and, in a sweet voice asked, "One for the road?"

"Knock yourself out," Brenda Brundtland-Govanni unenthusiastically answered.

Yes, life was back to normal. Brenda Brundtland-Govanni wondered why she had ever imagined that was a good thing.

ALTERNATE ALTERNATIVES

Wake Up and Smell the Chaos

SPECIAL TO THE ALTERNATE REALITY NEWS SERVICE
by ARTURO BIGBANGBOOTIE

I have learned how to communicate with a race whose language consists entirely of adverbs and the phrase "mac and cheese."

I have interviewed the developer of steel reinforced umbrellas in a world where flying electric sheep drop spent batteries on people's heads.

I have reported from a universe where consequences of actions were randomly passed on to strangers. If you overate, somebody else gained weight. If you committed a crime, somebody else went to jail. After 90 percent of the human population died, the remainder learned to treat each other with a great deal of respect. The Golden Rule turned out to be a great life philosophy; all it needed was an enforcement mechanism.

I have read lengthy *Cahiers du Cinema* articles explaining why Timothy Dalton was the best James Bond.

I once covered a world where only autistic children were allowed to become the CEOs of Fortune 500 companies. That may sound cruel, but their economy was doing much better than ours . . .

I know why the caged fluffnagel sings.

I have watched as Jimmy Carter and Menachim Begin held a contest to see who could stand on their hands the longest.

I was once sent to a barren universe where the rocks sing songs that are so sad that any single-celled life forms that develop immediately kill themselves. (When I got back, I had to spend six months in hospital, smartass.)

I was once sent to write about the avatar of a CFO who was selling the company's stock short behind his human counterpart's back. They'll be writing about this case in the business press for decades; a whole new business journal and several popular magazines were created just to report on it.

I have been in a world where human beings evolved with a third arm—it came out of the chest—which made breastfeeding easier, wrestling a very different sport and being left-handed a much less sinister condition.

I have met people whose Bible consisted entirely of Rorschach ink blots. You may scoff, but in over 2,000 years, they have never initiated a war . . .

Have you ever tried to speak Pig Klingon? It rips apart your vocal cords **and** hurts your brain! I know!

I've explored a universe where dreams go to die—it was a nightmare!

I've written about a reality in which X-Ray Specs actually allowed people to see through objects (walls, clothes, combustion engines, what have you). They were banned minutes after being made publicly available, not because they caused cancer of the eyeballs (that connection wouldn't actually be proven for 30 years), but because they "offended the common decency." After several years of futile effort, the United States of Vespucca legalized X-Ray Specs, but insisted that each one be sold with a chip that tested the skin of the wearer and would only work for those over 18. You don't want to know how it determined that they were over 18.

I have reported on gas giants—a race of people 20 feet tall who can't control their flatulence—who debated issues of environmental protection as drought was slowly killing their planet.

I have met Rush Limbaugh's inner child. I would strongly urge people with small pets to keep them away from it.

I once sold my left lung to get a story about political corruption on a world where selling your organs was legal. But, were the Alternate Reality News Service accountants willing to let me expense it?

I spent several months in a world where people went to the bathroom in public, but ate food in private. Or, did I see that in a movie? Or . . . both?

I was once in a universe where you could get anything you wanted . . . as long as it was green.

I remember when the robots designed to carve promotional messages in the lunar dust were hacked into and carved a huge pair of butt cheeks on the moon. Tabloid headline writers had a field day describing what had happened.

Yes, I've seen it all. And, I can't keep track of it anymore. When I'm riding on the bus, I expect a distinctly non-extinct, evolved dinosaur to sit next to me and try and convince me that the war in Iraq was necessary. When I'm making breakfast in the morning, I have to remind myself that the toaster will not report how many pieces I make to the Diet Police. No matter how often I remind myself that they do not exist in this reality, I see frustrums.

Can anybody tell me what, in this universe, is real? Please? Anybody?

Arturo Bigbangbootie, the Alternate Reality News Service's Transdimensional Traffic Writer, has been given an indefinite leave of absence for reasons of mental health.

Ira Nayman

When The Pleasure Principle Peters Out

by LAURIE NEIDERGAARDEN, Alternate Reality News Service Medical Writer

It happened when Shernold Telepatheur was coaching his eight year-old son's little league team, The Waxahachie Hatchetmen. They had a big game coming up against the Petaluma Native Stereotypes on the weekend, and he wanted to make sure they perfected their first to centre fielder to third double play.

As Telepatheur gently encouraged his son by shouting, "Throw it to Jimmy! To Jimmy! How hard can that be? Throw the [EXPLETIVE] ball to [EXPLETIVE] Jimmy!" his penis unexpectedly became erect. At first, Telepatheur tried to ignore the, uhh, extra bat on the field, but, when Jimmy shouted, "Hey, look! Coach Telepatheur's got a chubbie!" and the kids started giggling and pointing at his groin, he had to order himself to go to the showers.

At this point, the story could have just been another case of a man loving his child . . . and his child's best friend . . . and their right fielder . . . too much. However, without meaning to disappoint tabloid editors everywhere, the truth is more sciency: Telepatheur was one of the first patients to get a Love Zinger.

The creation of Smerck Industries, in collaboration with *The Playboy Network*, the Love Zinger is a computer chip implanted into the brains of men who have—my apologies to the squeamish, but I refuse to use a euphemism for this—erectile dysfunction. When the Love Zinger detects an amorous moment—the dim candlelight, the soft caresses, the insincere avowal of admiration for the music of Enya—it zips into action.

"Failure to get it up—what laypeople call "erectile dysfunction"—is the leading cause of divorce among the chronically insecure," Moira Hoeckbritsky, chief researcher assistant and ballbuster at Smerck Industries, explained. "The Love Zinger chip is the climax of over a decade of frenzied research that, we hope, will help men get it on by helping them get off.

200

"Ooh," Hoeckbritsky added, flushed, "I think I need a cigarette!"

The microchip had the usual side effects (including: swelling of the middle finger, nasal hair edema, beating of teeth and gnashing of breasts, baby navel, flash headaches, flash mobs, flashing, cholesterol immaturation, paisley lips, prolonged hardening of the nipples, Republicanism, roofing shingles and onomatopoeia). But, according to the satisfied customers in Smerck Industries' advertising campaign, it worked!

Unfortunately, the Love Zinger has a Love Bug: for reasons its creators have yet to find a plausible excuse for, it occasionally fires at random, usually at the most awkward, inconvenient times. Already, in addition to Telepatheur, there are reports of men with the Love Zinger implant having erections while fly fishing, watching C-Span and, most inexplicably, having root canal surgery.

"Yeah," Hoeckbritsky snorted, "men getting off at the wrong time. Big surprise, there!"

"Ah sense a suhtain lack of empathy heah," stated Harold "Gerald" McBoing-Boing. "Which ah would lahk the jury ta keep in mind—oh, ha ha, ah seem to have gotten a little ahead of mahself. Do pahdon me."

McBoing-Boing, an attorney with the firm of Leo Gazonga Bushmiller Trellice, has initiated a class action suit against Smerck Industries on behalf of all of the men with the Love Zinger implant who have suffered the embarrassment of awkward forwardness. "Ah figuh theah's gotta be at least a gabillion dollars wuth of sufferin' heah, yo honah—pahdon me, I mean, Mistuh Neidergaahden."

"Gerald McBoing-Boing?" Hoeckbritsky sneered. "Please! Isn't he the ambulance chaser who spearheaded the class action lawsuit against the McNaughton Ambulance Company? I'll take him seriously when hell starts licensing ice cream concessions!"

Telepatheur has not yet decided whether to join the class action suit. "My wife hasn't gotten over the whole Little League thing, yet," he admitted. "On the other hand, my regular call girl loves it . . . at least, she says she does . . . so, I'm torn.

"You really think," he added, "that there's a gabillion dollars worth of hurt here?"

Calls for Smerck Industries to recall the Love Zinger have started to be heard in Congress. "Hey, they approved the chip! They're just covering their asses!" Hoeckbritsky shouted. After a moment, she thoughtfully added: "By which, I mean, of course, that it has always been the policy of Smerck Industries to work with the government to ensure that our medical products are of the highest quality and most benefit to the public. And, by god, that's what we will continue doing!"

Santa's Little Helper Now On
The Naughty List

by SASKATCHEWAN KOLONOSCOGRAD, Alternate Reality News Service Fairy Tale Writer

Guess who's made Santa's naughty list?

Fyodor Rostenkowski-Flitwick, an elf who heads the—okay, look: the lede was actually a lot more clever before some nit used the idea in the headline. I don't write the headline—don't really have any say in what goes into the headline, usually don't even read it before an article goes to press—so, don't blame me if my lede now seems redundant, okay?

Fyodor Rostenkowski-Flitwick, an elf who heads the Northern Hemisphere offices of Christmas, Inc. left his laptop on a Yonge/University subway car some time in the morning of January 2. Two months later, Christmas Inc. CEO, Santa Claus, under investigation by *Sesame Street 2*, had to admit that the laptop had disappeared with his most important information: the naughty/nice list.

"Rest assured," Santa, who is famously camera-shy, said in a hastily written press release, "that we are doing everything in our power to find the laptop. In the meantime, Christmas, Inc. has taken steps to ensure that such a breach of security never happens again."

"This is a terrible invasion of privacy," responded Ontario Privacy Commissioner Ann Cavoukian. "The naughty/nice list doesn't just contain the names of children and their current status as children in good standing. It contains their addresses, the schools that they go to and a detailed list of all of the good and bad acts that they have committed throughout their lives.

"This is an open invitation to identity theft!"

Setting aside the question of who would want to steal a six year-old's identity, questions remain about the loss of the laptop. The *Smoking Gut* Web site has published a police report about an elf that was taken into custody on New Year's Day for drunk and disorderly conduct. According to the report, he had groped women on the subway while drunkenly asking, "Happy New Year! Wanna see my special little gift?" The elf gave the police the name "Fodor Flostenkowski-Ritwick," but his mug shots bear a striking resemblance to Rostenkowski-Flitwick.

Could one of Santa's helpers have lost the laptop with the naughty/nice list while on a bender?

Santa was unavailable for comment. Santa's lawyer, an elf named Germaine Grotowski-Amenable, however, was all too willing to comment. "You . . . you actually want my opinion? Nobody wants my opinion. You know, I only got my law degree to get some small measure of respect from the human beings around me. If I had known how little respect they have for lawyers, I would surely have stuck with my original training as an outdoor plumber. Still, you asked me a question—ME!—so that law degree might finally be paying off! You see . . ."

Fifteen minutes later, we gently tried to steer him back to the question. "Oh, this whole Rostenkowski-Flitwick/drunken elf losing sensitive information thing? Well, you gotta understand that it's a cold, cruel world for an elf. You ever had to work on an assembly line? It's mind-numbing physical labour, 18 hours a day—20 in November and December. And, the pay sucks: three pieces of bread a day and a bottle of wine every other week. On your one day off a year, you have to release a little steam. You see . . ."

That's when we gave up on Grotowski-Amenable as a source for this article.

"With losses of sensitive information," Cavoukian commented, "You often find that, no matter how good your security is, it is the human element that lets you down. Still . . . a drunken elf. Tsk tsk."

Timmy, aged five and a half, said, "Does this mean that Christmas will be cancelled this year? Who is liable if it is? I mean, what legal responsibilities does Santa have to supply Christmas presents to all of us who have been good this year?" Behind this statement was an unspoken question: if Santa can't give gifts at Christmas because he doesn't have a working naughty/nice list, why should I bother being nice?

To forestall parental panic, another hastily written press release from Santa was put out that claimed that Christmas Inc. is offering a reward of five years of being put on the nice list regardless of your behaviour and three fulfilled gift wishes (maximum value: $1,000) for information that leads to the return of the missing laptop. Christmas Inc. wants children everywhere to know that it is currently compiling a new naughty/nice list from backups it had at its North Pole headquarters, and that it should be able to satisfy the needs of at least 95% of its customers by the end of the year.

Speaking for children everywhere, Timmy commented, "Well, this just blows."

The Best Humanity Has to Offer

by FREDERICA VON McTOAST-HYPHEN, Alternate Reality News Service People Writer

Trade in Helium 3 was the most important issue dealt with by the various offshoots of humanity at the latest Intergalactic

Ruling Symposium and Oyster Bar. However, trade between star systems is such an arcane pursuit that even those who negotiate it have only a passing knowledge of its intricacies. (It is a well documented fact that Galactic negotiations are so deadly dull that only low level—read: not very bright—further reading: expendable—embassy workers are allowed to take part in them; this should explain why, to use but one example, terraforming of lifeless planets can only be conducted on alternate Thursdays.)

Let's be honest: galactic trade is boring. What everybody really wants to know is: did the Gee Stank Ambassador really get drunk and try to have sex with a Gallifreyan Puddle Fern?

Several witnesses claim that something funky was going on between Ambassador Wilson and the plant in a private room of the Arthur Dent Hotel (motto: "We always know where your towel is!"). The Gee Stank embassy has issued a statement denying the allegations. The Puddle Fern has remained stubbornly silent on the issue.

In the FP Bar and Oyster Symposium after the final day's deliberations, various strains of humanity gathered for the more serious business of mingling. As it always does (I flipped through dozens of universes to check, and it was true in every one of them), the conversation turned to the question of which branch of humanity was the original from which the others had springed. Spranged? Uhh . . . originated.

"My. People. Had. To. Develop. Great. Muscles. In. Order. To. Survive. Our. Gravity's. Crushing. Weight," stated Ambassador Kar'El Ror'Schach. "We. Are. Clearly. The. Template. For. Other. Specimens. Of. Humanity."

Ambassador Ror'Schach represented the P'Up'Py of Rinimbi Seven, the third planet in the Rinimbi star system. Due to the gravity on Rinimbi Seven, the P'Up'Py are short and squat, the sort of characters you expect to find underneath bridges demanding the sacrifice of small children to allow you to pass. But, very strong. Mind-boggling strong. So strong, in fact, that fighting and weightlifting events at the Galactic Olympics had to be cancelled because nobody could compete against them.

"Water people, are we," responded Ambassador Pulsate Slush-thrup of the Arklon Agonsutes. "Adapt to wet planet, had to we. A most graceful people, became we. First humans, were we."

Halsion, the planet of the Arklon Agonsutes, is 99 percent water. (At least, it was before the worst of global warming hit.) The Arklon Agonsutes developed gills, webbed appendages and an alternate breathing system in order to be able to live under water. All swimming events at the Galactic Olympics had to be cancelled because nobody could compete against them.

"Oh, pullleaze!" commented Ambassador Firefly of the Flauff of planet Esmerelda. "We have developed eyesight so advanced that we can pick the lint off a cashmere sweater at a mile and a half. You think we could possibly have evolved from the P'Up'Py? Are **you** blind? Oh, snap! And, the uniforms at the opening ceremonies of the Symposium? I needed three Gravol and an aspirin just to keep my lunch down! Oh, yes! I went there!"

Constantly changing atmospheric conditions on Esmerelda required the Flauff to develop extraordinary vision. It is said that their sight is so good that they can see three seconds into the future (except when distracted by reruns of *I Love Lucy*, which have only recently arrived in their star system). This ruled out baseball, basketball, hockey and just about every other team sport at the Galactic Olympics.

"Uhh, yeah," Ambassador (formerly Captain) Spalding added to the debate. "Hate to break it to you, but legend has it that the human race started on Urth."

Everybody in the bar made noises that, given their varied physiognomies, approximated laughter.

"You. Are. Weak," Ambassador Ror'Schach stated. "I. Could. Snap. You. In. Two. And. Use. You. As. A. Toothpick."

"Graceful, are not you," Ambassador Slushthrup added. "Please, laugh, do not make me."

"Oh, you didn't!" Ambassador Firefly screeched. "Honey, I know a poseur when I'm looking at one, and my poseur alert status is in ultraviolet!"

The argument went on well into the closing ceremonies the next afternoon. And, while all of the representatives continued to argue that their race, being superior, must have been the one from which all of the others developed, there was one thing upon which they could all agree: it definitely wasn't the Urthers!

A Robin Hood With Ambitions

by GIDEON GINRACHMANJINJa-VITUS, Alternate Reality News Service Economics Writer

According to his lawyer, Harunder Majrenkoi, CEO of International Local Industries Unlimited Ltd., is not responsible for the stock losing 99.347 percent of its value over the last 11 quarters.

"Harunder couldn't have been responsible," Samantha Meerkat said. "He's been dead for six years."

DNA tests of skeletal remains accidentally found in the legal department of the corporation (apparently nobody in management ever went into the legal department and the lawyers who worked there were used to much worse smells) confirmed that they belonged to Harunder Majrenkoi.

Of course, this begs the question—well, not so much begs as gently pleads or perhaps quietly and in a dignified manner asks for consideration of—yes, that's it—of course, this quietly and in a dignified manner asks for consideration of the question: who has been running International Local Industries Unlimited Ltd. for the past six years? And, this begs—well, not so much begs, but there isn't a term that captures the urgent neediness of the attitude with which the question needs to be posed, so we will have to settle for that word—the further question: what did that person do with Majrenkoi's substantial earnings during this period?

The answer to the first question: Majrenkoi's personal secretary, Marianas Tranche. "I don't deny that I've been running the company, pretending to be Harunder Majrenkoi," Tranche stated in a written . . . document. "And, I was getting an average return of over 30%, almost twice what Majrenkoi had gotten in the previous decade. Everybody was happy. I could have kept going for years if I hadn't invested so much of our cash reserves in AIG—bastards!"

Tranche got away with it for as long as he did because Majrenkoi communicated almost entirely by Twitter; he was a well known agoraphobic who only appeared in public for weddings, bar mitzvahs and Jimmy Buffett concerts. Tranche motion captured actors making speeches at shareholders meetings, then added Majrenkoi's face and voice.

"James Cameron was a consultant," Tranche proudly explained. "I had to scale back some of his most . . . excessive CGI plans. Still, it was good enough to fool the shareholders—thank goodness none of them had ever seen *Terminator 2!*"

Tranche's ruse was nearly exposed three and a half years ago thanks to a strange sequence of events involving seven hairy llamas, the world's largest hot tub and the entire cast of the Des Moines Dinner Theatre's production of *Annie Get Your Gun*. However, the events are so unlikely that readers wouldn't likely believe them, so they will not be described in this article.

Tranche is not suspected of foul play. The Coroner's report said Majrenkoi died of a massive brain hemorrhage brought on by trying too hard to make sense of David Lynch's *Inland Empire*. However, Tranche has been charged with 1,278,456 counts of xtreme identity theft.

As for the question with the urgent neediness that is close enough to begging without actually being begging? According to Florentine accountant (just as good as a forensic accountant, but also able to make a mean fettuccini) Bradford Queal, Tranche did not keep the money for himself.

"Tranche got himself a few small trinkets," Queal stated. "A basso harmonium, a lifetime subscription to the *Girls with Eyepatches* Web site, that sort of thing. Kinky with an odd taste in music, but not terribly extravagant."

So, where did the money go? Don't make me beg the question, because—

"Tranche gave it to people who had lost their jobs," Queal said. "Over 200 jobless people were each given $20,000 a year for the six years he was in charge of the company."

"I had always heard these stories of people whose grandmothers had died, but they hid the death so they could keep collecting pensions or social security or whatever," Tranche explained. "And, I thought, helping only one person in this way? Really? Don't you people have any ambition? Of course, this was when the market was booming and everybody was being encouraged to think big."

Police are not releasing the names of the people who received the money, but one, Tajuana Izetta, has come forward. "I'm a single mother with three children," Izetta told a world weary but teary eyed group of reporters. "I had just lost my job as a waitress in the shipping department of Toys 'R Us. So, when Marianas told me I had just won a sweepstakes, I didn't question him too closely. The fact that he had trouble naming the sweepstakes? Or, that I didn't remember ever entering a sweepstakes? I really didn't question him. Let's just leave it at that, okay?"

Police issued a hasty statement calling on people not to romanticize Tranche's actions. In part, the statement read: "Marianas Tranche is not a hero. Don't imagine Johnny Depp playing him in a movie about his life. Don't imagine the thrills of the times he almost gets caught. Don't imagine his doomed love for a single mother he helps, or the relationship he forges with her precocious but ultimately loveable children or . . . or . . .

"Umm . . . excuse me. I have to call my agent."

They Voted With Their Defeat

by ARTURO BIGBANGBOOTIE, Alternate Reality News Service Transdimensional Traffic Writer

The revelation was made clear: the world is a simulacrum in a vast computer-generated virtual space known as "The Matrix." It is run by machines for the power they can harvest from unconscious human bodies. Morpheus sent out the call to all who lived in The Matrix: join us in the real world.

So far, 37 of the over six billion humans in The Matrix have.

"Well, that was . . . anti-climactic," Morpheus commented.

"Are you kidding me?" derivatives collector Bart Rumbolo stated. "My shares vest in three years, six months, 27 days and . . . 41 minutes. You really think I'm going to give that up to become a rice farmer in some hellish, ecologically devastated futuristic landscape?"

"Well, actually—" Morpheus began.

"Oh, what I wouldn't give to be a rice farmer in some hellish, ecologically devastated futuristic landscape," sighed Gupti van Gupta, an Indian untouchable garbage scavenger in Mumbai who has the unenviable distinction of being rejected for the part of an untouchable garbage scavenger in *Slumdog Millionaire*. "But, no. Even out there, I would be an untouchable garbage scavenger. I just can't get a break in any reality, so why bother?"

"You are missing the point—" Morpheus tried again.

When asked why she decided to stay in The Matrix, house-wife Mona McRelevant simply answered: "I want to see who wins next season's *American Idol*. Is that so wrong?"

"I really thought that, given a choice between a false but pleasing prison and freedom in the difficult but real physical world, people would choose freedom," Morpheus mused. "How naïve was that?"

It gets worse. Many of those who did swallow the red pill—perhaps as many as 63%—were paranoid schizophrenics who had delusions that they were living in an alternate alternate reality. Although the details varied, a common theme among all of their stories was that there was a Force that bound all living things in their imaginary universe together.

Morpheus shook his head sadly and declined to comment.

The fact that powerful vested interests opposed the move to the real world didn't help. Fox News pundit Bill O'Reilly, for instance, argued that the world of illusion that everybody took for granted **was** real, and that The Matrix was just another plot by crackpot, extremist liberal intellectuals to undermine the supremacy of the United States.

"Trust President Obama to challenge the whole ontological basis of the existence of the country," O'Reilly bloviated. "Is this really change we can believe in?"

Dr. Phil had a different take on the subject: "I know you want to run away from the world as it is. We all want to run away from the world once in a while. It's a little thing I like to call 'Adult Responsibility.' That's right. Adult Responsibility. Capital letters and everything. Sometimes it can be overwhelming. When it is, who doesn't fantasize about an alternate world where freedom fighters battle the machines that have taken over and enslaved us all? I know I have. But, running away from the world as it is? That's just not what adults do."

"There is no need to go back into The Matrix now," Morpheus glumly stated, "but, if there were, one of the things I would be certain to do would be to slap Dr. Phil upside the head. Hard."

"You ask me, this Morpheus cat went about it all wrong, man" asserted advertising legend Bippi Folkstrell. "I mean, appearing as a voice in the head of every human being—who wouldn't kill for that kind of penetration? But, the message? Join me in a hellacious landscape *just because it's real*? Bubbelach, that was from hunger, that pitch was!"

Folkstrell said that if it had been up to him, he would have held an inter-cranial telethon for reality. "Coke, Nike, Sony, even Wal-Mart—they'd be in in a second," he claimed, trying to snap his fingers but making a feeble sound. "Get a couple of MTV VJs and, hey!—I hear Miss California is available—maybe get Tom Hanks to tell people that he's been to reality and it ain't as bad as you might think—man, I'm on fire, here! This could be big! This could be really, really big!"

Morpheus rubbed his forehead with the palm of his hand. "I'm too old for this shit," he said.

We tried contacting the machines that had created The Matrix, but we were approached by a giant metallic head. It was too scary to deal directly with, and we had to watch several hours of an *American Idol* marathon until the horror went away.

In The Family Way

by FRANCIS GRECOROMACOLLUDEN, Alternate Reality
News Service National Politics Writer

A bad toupee has led to the discovery of a plot by a religious
cult to take over Washington.

One day, Senator John Banner (R., Nevada) had a full head
of black, curly hair. The next, he had a raggedy mop of dark
brown hair.

"He looked like somebody had collected the furballs his cat
had spit up, somehow tied them together and plopped the resulting mess on his head," said journalist Jeff Sharlott, "It looked like
his grandmother had started knitting a sweater but stopped after
a couple of hours and he didn't know any other way to wear what
she had made. It looked like something the Coen brothers rejected
for Javier Bardem's character in *No Country for Old Men*.

"It didn't look normal."

Ordinarily, bad hair wouldn't elicit attention from the Washington press corps (not since Nixon, in any case), but Sharlott
began to notice other politicians with strange dos. Senator
James Inhoofe (R., Oklahoma), for instance, was starting to go
a little thin on top one day; the next, he seemed to have a mul-
let. Senator Jim DeMent (R., South Carolina) had a fro that
looked like a reject from a Melvin Van Peebles film. You could
use balding Senator Sam "Not James" Brownnose (R., Kansas)'s
new hair to mop up a tennis court. Words cannot begin to
describe the monstrosity on top of Representative Zach Wampum
(R., Tennessee)'s head.

What do these and at least 27 other Congressmen, mostly
Republicans but with a sprinkling of Democrats for exotic
flavour, have in common? They all belong to a little known
(until Sharlott's book on the subject, at which point it became
moderately poorly known) religious organization called The
Family Way.

The Family Way is a Jesusian group based on a few simple
concepts: Jesus was a free market advocate; Jesus believed in

infiltrating governments in order to promote the free markets he believed in; if you promoted free market economics in strict accordance with his teachings, you were an okay guy in Jesus' books.

"It was this last one that got them in trouble," commented Sharlott, who spent a month living at the group's EC Street compound in Washington as research for his book.

Being in tight with Jesus because you were doing his good works meant that you were forgiven for anything else you may have done in your life. While in office, both Senator Banner and South Carolina Governor Sanford N. Sonne, for example, had such absurd affairs that they defy description, much less satire; but, because they were made guys in the eyes of Jesus, the consequences were minimal.

"Any conduct could be forgiven as long as they were chosen," Sharlott explained. "Just like jocks in high school. Still, the affairs brought embarrassing public attention to The Family Way. You have to understand: these guys are so secretive, they make *The Da Vinci Code* look like *Where's Waldo?* Although they made no public statements, it was clear they had to do something."

What they felt they had to do wasn't clear until a windy day in the Beltway. Inhoofe, rushing to catch a meeting on crushing health care reform—bipartisanally—was caught by a gust that blew the lid off his head and the conspiracy: many pictures were taken of the scar on his bald pate.

"They had lobotomies!" Sharlott exclaimed.

"Actually, they were only partial lobotomies," CNN's Doctor Sanjay Gupta corrected him. "The point was to sever the part of the brain that controls will from the part of the brain that controls rational thought. The theory that had been circulating the medical profession was that if you could do something like that, you could create a completely controllable person. But, it took a crazy religious sect to pull it off!"

The Family Way had apparently been experimenting with lobotomizing its politically connected followers as early as the 1970s, when it fully lobotomized Senator Throb Sturman (R.,

South Carolina, D.). This caused Sturman to blurt out non-sequiturs and drool uncontrollable, but journalists chalked this up to his age.

Experimentation led to the partial lobotomies, which are carried out using laser scalpels. Patients are "bent to god's will" (totally compliant) without becoming obvious drooling shadows of humanity ("devout").

"It's actually quite brilliant," Dr. Gupta commented admiringly, "if you can overlook the strange influence of a small religious cult on the political culture of the nation. Fortunately, being a medical correspondent, I can!"

Many of the Senators and Representatives connected to The Family Way have issued statements denying having any medical procedures done on their brains. "The led [sic] in the water in Washington may have caused some hair loss," every single statement claimed. "Otherwise, nothing unusual is going on hear [sic]. The Senator/Representative looks forward to serving the people of his state."

Sixteen identical statements, right down to the typos. Nope. Nothing suspicious here.

"Still, we shouldn't make too much of this whole 'lobotomization' thing," Sharlott advised. "It's not like any of the Congressmen involved were the brightest bulbs in the chandelier to begin with!"

Explosive Testimony At GM Love Child Trial

by HAL MOUNTSAUERKRAUTEN, Alternate Reality News Service Court Writer

The palimony trial between Jane Doe (not a pseudonym—her real name) and General Motors Corporation took a dramatic turn this afternoon when Doe was accused of infidelity.

"Ain't it true," Marcello Defibrillatore, lead counsel for General Motors Corporation, demanded, "that for the final six months of your alleged relationship with General Motors Corporation, you was actually involved with McDonald's Restaurants of Canada Limited!"

"It's a lie!" Doe sobbed. "Me and McDonald's Restaurants of Canada Limited, we . . . we were just good friends!"

Pandamonium broke out in the courtroom, forcing Judge Veronica Tederoscoe to order a recess until the Chinese bears could be removed and order could be restored.

This, the second day of Doe's testimony, was in marked contrast to that, the first day of her testimony. During that, exchanges like the following were not uncommon:

DEFIBRILLATORE: How is it possible that you had a child with General Motors Corporation?

DOE: We were young and in love. Or, at least, I thought we were.

DEFIBRILLATORE: But, General Motors ain't a human being. It's a corporation.

DOE: But, a corporation **is** a human being. The Supreme Court said so.

DEFIBRILLATORE: For, uhh, purposes of the law, Miss Doe. For purposes of the law. That don't make it possible for you to have a child with it.

DOE: Are you prejudiced, Mister Defibrillatore?

DEFIBRILLATORE: Wha?

DOE: You don't believe in mixed human/corporation relationships, do you?

DEFIBRILLATORE: It ain't about what I believe in! You can't have a child with a corporation! It ain't natural!

DOE: Oh! You are! You are prejudiced!

Try as he might during that, Defibrillatore could not shake Doe from her position that she had had a child with General Motors Corporation. Obviously, he met with his team overnight, and, after they decided on a sushi, artichoke and anchovy pizza with a side vat of Tums, they decided to take a different tack on this.

When the court returned from its recess, Doe's lawyer, Jeremiah Icky, wiping the dirt from the playground off his otherwise immaculate suit, objected to Defibrillatore's new line of questioning.

"Ms. Doe's relationship with General Motors Corporation was well documented in the tabloid press," he stated. "Is my colleague trying to argue that Ms. Doe is not allowed to have any friends outside of the relationship? Your Honour, Judge Landers determined this to be 'the sign of a weak and controlling ego' in *Doe v. Smith* (not his real name, but as good as we're going to get, so suck it up)."

"I got three words for my esteemed colleague," Defibrillatore responded. "Alienation of freaking affection!"

Judge Tederoscoe ruled that she would allow the line of questioning, but that she would keep it on a short leash because she was really into S/M.

The stakes are high in *Doe v. General Motors Corporation*. Although conceded by most economists and surgical interns to be bankrupt, General Motors Corporation is in line for a honking large sum of bailout money, rumoured to be in the tens of billions. Since Jane Doe is asking for half of General Motors Corporation's earnings past and present, real or imagined, fiduciary or . . . whatever the opposite of fiduciary is, this could turn into a fight for a tweeting large sum of money.

The government has filed an *amicus* (literally: "Am I allowed to swear?") brief with the court, siding with General Motors Corporation. Boiled down to its essence, the brief asks the court to consider that it is already embarrassed by how much the bailout is costing and would the court please, please, please not make matters worse by giving a private citizen such a tweeting large amount of money, money that by rights should be going to bad corporate managers?

This is just the latest in the strange twists this case has taken.

Defibrillatore had asked for a DNA test of Jane Doe's child, Janet Doe (not her real name, but an amazingly lifelike recreation), but experts say he isn't likely to use it. For one thing, General Motors Corporation doesn't have a physical body, which makes testing it for DNA problematic. For another thing, Janet Doe's DNA showed markers of greed, arrogance, short-term thinking and disregard for the natural environment; although having no scientific validity, the jury may have seen these things as evidence of General Motors Corporation's paternity.

The rest of the afternoon's cross-examination degenerated into a "she said/it said" argument over who picked up the tab for dinner at Sardis 18 months ago. Court watchers agreed that it was one of those exchanges that doesn't add anything to either side of the case, but does allow lawyers to pad their fees.

The trial continues.

Opposition To Unorthodox Cure Grows

by LAURIE NEIDERGAARDEN, Alternate Reality News Service Medical Writer

Clowns. Sure, they make some people laugh, but at what cost? They scare small children and haunt the dreams of impressionable adults. Most people, according to Statistics Canada's Department of Vague Generalizations, consider clowns to be psychologically damaging and a drag on the economy. Is there anything that can tip public opinion back in favour of these once lovable scamps?

How about curing sexually transmitted diseases?

"Ve haff been getting ze most amazing results from our researches, jah?" claimed Jully Swedenborger, head of the Straneaushanswurst Institute in Redondo Beach, California. When it was pointed out to Swedenborger that he didn't appear to be

German, he dropped the outrageous accent and said, "Yeah, okay, but that doesn't change the fact that our research has shown some amazing results, okay?"

How can clowns affect other people's health? Apparently, their tears have healing properties not found in the tears of "straights," non-clownic citizens. In clinical tests conducted over the past five years, researchers at the Straneaushanswurst Institute have shown that the tears of clowns ameliorate the symptoms of syphilis, gonorrhea and three different kinds of Herpes.

"Three types!" Swedenborger enthused. "Zat's more zan— sorry, that's more than antibiotics!"

According to Swedenborger's research, you can't just put on big shoes and a red nose and call yourself a clown for your tears to have any effect on people with sexually transmitted diseases. You have to have been a practicing clown for at least 6.37 years for your tears to have any effect. The most potent cure comes from the tears of people who have been clowns for over 20 years.

"We call this a high clownic," Swedenborger dryly stated.

Swedenborger is waiting for approval from the Food and Drug Administration to begin offering the tears of a clown cure to the public. He envisions a system of tear banks where clowns anonymously donate their lacrimal emissions. The clown donor would enter a small room with a cup; the room would be filled with sad novels with unhappy endings and unfunny comedies on DVD. The clown would be encouraged to avail himself of the media and do what comes naturally until the cup is filled.

"Uh, yeah, I . . . I . . . I would be totally into, uhh, that," commented a clown who asked to be identified only by the name Shakes. "Cry into a . . . a . . . a cup? I can, uhh, do that. How much does it pay?"

"Oh, no, no, no, no, no, no, no," responded Claire Kane, noted children's performer and woman considering starting the group Stop Clowning Around, a clown's rights organization. "Selling our tears for money? That's exploitation, that is. It . . . isn't right."

"Okay, so we don't give them any money," Swedenborger conceded.

"What?" Shakes shouted. "You, uhh, expect me to watch *Pagliacci* and . . . and . . . and cry into a cup **for nothing?**"

"Ahhh . . . uhh . . . I'm sure we can come to some reasonable accommodation on this," Swedenborger unconvincingly replied. "Think of all the people who will lead happier, healthier lives thanks to this cure."

"Think of the poor clowns," Claire Kane asserted, "driven by economic need to sell their own tears. Month after month—"

"Day after day," Shakes interjected.

"On a regular basis subjecting themselves to sadness," Claire Kane smoothly continued. "How could this not stunt their—our emotional growth?"

"Stunt our emotional growth? Oh, please!" stated another clown known as Pennywise. "Clowns are inherently depressed— why do you think we have this insatiable need to make other people laugh? And, why do you think most children fear us? They know that deep down we're miserable people. THEY KNOW."

The Vatican issued a statement opposing the use of clown tears as a cure for sexually transmitted diseases. Cutting through all the rhetoric about the "sanctity of beloved comedic characters," the underlying rationale for the Vatican's position seems to be that sexual activity is immoral and those who engage in it deserve to suffer painful and lingering diseases.

"MIND YOUR OWN BUSINESS!" responded Shakes, Claire Kane and Pennywise.

While the issues play out in the court of clown opinion, science marches on. Early results of new research at the Straneaushanswurst Institute indicate that the snot of mimes has much promise as a cure for advancing dementia in the elderly.

"But, uhh, that's kind of gross," Swedenborger allowed, "so let's wait until all of the tests come back before we get too excited about it."

Much Hell Breaks Loose

by FREDERICA VON McTOAST-HYPHEN, Alternate Reality
News Service People Writer

Satan looked resplendent in his Armani suit and mirror
shades. One didn't have to be a trained exorcist to see, though,
that his rough red features were troubled.

"No, I'm sorry, this is not working for me," he told his mark,
a suburban housewife he was in the process of seducing.

"Don't . . . don't you find me attractive?" asked Name Withheld By Request.

"It's not you, it's me," Satan lamely said.

Name Withheld By Request threw her drink in his face and
stormed away from the table in the chic restaurant.

"I always deserve that," Satan commented, as much to himself as to anybody around him. "Yet, you would be surprised
how infrequently it happens."

Satan. Lucifer. Beelzebub. The Devil. The Prince of Lies.
The Prince of Flies. The Prince of Darkness. Stan. Over drinks
at Lilith, a trendy wine bar, the personification of evil told me
he hasn't gotten any job satisfaction in decades.

"There are no challenges any more," The Devil confided.
"The Dark Ages? When everybody had the fear of God in them?
That was when harvesting souls was great sport. But, now—"

Satan was interrupted by a boy in a Black Sabbath t-shirt
with a mop of unruly hair and a stud in one ear. "Are you . . . ?
You are, aren't you? Oh, man, I'm your biggest fan!" the boy
enthused. "Can I have your autograph?" Satan graciously signed
a napkin in blood and handed it to the boy. Then, he gently nodded towards the waiter, and a couple of staff members respectfully escorted the boy out of the establishment.

"There was a time when only the most crazed, hardened
old men worshipped me," Satan sighed. "Now, any 15 year-old
who has heard an Ozzy Osbourne song thinks we're friends. It's
pathetic, really."

Although he condemned the usual suspects—secularization, abortion, the Internet (started as a lark, he had abandoned his Facebook page in disgust after he got his millionth friend)—Satan saved his harshest condemnation for evangelical Christians who preached a gospel of selfishness, greed and power.

"The meek shall inherit the earth? Hello? Ring any bells?" Satan groused. I would have thought it was the alcohol talking, but he assured me that it had no effect on him, that he just drank to be sociable. "Camel through the eye of a needle? Have you even read the New Testament? When religious leaders are taking millions of their followers down the wrong path, what is there left for me to do?"

Satan noticed a couple of girls outside the window giggling and pointing at him. He said he knew what they wanted of him, and they weren't going to get it.

"Just because I have horns," Satan sourly observed, "does not mean I'm horny."

Politicians. Rock stars. Darter snail researchers. Satan ticked off a list of professions that at one time may have posed some kind of challenge to his ability to corrupt the innocent. Then, he explained why they have already become corrupt. "Nobody is innocent any more," he observed.

I asked The Devil if, perhaps, he wasn't being too pessimistic. He started to say something about negativity being one of his greatest weapons, then suddenly stopped and looked at me piercingly. I know it's a cliché, but it was like he was looking into my very soul.

Satan asked me what I wanted out of life. I demurred; I had heard stories about how slippery he could be, and I thought it for the best to keep our relationship purely professional.

"A smart, talented woman like you? Surely, you don't plan on being a . . . 'people writer' for the rest of your life." The way he said my current beat, I could picture myself with grey hair, using a walker to get to my next interview, a narcissistic rock star who can't get my name right and throws up in my lap halfway through. Then, I go home to my 37 cats.

Satan must have taken encouragement from my shudder, for he lowered his voice and asked, "How would you like to be the Editrix-in-Chief of the Alternate Reality News Service?" He positively purred.

"You . . . you can do that?" I asked, enthralled.

Satan smiled Mona Lisaly. "I could make a few calls," he said. I licked my lips with eager sensuality. I was about to say, "Yes! Yes! Make those calls, big boy!" when Satan waved his hand.

"You see how easy it is?" he said, shaking his head. When I realized what had happened, I felt nauseous, not that Satan noticed. I began to understand where his negative reputation had come from.

"If this is winning," Satan stated darkly, "I fear eternity is going to be quite boring."

How to Get a Head in Life

by ARTURO BIGBANGBOOTIE, Alternate Reality News Service Transdimensional Traffic Writer

"Express vernacular recon."

At 12:37am EST, The Big Floating Heads (BFH) that appeared over 30 major cities across the world (and Paris) precisely six years and one month ago spoke. And, as we should have expected (although few of us did), what they said was complete nonsense.

Perhaps surprisingly for heads the size of hot air balloons, the BFHs did not speak in a booming bass, but a soft whisper. "I had almost forgotten the big fat head things were there," said citizen Marilyn Monroachkillah. "It was like . . . the time grammy came to stay with us. Most of the time, she sat in her corner casting doom and gloom predictions about the family with yarrow stalks. Then, just when you had almost forgotten she was there—BLAM!—she'd say something like, 'When the sun is benign, search out Consadine.' Nobody ever had the nerve to ask her what she was talking about."

"Concertina goiter verbosity."

"Naah—grammy Monroachkillah never said that."

What, exactly are the Big Floating Heads? Three different answers are given by different groups of Headologists, those who study the BFHs. The first group believes that the BFHs are projections of the consciousness of people who live in another dimension. For this group, the words are their attempt to communicate with us, although they are either really dumb or very bad at learning languages.

"Some people initially thought they were manifestations of a deity," said Monique Mercury, an Economics professor at Wellington College with an amateur's interest in the Big Floating Heads. "Many of them found peace in the knowledge that they were constantly being watched. In cities where the Heads appeared marriages were saved. Crime rates went down. Jim Carrey movies couldn't be played in theatres. They believed that theirs was a loving god . . .

"Of course, they don't know what to make of the recent statements. Some followers have become disenchanted with the incomprehensibility of the Heads, others are tracking down as many of the statements as possible, hoping to eventually come up with enough to fill a holy book.

"Good luck with that."

According to Mercury, Headology was developed as a rational response to this irrational belief, and she expects Headology will supplant it. "Headology," she explained, "is superior. Headology is scientific."

"Citywide wagering floorboard."

The second group of Headologists argues that the first group has to be wrong. They point to the dozens of Headcams set up to capture the existence of the BFHs, which show that they never take a break, never blink, never appear to breath, never even move their eyeballs.

"Yeah, kids will train their Webcams on the strangest things," chuckled Aloysious Pasha Krugg-Mann, hea—err, primary

Headologist in the Sociology Department of the University of Toronto. "As a parent, I should be appalled at the way my children are wasting their time, but, as a scientist, I find myself exhilarated by the research potential!"

Krugg-Mann believes that the BFHs are actually computer generated projections, possibly from another dimension, but just as possibly from another planet in this dimension. "The fact that they don't blink could be a programming error," he stated. "Or their programmers might have felt it wasn't worth the bandwidth. Lord knows, we've all had to deal with less than optimal software that was shipped imperfect to make a deadline!"

"Bored stripe liniment."

The third group uses Occam's razor to reject both theories. "We don't need to posit other dimensions or life on other planets," Carl Rorschach, a freelance Headologist currently on a two and a half week limited contract with the Gotterdammerung Institute of Sri Lanka, commented. "They are actually projections from the unconscious of the human race. At first, we thought they represented our collective superego, but, now, whoa—what they said seems to come directly from the id!"

To say that the three camps do not get along would be to understate the nature of understatement. Two years ago, at the third Biennial Headology Conference and Talent Show (dubbed the Headcaseology Conference by Tokyo businesspeople who, in the current economy, were nonetheless happy for the business) Rorschach and Mercury got into a heated debate about whether the transdimensional projection was responsible for a distortion in the sizes of the Heads, or whether the aliens were really that big. Interpretations of what happened differ, but most versions of the story agree that Mercury had to have surgery on her left eye to remove a canapé that had lodged there, while the possibility that Rorschach would be capable of having children had decreased by over 23.4763 percent.

"Mental mauve strawberry."

"Yeah, I heard all about the fighting between all the Headologists," citizen Monroachkillah sadly stated. "I wish they'd get their shit together. I mean, if smart people don't know what's going on, how are ordinary people like me ever supposed ta know?"

But, What If The Committee Had Set Out To Make a Camel?

by FRED CHARUNDER-MACHARRUNDEIRA, Alternate Reality News Service Science Writer

Bonita Verklempt wanted an animal that had the power of a horse. Gerald McFlecktone wanted an animal with the grace of a cat. Arnold "Just Arnold" Compote wanted an animal with the nose of an anteater. What they got was an animal with the excretions of a horse, the skittish temperament of a cat . . . and the nose of an anteater.

What they got was a flutz.

About the size of the OED, the common flutz has the body of a raccoon which appears to have been put through a blender, an outsized head, four eyes (two on its head and one on each of its tails), human hands on two of its four legs and the underhanded cunning (not to mention IQ) of a Rush Limbaugh dittohead. The rare pink-nosed flutz is so disgusting we'd have to password protect our site just to describe it.

"I thought the hands would be useful for the flutz because it could use them to pass researchers the medical equipment they needed to experiment on it," McFlecktone ruefully stated. "Instead, it mostly uses them to scratch its bum and make rude gestures at us! I can't imagine where it learned *those*!"

Verklempt, McFlecktone and Compote are members of the Next Stallion Working Committee of International BioScien-Tech, a wholly owned subsidiary of MultiNatCorp.

"Horses are amazingly useful animals," Verklempt stated. "You can ride them. They can pull plows or carts. They star in western movies. You can use them to count when you don't have an abacus handy. In bad economic times, they make a tasty burger. Our committee was tasked with finding a new animal with the same or greater versatility."

When it was pointed out that task is a noun, not a verb, Verklempt responded, "Obviously, you know nothing of the scientific method."

By combining genetic material from different animals, International BioScienTech has become a world leader in creating new species. It's sort of like mixing a cocktail, only with meat instead of alcohol. Lots and lots of meat.

The Next Stallion Working Committee was given the task (I do so know the scientific method—I slept with it on and off for four years!) of creating an animal that could be used in a wide range of medical experiments. "We thought we would be getting a mouse with the digestive tract of a giraffe and the spleen of a black widow spider," explained International BioScienTech President Guy Flighty. "Now, that would have been an animal you could experiment on!

"Instead, we got . . . this."

The flutz was named after the co-chairs of the Next Stallion Working Committee, Gordie Fleetermauss and Gerhardt Pavel Utz. Neither of them has been seen in public since news of the creature's creation was first reported. Utz is rumoured to be taking a walking tour of Hawaiian volcanoes.

"The mottled and folded skin—like a flakey shar pei—was supposed to help in developing certain kinds of cancer," Compote defended the committee's creation, although he conveniently couldn't remember whose idea the skin design was. "And, it probably would have, too, if any researchers had been brave enough to actually experiment on the flutz, even though it did make the animal next to impossible to clean."

Although it is a bust in terms of medical research, International BioScienTech is looking for other ways to exploit the flutz. Owing to the unfortunate decision to give the animal the teeth of piranhas, marketing it as children's toy was a no go. The unfortunate tendency of the flutz to defecate often and in awkward places (playpens, pianos, luggage that you thought had been safely put away in the closet until your next family vacation) made it an unlikely candidate for family pet.

The obvious next step (the next time you see the scientific method, tell it I want my mix tapes back—I put a lot of thought into what I was going to put on those tapes, and I want to give them to somebody who will appreciate them!) is to declare the flutz a failure and move on to the company's next project. However, after eight years and a rumoured expenditure of over $10 million, that seems unlikely.

Could the dozen or so prototype flutzes be headed for a zoo near you?

The Customer Is Always Wrong

by GIDEON GINRACHMANJINJa-VITUS, Alternate Reality News Service Economics Writer

Gideon Alice was driving his 2005 Ford Wildebeest down the highway while watching C-SPAN on the 25 inch flat screen television in his control panel. The soporific effect of a debate on corn subsidies to small flange manufacturers kept him from noticing that his up turn signal was flashing. This went on for over 10 miles, until Alice changed the channel to *Die Hard IX: Dying Me Softly With His Song*, noticed the flashing signal and turned it off.

A week later, the Ford Motor Company and Shakedown Brokerage served notice that it was suing him for $765,000.

Page 17 of Alice's licensing agreement with Ford clearly states: ". . . powdered donuts, except Valvoline crullers, driving under the influence of exotic perfumes, aphrodisiacs, skin cleansers or shampoos, wearing thong underwear while sitting on the car's lovely suede interiors, allowing right turn signal to flash for more than seven miles, showering while driving, playing billiards while driving, supporting the military coup in Honduras while driving, daydreaming, nightmaring, questioning the existence of a beneficent all-knowing god, allowing up turn signal to flash for more than four miles, removing all your clothes and . . ."

This paragraph ends on page 198 with the ominous conclusion: ". . . if the elephant is more than two months pregnant without the express written consent of the commissioner of major league baseball, licensee shall be considered in breach of contract and shall be prosecuted to the fullest extent of the law. Sucker."

"I can accept the lawsuit," Alice commented, "but the taunting was a bit much."

This is the latest in a series of lawsuits brought by corporations against individuals. Specific Mills, for example, sued a suburban Yellowstone Park woman who was seen eating Vamp Strawberri cereal with chocolate milk, a clear violation of the instructions at the bottom of the box. Panasonic sued a 14 year-old Milwaukee man for using his boombox in the privacy of his own home rather than on the street, a condition of its purchase. Brita sued famous Harvard law professor Henry Louis Gates for using one of their filters on his pet cat.

These and other companies seem to be following the template laid down by Rottenman School of Economics professor Carmella Hwang-Cheung in her book: *Customer as Criminal: A New Approach to Economics*.

Hwang-Cheung, an expert on macroeconomic voyeurism, begins her book with an analysis of economic trends, noting that the drive to lower wages to pre-Dark Ages levels leaves fewer and fewer consumers with money to spend. Her solution to this problem is to turn the traditional economic model on its head: instead of selling a large number of products with a low profit margin, sell a small number of products with a honking large profit margin.

But, how can a business ensure sales of large profit margin items? Hwang-Cheung, an internationally respected smarty-pants, recommends creating incomprehensible contracts that consumers sign upon purchase, then building surveillance technologies into your products (the Wildebeest, for instance, multiplies the number of turn signal flashes by the number of tire rotations per second to determine the distance you have your turn light on, then sends this information to a Blackberry in Ford's Manassas, Saudi Arabia headquarters) to catch transgressions.

"Let's face it," Hwang-Cheung writes, "your customers are thieves who will steal value from you every chance they get. Why not use this to your advantage?"

"Besides," Hwang-Cheung added 17 years later, "it worked for the recording industry, so why wouldn't it work for you?"

So far, American courts have favoured corporations, using the time-honoured judicial principle of *Gentlemen's Rea Quarterly* (almost literally: "Eh! A contract's a contract. Whaddaya gonna do?") However, only seven of the nine Supreme Court justices were appointed by Democratic Presidents, and only one more could tip the scales back in favour of consumers.

Isn't there a risk, though, that potential customers, wary of being subject to curt action [EDITOR'S NOTE: Gideon, did you mean "court action?"], will simply stop buying things?

"Naah," Hwang-Cheung, clearly anticipating this objection, wrote. "We love our shit. Sooner or later, the evolutionary imperative to buy something will overcome somebody, and **BAM!**—we've got them!"

Then Alice—remember Alice? This is a news article about Alice. Then, Alice worried about whether or not he could afford to fight Ford's lawsuit. However, since the company's settlement offer only knocked five cents off their asking price, he figured it wasn't worth accepting. "Wow," Alice asked, "who knew that the freedom of the road would end up costing so much?"

Border Skirmish Escalates . . . Maybe

by INDIRA CHARUNDER-MACHARRUNDEIRA, Alternate Reality News Service Fine Arts Writer

With their lobster-shaped turrets and lip treads that seem to have a tongue moving back and forth in them when they're rolling, you'd be hard-pressed to recognize the vehicles as tanks.

Ira Nayman

Nonetheless, the fact that they are being massed on the border between West Surrealisma and The Dada Nation is being seen by many as a provocative act.

The Dada Nation has responded by sending three platoons of performance artists, including the much feared Seventh Cabaret Voltaire Infantry, to the border. Should the tanks cross the border into Dada, the performance artists will don masks and recite nonsense poetry at them.

"The Dada Nation may seem overmatched," analyzed eager Military art historian Brendan Boomish, "but you may recall that in the Battle of the Brunch, they caused the Fauvist Fourth Soft-Focus Tank Brigade to laugh so hard that they fired on each other, decimating their own forces. The Dada Nation military is an awesome fighting machine!"

Since their founding, there has always been tension between West Surrealisma and The Dada Nation. The Dada Nation constitution (written in smoke and mirrors) claims nonsense as the country's highest value; they believe that the West Surrealismists have abused the power of the subconscious for material gain. The West Surrealismists, for their part, reject the use of nonsense for its own sake, arguing that without a radical agenda to alter people's consciousness, it's just fun, and we can't have any of that.

Despite these differences, the countries managed to maintain a fragile peace until two weeks ago when Andre Breton, President in Chef of West Surrealisma, sent a sternly worded communiqué to the government of Grand Self-inflicted Leader in Chief of Distracted Integrated Nationalist Pig Farmers Tristan Tzara which read: "Fishtail antagonists tread blue criminal through bleeding feeding trout."

"This is a classic Breton diplomatic maneouvre," Boomish said enthusiastically. "It was probably written using the Exquisite Corpse method taught to all of the country's diplomats."

The response was not long in coming. Two days layer, Tzara wrote back: "trout. tread bleeding blue Fishtail through antagonists feeding criminal"

"Tzara cut up Breton's message, rearranged the pieces and sent them back to Breton!" Boomish was so excited that he practically vibrated. "It was a stunning counterstroke! They'll be studying this move in political science art classes for decades to come!"

Two days after this harsh exchange of diplomatic rhetoric, Dada Nation Minister of Foreign Affairs, Internal Affairs, May-September Romances and Assorted Other Emotional Entanglements Allen Ginsburg amusedly mused to the *L. A. Times* that the government had been developing plans to levitate the Pentagon. "That would be, like, a really groovy way to let the West Surrealismists know how seriously we take them, which is, like, not at all, man," Ginsburg considered considerately.

The West Surrealisma response was quick and, if the Dada Nation had actually been paying attention, would have been devastating: Minister of Warts Christo told the *Washington Post* that troops of visual artists could be deployed to wrap the San Francisco Bridge with paper at a moment's notice. "Not only would this cripple West Surrealisma by effectively halting all civilian traffic between the island and the mainland," Christo explained, "but it would also recontextualize large scale engineering projects so that we might think more deeply about how we create the environments in which we live!"

So far, the military of Midwest Futurista, a country that borders on both West Surrealisma and The Dada Nation, has not gotten involved in the dispute. Considering how much value the Midwest Futuristans put on speed, the sleek lines of our modern vehicles and, frankly, disastrous military adventurism, this seems to be out of character. However, it is rumoured that Midwest Futurista is supplying cubist tanks to both sides, which is totally in its character.

How serious is the confrontation? "Well, the older European nations—countries like the United Kingdom of Representationists and Central Religious Iconographia—are unlikely to get involved," Boomish, his excitement having left him drained, quietly explained, "which would keep the fighting local—"

Well, no. What we meant was: how much damage can lobster tanks and donning masks and reciting nonsense poetry really do? "Physically? Not much, perhaps," Boomish allowed. "However, to the extent that they can change people's conceptual frameworks, forcing them to see the world in a new way, this war could be devastating!"

Bunny Lakaida is Missing

by ARTURO BIGBANGBOOTIE, Alternate Reality News Service Transdimensional Traffic Writer

When somebody says, "It's like he vanished into thin air," what they're really saying is usually, "When it came time to pay the bill, he scarpered." When a police liaison representative says, "It's like he vanished off the face of the earth," what she is usually saying is, "He's either dead and buried in a shallow grave somewhere or he has skipped the country—either way, we don't have the resources to look for him."

Lakaida "Bunny" Chan Aikida vanished off the face of the earth into thin air. That is not a metaphor. It is not a euphemism. He disappeared in front of a dozen people, at least three of whom were not completely demented.

Lakaida, who was 87 years old, was living in the Chairman Mao Rest Home and Dance Studio. He spent most of his days sitting in a corner of the common room, looking at the window and talking loudly about an incident in 1947 when, in order to teach Chang Kai Shek a lesson about the re-education of the ruling classes, Lakaida spit into his beer.

"The first thing I noticed was the room got an awful lot quieter," Nigiri Seet En-lo, another resident of the home, stated. "I enjoyed the quiet—it gave me time to plan how I was going to smuggle the contents of my pants past the guards at the front door. After a while, I got a little . . . unnerved by the quiet, and, looking around, I noticed that Bunny was not in his chair."

Security tapes, verified by police experts, show that one moment Lakaida was sitting in his chair, the next moment it was empty. Empty, curiously, save for 27 American pennies.

"Oh, he didn't disappear," Koari Watanamaker, Chief Obfuscations Relations Officer of the Chairman Mao Rest Home and Dance Studio claimed. "Our residents often wander off on their own, unattended, without anybody really knowing where they are. But, they always turn up, so there's nothing to . . . worry . . . a . . . uhh, could I maybe rephrase that answer a bit?"

What about the tape? "Oh, pfah!" Watanamaker waved her hand dismissively. "The police have investigated the Rest Home and Dance Studio several times for code violations, and they never made a charge stick. Well, okay, except for that one time. But, my point is that I wouldn't trust the judgment of the po— police . . . umm, you know, I think I need some time to think my answer to this question through more carefully."

What about the pennies found on Lakaida's chair? "Oh, we don't allow residents to have money," Watanamaker stated. "The orderlies will steal anything of value from their rooms. So, we tell their families not to let them have—you know, today is just not my day."

Not impressed with Lakaida's vanishment? Consider this: he had a C-chip implanted in his skull. The C-chip was, of course, designed to be implanted in youngsters to give parents the comfort of knowing that if their children were kidnapped and killed, authorities could recover the bodies. Oddly enough, parents were not comforted by this thought, and their protests effectively killed the programme.

The company turned around and sold the C-chip to old folks homes (changing the concept from "Child-chips" to "Coot-chips"). The tag line for the company's ads in *Septuagenarian Care and Mortuary News Monthly* was: "You keep track of your residents, we don't have to deal with obstructionist lobby groups—it's a win/win!"

Lakaida "Bunny" Chan Aikida's C-chip stopped sending out signals the moment he vanished.

Could Lakaida's C-chip have failed the moment he disappeared? "Oh! Oh! I know the answer to this one! Ask me! Ask me!" Watanamaker shouted. I nodded my head, and she responded: "The whole point of the C-chip is to locate bodies after they have . . . become bodies. So, it is highly unlikely that the C-chip would stop working."

Clapping her hands, Watanamaker added: "That was the right answer, wasn't it? Oh, I'm good—I'm really good!"

Beijing authorities, sensing that this was over their heads, called in the Multiverse Police Force. Blue Officer Chiang Ku Lio, who has been assigned to the case, stated, "We were asked to investigate the possibility that Mister Lakaida had been kidnapped to another universe. We will be happy to answer any questions that reporters may have."

Why kidnap an 87 year-old man?

"No comment," Chiang responded.

Had there been a ransom note?

"No comment," Chiang answered.

What's up with the pennies?

"No comment," Chiang replied. "If any further questions occur to you," he added helpfully, "please feel free to ask."

The investigation continues.

The Horror Starts With
Home Made Desserts

by FRED CHARUNDER-MACHARRUNDEIRA, Alternate Reality News Service Science Writer

Given how deeply our lives are enmeshed with technology, how things like the Internet, iPhones and the Waterpik are such an integral part of our everyday existence, anybody who chooses to live without the latest high tech has to be considered anti-social, at best, and downright revolutionary at worst.

This is the position of the Cozy Tea Society. Don't be fooled by the soporific name: the Cozy Tea Society are a rabid bunch of eco-anarcho-Neo-Luddite throwbacks who reject technology when it doesn't suit their purposes. In short: they oppose everything you hold dear in your life.

I recently spoke with the president of the Cozy Tea Society. She asked to be identified only as Mrs. Harriet Benchley of 21 Sussex Drive, Norfolk, a handsome woman of a certain age with sparkling eyes behind her horn-rimmed glasses who is slow to anger and quick with a smile who likes to spend her Fridays around the corner at the Queen and Commoner Pub and wouldn't say no to a pint and a game of darts if the right man asked if you know what she means. Harriet's a wicked one for the darts. Given the radical agenda of the organization she heads, it is understandable that she wouldn't want to give information that could help authorities identify her.

This is a partial transcript of our interview.

ALTERNATE REALITY NEWS SERVICE: Why do you want to destroy society?

HARRIET BENCHLEY: I do?

ARNS: Do you have any idea where we would be without toaster ovens?

HB: In a pretty sad state, I should imagine.

ARNS: I couldn't disagree more. The world would fall ap— what?

HB: I do a lot of baking in my toaster oven.

ARNS: Maybe the toaster oven is a bad example. I mean, you hate technology, right?

HB: Weeeeelllll, not really, no. I just think that we shouldn't pursue every technology just because we can.

ARNS: AHA!

Ira Nayman

HB: Aha?

ARNS: If we didn't pursue every technology just because we could, our society would fall apart.

HB: I highly doubt that. Still, What the Cozy Tea Society advocates is that every person should weigh the pros and cons of each new technology and only use the ones which they feel will make their life better.

ARNS: And, reject the ones that won't.

HB: And, reject the ones that won't.

ARNS: AHA!

HB: Again with the 'Aha!'?

ARNS: Technological innovation is the driver of the new economy. If people had a choice, they might choose not to use it. The whole system would collapse!

HB: That seems a bit extreme.

ARNS: It is! It's very extreme! It's as extreme as it gets!

HB: Well! If we're going to be contemplating complete social collapse, I need some tea. Would you like some tea?

ARNS: Tea? That would be . . . nice of you.

HB: You seem surprised that I could be nice. Why not? You didn't expect when you came to interview me that I would have fangs, did you?

ARNS: Yes. Maybe. You know. Little ones. Little fangs. But, uhh, pronounced.

HB: Ah. Well. I think I really do need that tea, now.

(Pause while Harriet Benchley makes tea.)

HB: There. That's better. I find that everything seems to be easier with a nice, relaxing cup of tea.

ARNS: AHA!

HB: What now?

ARNS: You made tea!

HB: Yes . . . ?

ARNS: With a kettle!

HB: Right . . .

ARNS: On a stove!

HB: I'm sorry, but I don't see your point.

ARNS: You haven't rejected technology entirely. If you had, you wouldn't be using a pot on a stove. You would boil the water for the tea over a wood fire in a pit using a . . . a hollowed out coconut!

HB: That sounds positively barbaric.

ARNS: THAT'S WHAT I'VE BEEN TRYING TO SAY!

HB: But, that's not what I believe.

ARNS: I'm sorry?

HB: The Cozy Tea Society believes in appropriate technology, appropriateness to be determined by each individual.

ARNS: Anarchy!

HB: That's a bit of a stretch.

ARNS: Well, with your radical reasonableness, you're not helping.

HB: Mmm. Would you like some cookies?

ARNS: Are they factory made?

HB: No. I'm sorry—I made them myself. Fresh out of the oven.

ARNS: You bastard. You sick . . . sick bastard. Will you stop at nothing to score political points?

HB: Sorry. (Pause.) They're chocolate chip.

ARNS: Well . . . maybe just one . . . or two . . .

That's the problem with radical belief systems—they can be highly seductive. And, actually, quite tasty . . .

ALTERNATE QUIZ

What the Heck Do You Know?
About Alien Life

Have you been keeping up with our reports from alternate realities? The staff of the Alternate Reality News Service has put together the following quiz to test your knowledge of alien life forms that have recently made the headlines.

1) Instumbrek vi la yclempt George W. Bush versnicket oxytocin. Versnacket innim annus illustrationacum George W. Bush inducticum Al Gore ol. Cicoletti sa di nadium prelectunu Bush antrobis Gore antrobis Barack Obama dreisenu bumfuzzlin macheno?
   a) Barack Obama ni bumfuzzlor echt. Al Gore antrobis denatttttt plundum. George W. Bush . . . fid . . . fid . . . regnoggbin!
   b) regnoggbin mi grunderplexis! George W. Bush ish plat gegunnim bairuntnew! Gegunnim bairuntnew!
   c) 2012

2) Why did President Maddow urge Americans to support a war on the Frenglippe Empire?
   a) despite having three hearts, the Frenglippe only have a third of the compassion of human beings, which makes them ruthless businesspeople
   b) a Frenglippe ambassador insulted the president's mother, and things quickly turned ugly
   c) the Frenglippe war armada circling the globe strongly suggested to the president that their intentions were not friendly

3) Klaatu berada nictu?
   a) I'm sorry—Klaatu's been a naughty boy and he can't come out and play
   b) berada . . . berada . . . bera—wasn't that a cop show in the 70s?
   c) the Apocalypse is not in right now. At the sound of the tone, please leave your name, phone number and a brief mess—oh, wait. Is that someone knocking on your front door?

4) What finally ended the Gramarzcy Uprising on N'e'bu'lo'n IV?
   a) patching Howard Jones' "What Is Love?" into the headphones of the Gramarzcy Grazsnozty D-57 Fighter craft as they were about to attack the Starfleet Ship Space Guppy
   b) projecting a giant hologram of Howard Jones singing "What Is Love?" over the major Gramarzcy cities of Glornitz, Flornitz and Pagagagagarog
   c) after 17 revolutions, the Gramarzcy realized that they were actually in charge of N'e'bu'lo'n IV and, therefore, really didn't have anything to rebel against

5) Considering how vulnerable they are in battle, why do so many alien races have eyestalks?
   a) Darwinian evolution was a local phenomenon
   b) when your eyes are so exposed, you develop effective, if exotic methods of coping . . . yeah, that sounded lame to me, too—if I were you, I'd go for answer a)
   c) it's just the universe's way of teaching humanity gemunstlichnuggen

6) According to *Galactic Diplomacy for Beginners*, what is the first thing representatives of the Galactic Federation should do upon encountering a new race of aliens?
   a) build a sports stadium on its home planet as a show of goodwill
   b) destroy several of its major cities as a show of strength
   c) have sex with its least loathsome member of the opposite sex (or, if it has more than two sexes, have sex with n-1 of its least loathsome members of n sexes; either way, defining "opposite sex" is a judgment call)

7) Il gafleebin esse vanatu vinatius claptorum. But, then you are confronted with the vacuum of space, and you locked the keys to the door inside the capsule! Echbladd qraqtaq drbbblin qa wa verblemt Ryker wa qa delphinium. Of course, you didn't know that when you flushed the ship's waste out onto their planet. Still, uddle peewatish qwerff?
   a) k'flort! K'flort! K'flort! Then, let the lawyers sort it out
   b) ambrigorgon fuzzlchut in set quaqua pel strort schleppenzie hult. Of course, if you do, it will be too late to let the lawyers sort it out
   c) that depends upon Admiral Ryker's estimation of the situation, but you are guaranteed of one thing. Awqstwerdly tu ta, primitaa tu ta

8) A rocket traveling at .237 light speed leaves earth at 8:32 Galactic Standard Time on a path for Tau Ceti. A second rocket traveling at .327 light speed leaves Andromeda on a path for Tau Ceti at 2:36 GST. How stupid must the pilots be to crash in space?
   a) fleigeltron stupid (the fleigeltron, you will recall, were so stupid that they went extinct because they collectively forgot to eat)
   b) punching a blastronicom in the snatchblort stupid
   c) forgetting to zip up the fly of your spacesuit before an EVA stupid

9) What is the first thought that comes to mind when you find out that the universe you believed you lived in is actually a computer simulation run by sentient machines?
   a) "If only I had known, I wouldn't have worried about eating that extra blintz at lunch!"
   b) "If only I had know, I wouldn't have worried about having that affair with Margot!"
   c) "Well, that explains the popularity of Miley Cyrus!"
   d) other

10) Why should you never eat Marulian wombat eggs?
    a) you'll have gas until the end of the Hyperbolean Era
    b) have you ever seen a Marulian wombat's mother? If you had, you wouldn't need to ask this question
    c) the eggs of Archsockl combustion engine worms are much cheaper (and only marginally less edible)

11) Hooga hooga paradigm gort febluchen esta socket wrench paromachid wer tas ichnibbin foam insulation. Foam insulation? Backschnabble. Assuming ichy brit clob gesundheit, what horcking blastoma glorb fram de insecticide maclatchet?

    a) ichorizing hort trenchcoat mirt virt Seth Rogen boblinc mercathozine

    b) indelible edubkle: "Doctor! Doctor! Paromachid wer Tardis gezundheit! Glug impen tas wer gezundheit? Aah . . ."

    c) only with a machete at high speeds

12) What guidebook must Alternate Reality News Service reporters carry with them at all times?

    a) *The Hitchhiker's Guide to the Multiverse*

    b) *Universal Diplomacy for Beginners*

    c) Alternate Reality News Service reporters are given a guidebook before being sent into different universes? Really? I think I have to have a little talk with Brenda Brundtland-Govanni . . .

13) How superstitious are the Beldar Ganoush of Zyklotron III?

    a) they would declare total war against my home planet if they knew that they were referred to in question 13 of this quiz (so, please, for the sake of my children, don't tell them)

    b) one time, one guy threw salt over his shoulder, only to hit the guy standing behind him, who threw salt over his shoulder and hit a woman standing behind **him**—before you knew it, half the citizens of the planet threw salt over their shoulders in a daisy chain of superstition that lasted a week and a half, and the best part is that they had to import the salt from earth because **it isn't even their superstition**

    c) they refused to make their sidewalks out of concrete in order to save their mother's backs

14) Sssssssss ssssss sssssssssss sssssssssssss ssss sssssss sssssss sssssss sss sss ssssssss?

    a) sssssssss ssss sssssssssssssssssssssssssssss!

    b) sssss sssssss sssssss sssssssss ssss sss sss sss . . .

    c) sorry—we don't negotiate with terrorists

15) Do Jedi Knights go to the bathroom?
   a) yes, but only when the camera is not on them (it would diminish respect for The Force . .)
   b) no: they use the power of The Force to excrete sunshine through their every orifice
   c) you have way too much time on your hands, you know that?

16) Fill in the blanks: If _____ were _____, _____ would ride.
   a) Foofnarrons; Heirarchqets; pantsuits
   b) Cholesterons; effeminate; Monosorbates
   c) wishes; horses; Gobstilliards

17) Why did the Fuffnapoli of Bart Prime die out?
   a) they discovered invisibility, and ended up not being able to find partners to mate with
   b) they were not immune to ITDs (Internet Transmitted Diseases)
   c) the Fuffnapoli of Bart Prime only ever existed in the mind of a cruel writer who thought that asking a question about killing them off would be funny

18) When your starship is attacked by the Floogly Bombs of a Dalhous Battle Cruiser/Bed and Breakfast, what do you have to do to keep your reactor core from exploding?
   a) throw half a ton of quadro-triticale, 50 gallons of water and a pinch of salt into the reactor. Not only will this cool it down, but it will also make bread for a crew of 3,000 for 10 weeks
   b) wait until the last possible moment and give your onboard computer the code that will stop the core explosion
   c) tell your chief engineer to fix it—he'll bitch and moan that it canna be done, but in the end he'll do it

19) Fart faaaaaart squeak fart fart fart aaaaaaaaaaaaaaaaaaaaaa aaaaaaah?
   a) I'm sorry, I don't speak 3 year-old
   b) toot squeak fart FAAAAAAART! And, you'll be hearing from my attorneys!
   c) I wouldn't say that near a Flaming Sambuca if I was you

20) How much of the Alternate Reality News Service's reporting on alien creatures do you actually believe?
   a) are you kidding? I went to school with Frederica von McToast-Hyphen—practically lost my virginity to her, if you must know—and I believe every word that comes out of her processor
   b) are you kidding? I served on the Starship Floating Budget Bloat with Majumder Sakrashuminderather, and I wouldn't trust him as far as I could throw a Silurain Barfsnaggle!
   c) I only believe the words that I don't understand

INDEX

ALTERNATE AUTHOR BIO

Ira Nayman has written radio plays, film and television scripts, produced a short film and is the creator of the off-beat humor website *Les Pages aux Folles*. Mr. Nayman received his M.A. in Media Studies from the New School for Social Research and his Ph.D. in Communications from McGill University. He grew up in Toronto, Ontario, Canada. When he is not being funny all over the place, Mr. Nayman teaches New Media at Ryerson University.

LaVergne, TN USA
24 March 2010

177068LV00001B/21/P